"Mr. Brookfield, there are several other ladies to choose from…"

Millicent turned to face Nicholas. "Before we say anything more, I feel compelled to point out that I'm merely the one who composed the advertisement. I assure you, it's quite all right if you find you prefer another of them."

So Miss Matthews had a sense of fair play and generosity. Nick liked that about her. But somehow he knew her suggestion was something he didn't even want to consider. It was incomprehensible how he could sense that already, but there it was.

"I know you will find this difficult to believe, since we've only just met, and we really don't know each other at all," he said. "I can well understand that it appears I'm making a snap judgment, and perhaps I am, but I would like the opportunity to get to know you better. I—I find you very attractive indeed, Miss Matthews, and that's the simple truth…."

Books by Laurie Kingery

Love Inspired Historical

Hill Country Christmas
The Outlaw's Lady
*Mail Order Cowboy

*Brides of Simpson Creek

LAURIE KINGERY

makes her home in central Ohio, where she is a "Texan-in-exile." Formerly writing as Laurie Grant for Harlequin Historical and other publishers, she is the author of eighteen previous books and the 1994 winner of a Readers' Choice Award in the short historical category. She has also been nominated for Best First Medieval and Career Achievement in Western Historical Romance by *RT Book Reviews*. When not writing her historicals, she loves to travel, read, participate on Facebook and Shoutlife and write her blog on www.lauriekingery.com.

LAURIE KINGERY

MAIL ORDER
Cowboy

Steeple
Hill®

Published by Steeple Hill Books™

STEEPLE HILL BOOKS

Steeple
Hill®

Recycling programs
for this product may
not exist in your area.

ISBN-13: 978-0-373-82847-0

MAIL ORDER COWBOY

Copyright © 2010 by Laurie A.Kingery

www.SteepleHill.com

Printed in U.S.A.

What doth the Lord require of thee,
but to do justly, and to love mercy,
and to walk humbly with thy God?
—Micah 6:8

To my wonderful editor, Melissa Endlich,
who always makes me strive to be the best writer
I can be, and always, to my husband, Tom

Prologue

Simpson Creek, Texas, July 1865

"The problem, as I see it," Millicent Matthews announced in her forthright way, looking around the edges of the quilt at the members of the Ladies Aid Society, "is that we unmarried ladies are likely to remain so, given the absolute lack of single men who've come home to Simpson Creek from the war. The few men who did return were already married, and while I'm very happy for their wives, of course—" she added quickly as one of the town's matrons looked up "—the rest of us will have to leave or remain single unless Decisive Action is Taken."

"Oh, I don't know, Milly," said her sister Sarah, staring down at the Wedding Ring pattern as if it held the answer to their dilemma. "Perhaps not all of our men are able to travel yet from wherever they were when the war ended. They might be recovering from wounds, or the effects of confinement in northern prisons…"

Milly felt a rush of compassion for Sarah, whom she knew was still holding out hope that her beau would yet return, despite the fact he had been reported missing in action late last year. Since then, they'd heard nothing more.

"Sarah, it's *July*," she pointed out gently but firmly. "The war was over in April. We've seen the casualty lists. All the other Simpson Creek men have been accounted for, one way or the other. The ones who survived have managed to make it to Texas. If Jesse was still recovering elsewhere, surely he would have sent word by now." She let the statement hang in the air.

Sarah's gaze fell to her lap and her lip quivered. "I…I know you're right, Milly. I just keep hoping…"

Across from them, Mrs. Detwiler pursed her lips.

Milly laid a hand comfortingly on her sister's shoulder. She was sure the color of Sarah's dove-gray dress was a concession to her uncertainty as to whether she was mourning or waiting.

Milly was just about to say "Jesse would want you to move on" when Mrs. Detwiler cleared her throat.

"We need to accept the lot in life that the Lord sees fit to give us," the woman said heavily, clutching the mourning brooch on her bodice. "I lost my own dear George ten years ago, God rest his soul, and I have learned to resign myself to my widowhood, even—dare I say it—*treasure* my single state." Her expression indicated Sarah would do well to be so wise.

"Mrs. Detwiler, I admire the way you've adapted to your loss," Milly began tactfully, not wanting to offend the widow of the town's previous preacher. "But you had many happy years with Mr. Detwiler, and raised several children."

"Seven, to be exact." Mrs. Detwiler sniffed, and raised her eyes heavenward.

"Seven," Milly echoed. "But Sarah and I and several others here—" she saw furtive nods around the quilt frame "—are young, and have never been married. We'd like to become wives and raise children, too. And there are others who were widowed by the war and left with children to raise and land to work or businesses to manage. They need to find good husbands again."

"In my opinion, you would do better to devote yourselves to prayer and good works, Miss Matthews, and let the good Lord send you a husband if He wishes you to have one."

Milly could feel Sarah tensing beside her. Sarah never liked confrontations. But Milly had seen the spark of interest and approval in the eyes of half a dozen young ladies plying their needles on the quilt, and their silent support emboldened her.

"I agree that prayer and good works are important to every Christian, of course, and I *have* been praying about the matter. Sometimes I think the Lord helps those who help themselves."

At this point Mrs. Detwiler cleared her throat again. Loudly. "I hardly think this is the time or place to discuss such a frivolous topic." From her pocket, she pulled out a gold watch, a legacy of her dear departed George. "I must return home soon, and we have not yet discussed the raffle to be held for the Benefit of the Deserving Poor of San Saba County. If we don't stop chattering and keep stitching, ladies, this quilt will not be ready to be raffled off at the event."

Milly tucked an errant lock of dark hair that had

escaped the neat knot at the nape of her neck and bit back a sigh of frustration. As president of the Ladies Aid Society, Mrs. Detwiler had an obligation to keep the meetings on track, but she suspected the widow was all too happy to have an excuse to stifle the discussion.

"You're right, Mrs. Detwiler, of course. I'm sorry if I spoke out of turn," she said in the meekest tone she could manage. "Perhaps it *would* be best to discuss this subject at another time, with only those concerned present. So why don't the unmarried ladies who are interested meet back here again tomorrow, say at four o'clock? We'll serve lemonade and cookies."

Chapter One

"Sarah, thank you again for making the cookies and the lemonade," Milly whispered as the ladies began to arrive in the Simpson Creek Church social hall. It must have been the dozenth time she'd thanked her sister since volunteering to supply refreshments, knowing it would be Sarah who actually made the cookies. Milly's baking efforts always ended up overbrowned, if not completely charred.

"I told you, you're welcome," Sarah whispered back, smiling. "I couldn't run a meeting the way you're about to. We all have our gifts."

Milly was none too sure she had any gifts worth boasting of, but what she was about to propose to these ladies *had* been her idea.

"Sarah, we're going to need more chairs," she whispered again, this time in pleased astonishment as women kept filing in. They had set out only half a dozen, including the ones for her and Sarah. The next few minutes were a busy bustle of carrying chairs and making a bigger circle. Finally, in all, there were ten never-married ladies and two widows, plus the mother of

Prissy Gilmore, who probably wanted to keep a careful eye on what Milly Matthews was proposing—especially because Prissy's father was the mayor.

"Ladies, I want to thank you all for coming," Milly said, pitching her voice louder than the buzz of conversation as everyone settled themselves in their chairs and greeted one another. "I'd like to open this meeting with prayer." She waited a moment while everyone quieted and bowed their heads.

"Our heavenly Father," Milly began, "we ask You would bless us this day and direct our efforts as we seek to find an answer to a problem. Guide us and bless us, and keep us in the center of Your will. Amen." She raised her head, and as the others raised theirs and opened their eyes, she saw them looking expectantly at her.

Milly took a deep breath. "As I was saying two days ago as we worked on the quilt, we single women in Simpson Creek face a problem now that the war is over and there are no single men here—"

"So what are you proposing we do, Milly?" interrupted Prissy Gilmore impatiently. "Become mail order brides and leave Simpson Creek?"

Milly laughed. "Merciful heavens, no! *I'm* not going to, anyway. I love this town. I don't want to leave it and Sarah and go marry, sight unseen, some prospector in Nevada Territory or a widower farmer with a passel of children in Nebraska. I want a husband who can run the ranch Papa left us and defend it against the Comanches if they come raiding. Y'all know Sarah and I have been coping—" barely, she thought "—with only our foreman, old Josh, and his nephew Bobby to help us."

Josh and Bobby weren't enough, she knew. Once, the Matthews bunkhouse had housed six other cowhands, with more hired at roundup time. Josh was old and becoming more and more crippled with rheumatism, while Bobby wasn't even shaving yet.

Josh had taken her aside only the night before and explained that if they didn't find a way to make the ranch productive again, they might lose it to taxes. They were already losing cattle left and right to thieving Indians and rustlers, but there was no way an old man and a young boy could protect the place.

"Maybe y'ought to sell out and move into town, Miss Milly," Josh had said. "Don't worry 'bout me 'n the boy. We'll find a place somewhere." But who would hire such an old cowboy and a boy still wet behind the ears?

"I'm sure you could interest some Yankee soldier or his carpetbagger friend in your ranch," Martha Gilmore, Prissy's mother, suggested with a smirk. "They'd be only too willing to marry you to get their hands on a good piece of Texas ranch property."

Several of the young ladies looked dismayed. "Y-you wouldn't do something like that, would you, Milly?" asked Jane Jeffries, a young widow who still wore black despite losing her husband midway through the war.

"Of course not, Jane," Milly assured her. "I'm looking for a good Texas man, or at the very least, a Southerner. I do realize there are *some* things worse than being an old maid. Marrying a Yankee soldier or a carpetbagger certainly falls into that category."

"I'm relieved to hear you say so," Emily Thompson said from across the circle. "So what course of action *did* you have in mind?"

Milly stared out the open window of the church social hall. "I thought perhaps we could place an advertisement in a newspaper, not the *Simpson Creek News,* of course, but a larger city's newspaper such as the *Houston Telegraph.* It just so happens our Uncle William is the editor of that paper, so I'm sure he'd help us." She smiled at the other ladies. "We'll include a post office address where interested bachelors could reply. Of course they'd be required to send references, and a picture, if at all possible."

"You mean," asked Martha Gilmore, "to enlist mail order *grooms?*"

Milly blinked, startled to hear her idea summed up that way, as several around the circle tittered. She considered the phrase. "Yes, I suppose you could call them that."

"Oh, Milly, I don't know…" Sarah murmured uneasily.

Milly pretended she hadn't heard. Sarah was always apprehensive about daring new ideas. "Who's with me?" she asked, making eye contact with each in turn—Prissy Gilmore, Jane Jeffries, Ada Spencer, Maude Harkey, Emily Thompson, Caroline Wallace, Hannah Kennedy, Bess Lassiter, Polly Shackleford, Faith Bennett. And they met her gaze, some shyly, some boldly, but all with interest.

"How would such an ad read, Milly?" asked Ada Spencer curiously.

Milly thought back to what she had begun composing in her mind at the meeting once Mrs. Detwiler had redirected the conversation. "I'm open to suggestions, of course, but here's what I had so far," she said, pulling a folded sheet of paper from her reticule. "Wanted: Marriage-Minded Bachelors," she read aloud. "Quality Christian gentlemen who desire to make the acquaintance of refined, genteel young ladies with a view to matrimony are requested to send a letter to—and here we would need a name for our group, ladies—References are required, and those sending photographs will be given preference. Drunkards, Yankees, Carpetbaggers and other riffraff need not apply."

"I think that's excellent, Milly!" Maude Harkey cried, clapping. "Bravo! You've certainly covered everything."

Some of Milly's apprehension left her in the face of Maude's enthusiasm and the approving glances of several ladies around the circle. "Thanks, Maude," Milly said. "But we need a name for this group. What shall we call our organization? The Marriageable Misses? The Wedding Club?"

Mrs. Gilmore looked as if she wanted to say something but she held her peace.

"How about The Simpson Creek Society for Promotion of Marriage?" Caroline Wallace suggested.

It was a more formal name than Milly would have preferred, but she wanted each lady to feel she had a say in the formation of their organization, and everyone seemed to like this one.

"All right, that seems to be the consensus," Milly said. "That's what we'll call ourselves. The rest of the advertisement could read, 'Inquiries should be directed to the Simpson Creek Society for the Promotion of Marriage at post office box number—' Caroline, can we arrange for a post office box before we leave town so I know what number to put in the ad?"

Caroline, the daughter of the postmaster, nodded. "I happen to know number seventeen is empty. I'll tell Papa."

"Will you need any money for the advertisement, Milly?" asked Jane Jeffries. Several of the ladies' faces registered dismay. If there was one other thing the unwed ladies of Simpson Creek lacked, it was ready cash.

"I don't think so," Milly said, and hoped it was true. "I'll write to my uncle this very day, sending our advertisement copy." She was counting on Uncle William to run the advertisement gratis, or at the very least run it at a discount.

"Well, I think that went well, don't you?" Milly said, after the last of the ladies had gone home and she and Sarah were alone in the social hall. She munched on one of the few cookies that hadn't been devoured by the Simpson Creek Society for the Promotion of Marriage.

"Yes...yes, it did," Sarah said, her tone thoughtful as she scooped up the plates and cups filled with crumbs and remains of the lemonade. "They all seemed very excited about your ideas."

"But what about *you,* Sarah?" Milly asked. She hadn't been able to gauge Sarah's reaction during the meeting. "Are you going to be one of us, or do you think it's a foolish idea? Would you rather I hadn't suggested it?"

Sarah's green eyes lost focus. "I...I don't know.

Won't it look as if we're somewhat…oh, I don't know… *fast?*"

"Oh, I don't think so, not if the advertisement is worded properly, as I believe it is," Milly said. She had been very satisfied when the group agreed that the words she had composed in her head were perfect as they stood. "We'll be able to tell by the tone of their letters if they've gotten the wrong impression, I should think, and we simply won't extend an invitation to come and meet us."

"I suppose you're right…" Sarah said, but her tone was far from certain. "But Milly, what if—what if the men who answer the advertisement lie about their qualifications? What if they turn out to be men of bad character? Why, a man could say anything about himself on paper, and turn out to be quite the opposite," Sarah said, twisting a fold of her apron. "Why, he could be an outlaw, or a cardsharp—or a *Yankee!*"

"That's true," Milly admitted frankly. "But if we find that to be the case, we'll send them packing. And you know, there are no guarantees when one meets a man in the usual way either," she pointed out.

Sarah looked puzzled. "Whatever do you mean?"

"Just look at that woman in Goliad we heard about, Bertha McPherson," Milly said, with a wave of her hand, as if the woman stood before them. "She married that fellow from Goliad who courted her for six months, and once they tied the knot, she found out he still had a living wife back in St. Louis."

Sarah sighed. "I always thought we'd marry boys from Simpson Creek, boys we'd known all our lives."

"I know…" Milly had thought so, too. Just as she

had believed the brave talk of the boys who'd marched off to war, promising they'd be back, victorious, in six months. "Yes, what we're doing is a leap of faith," she admitted. "But would you rather take a chance, or die an old maid? *I* don't want to be called 'Old Maid Milly Matthews,' thank you very much."

"They're already calling you 'Marrying Milly'," Sarah said, then put a hand over her mouth as if she hadn't meant to say it.

Milly blinked. "Who's 'they'?"

"Folks in town," Sarah said, facing her sister as Milly also sank into a chair beside her. "I overheard Mr. Patterson talking to Mrs. Detwiler in the mercantile yesterday. They hadn't seen me come in. She was telling him what you'd said in the Ladies Aid Society meeting the other day. Folks in town are already calling us the Spinsters Club."

Milly winced but reached out and put an arm around her sister's shoulder. "We mustn't mind what people say, Sarah. People will always gossip." She hadn't missed the fact that Sarah had said *us,* and her heart glowed with love for her. Worried as she was, her sister was joining her in this project.

"Have you prayed about this?" Sarah asked. "I mean, I know we opened the meeting with prayer—that was a lovely prayer you said, by the way—but have you been praying about this? A lot?"

"Of course," Milly said. "I've been praying for months, ever since the war ended and those first few men started returning, and none of them were the single men on the Missing in Action lists. But I suppose we'd both feel more confident if we prayed now, right?" They had always prayed together, first as a family and now just the two of them, after losing first their mother and more recently their father. Milly had always found it a source of strength.

Sarah nodded. Milly took her hand, and they bowed their heads and sought the Lord's blessing on their enterprise.

Chapter Two

Nicholas Brookfield, late of Her Majesty's Bombay Light Cavalry, reined in the handsome bay he had purchased after leaving the stagecoach and studied Simpson Creek. A small town, more like a village really, consisting of one main street, with a sprinkling of buildings on both sides of the dusty thoroughfare. Signs proclaimed the presence of a saloon, a boardinghouse, a general store, a livery, a combination barbershop-bathhouse, and at the far end of the street, a church. Branching off from the middle of the main street was another road with several houses of various sizes, some sturdy-looking fieldstone or brick two-stories, others smaller and of more humble construction, wood and even adobe cottages.

He wondered if Miss Millicent Matthews lived in any of these, or if her home was out on one of the ranches he'd passed on the road into Simpson Creek. And for the twentieth time, he wondered if he was on a fool's errand. Had the intermittent fever he was prone to, and which had laid him low once again when he arrived in Texas a week ago, finally seared his brain, rendering him mad? What else explained why he'd let curiosity take control and come here in search of the writer of that intriguing advertisement, instead of going straight to Austin to the job that awaited him?

He glanced at his clothing, deeming it too dusty from his travels to make a good impression on a lady. Pulling out his pocket watch, a gift from his brother when Nicholas achieved the rank of captain, he discovered it was only eleven. He would do well, he decided, to bespeak a room at the boardinghouse and visit the barbershop-bathhouse before paying a call on Miss Matthews, assuming someone in this dusty little hamlet would tell him where he could find her.

"Have there been any inquiries about our advertisement?" Prissy Gilmore asked, after all the ladies of the Simpson Creek Society for the Promotion of Marriage had settled themselves in a circle in the church social hall.

"Not yet," Milly admitted, as cheerfully as she could manage. "But it *has* been only two weeks. It would take time for a man to read the advertisement, compose a letter, perhaps have a tintype taken if he doesn't have one ready, and for that letter to reach the Simpson Creek post office." Afraid of discouraging her friends, she wasn't about to admit she had made a pilgrimage to the post office every other day this week, and her only reward had been the letter she now brought out from her reticule.

"However," she said, smiling as she drew it out of the envelope and unfolded it, "I do have this note from our

Uncle William, who you will remember is the editor of the *Houston Telegraph*."

"Dear Millicent and Sarah," she read, *"I hope this letter finds you well. I wanted you to know I am in receipt of your rather interesting advertisement copy and have published it (though I must confess with some trepidation as to what your late father would have thought of your scheme) in accordance with your request. I have to say this advertisement caused no small amount of talk in the* Telegraph *office and around the town. Word of it and of your group has spread to those cities with whose newspapers we share articles, so it may be possible that you will receive inquiries from as far away as Charleston, South Carolina, and even New York City."*

Milly folded up the letter and stuck it triumphantly back in her pocket without reading the paragraph that followed, in which her Uncle William implored her to be very cautious in meeting the gentlemen who would write in response.

"So you see, ladies," she said, infusing every word with confidence, "our advertisement has made a stir. I'm sure we will begin receiving inquiries any time now—perhaps even in today's post!"

A pleased hum of excitement rose from the ladies sitting around her.

Maude Harkey raised her hand. "Milly, assuming these letters start arriving, we've never discussed how it will be decided who gets matched with whom. How will that take place?"

"That's a good question, and one I think the Society should decide as a group," Milly responded, settling her hands in her lap. "What do you think, ladies?" She watched as they all looked at one another before Jane Jeffries raised a timid hand.

"I think we should let the gentlemen decide," she announced, then ducked her head as if astonished at her own audaciousness.

"Yes, but how?" Milly prodded.

Jane shrugged.

"We could have a party," said Prissy Gilmore, who'd managed to avoid bringing her mother. "With chaperones, of course, so Mama won't have a fit—and the gentlemen could be presented to all of us. They could decide whom they preferred." She smoothed a wayward curl that had escaped her artful coiffure.

"Yes, but what if only one of them comes at a time?" Sarah asked. "Won't he feel awfully uncomfortable, as if he's on display like a prize bull at a county fair?"

"Well, he would be, wouldn't he?" Emily Thompson tittered. "Poor man. But perhaps it won't have to be that way. From the sound of that letter, it seems as if they might well come in *herds!*"

"Wouldn't that be wonderful? Then each of us could have our pick!" Ada Spencer said with a sigh, and everyone laughed at her blissful expression.

"Maybe the gentleman will express a preference as to the type of woman he's seeking," Maude Harkey said. "He might have a decided interest in short redheads, such as myself."

There was more laughter.

"Don't forget, ladies," Milly reminded them, "as more and more matches are made, the number of ladies looking over the applicants will be fewer and fewer.

Eventually there will be no more need for the Society,
God willing, for all of us will be married."

"Amen," Ada Spencer said. "But the fact remains, we
have yet to receive the first response to our advertisement. I hope we don't end up as the laughingstocks of
Texas."

Her words hung in the air, and once more the ladies
were glancing uneasily around at each other.

"I think we ought to pray about it now," Milly said.
"And you've all been praying about it at home, haven't
you?"

There were solemn nods around the circle.

"Very well, then," Milly said. "Who would like
to—"

Sarah raised her hand. "I think when we pray, we
ought to include something about God's will being done.
I mean, it might not be God's will for all of us to be
married, you know."

Milly opened her mouth to argue, then shut it again.
The idea that the Lord might *intend* for her to go through
life as an unmarried lady for whatever reason He had
was startling, but it could be true.

"You're right, Sarah," she said, humbled. "Would
you lead us in pr—"

Before she could finish her sentence, there was a
knock at the door of the social hall. Then, without waiting to be invited in, a tousle-headed boy flung open the
door.

Milly recognized Dan Wallace, Caroline's brother,
and son of the town postmaster.

Caroline called out, "Dan, is anything wrong? We're
having a meeting here—"

"I know, Caroline," Dan said. "But Papa said to show this gent where to go."

Caroline's brow furrowed, and Milly saw her look past her brother. "What gent?"

"He's waitin' outside. He came t' the post office. Says he's come in response to the advertisement y'all placed in that Houston newspaper. He's lookin' for Miss Milly, an' I knew she'd be here with you 'cause a' the meetin'."

Milly felt the blood drain from her face. It shouldn't be happening this way. A man couldn't have just *shown up*.

She looked uncertainly at the others. "But…but he was to have written a letter first," she protested, "so we could evaluate his application, then send him an invitation if we agreed he was a good candidate."

"Perhaps his letter got lost in the mail or delayed," Sarah pointed out, reasonable as always.

She supposed what Sarah had said *was* possible, Milly had to admit. Stagecoaches carrying the mail got robbed, or his letter could have fallen out of the mail sack and blown away, or gotten stuck to another going elsewhere…. But the man should have waited for a reply from them.

"I say an applicant is an applicant," Maude Harkey said. "He must have come a long way. Least we can do is see him and hear what he has to say."

Milly couldn't argue with that, she decided. They had prayed fervently that their advertisement would be answered, and it had been, though not in the way she had planned.

Now that the moment had come, though, she felt a

little faint. Her corset suddenly felt too tightly laced. It was hard to get a breath. She rose, wishing she had worn her Sunday best instead of this green-and-yellow-sprigged everyday dress, wished that she had time to pinch her cheeks…. Darting a glance at the others, she saw that all of them appeared to be wishing much the same.

"Well, by all means, invite him in, Dan," Milly said with a calmness she was far from feeling.

The boy looked over his shoulder at whoever stood beyond their sight and said, "You kin come in."

He was tall, taller by a head than Milly, which must put him at six feet or so, she thought absently, and so darkly tanned that at first Milly thought he was a Mexican. But then he doffed his wide-brimmed hat, and she saw that his hair gleamed tawny-gold in the light shed by the high window just behind him. His eyes were the blue of a cloudless spring sky, his nose straight and patrician. He wore a black frock coat with a matching waistcoat over an immaculate white shirt. He looked to be in his early thirties.

He was easily the most compelling man Milly had ever set eyes on.

He bowed deeply from the waist, and when he straightened, he smiled as his gaze roved around the circle of thunderstruck ladies.

"Good afternoon, ladies. My name is Nicholas Brookfield. I am looking for Miss Millicent Matthews." His eyes stopped at Sarah. "Are you Miss Matthews, by chance?"

"I—uh, that is, I'm S-Sarah Matthews, her s-sister…" Sarah stammered, going pale, then crimson. She gestured toward Milly. "That's Millicent."

The woman she pointed to was nothing like the image Nick had formed in his mind of Miss Millicent Matthews, being neither blonde nor short. She was tall and willowy, her figure hinting at strength rather than feminine frailty. Her hair gleamed like polished mahogany, so dark brown that it was nearly black, her eyes a changeable hazel under sweeping lashes, her lips temptingly curving rather than the pouting rosebud he had always thought the epitome of female loveliness.

In that instant, Nicholas Brookfield's ideal image of beauty was transformed. Millicent Matthews was the most striking woman he had ever encountered. He couldn't imagine why he had thought, even for a second, that she was blonde. Why on earth had *this* woman needed to place such an advertisement? Were the men of Texas blind as well as fools?

"Mr. Brookfield, I'm sorry, we weren't expecting you. In the advertisement we placed, we indicated that an interested gentleman was to send a letter. Is it possible your letter got lost in the mail?"

Nick had wondered if the woman would confront him for not following directions, but she had given him a way to save face, if he wanted to use it. Nick wouldn't take refuge in a lie, however, even a small one.

He gave her what he hoped was a dazzling smile. "I'm afraid I didn't want to wait upon an answer to a letter, Miss Matthews, the post being so slow, you understand. I'm here in Texas to take up a post in Austin, but I happened upon your advertisement and found it so intriguing that I rode on to Simpson Creek, purely out of curiosity."

"'Purely out of curiosity?'" she echoed, narrowing her eyes. "Does that mean you're *not* interested in marriage, sir? That you just came to see what sort of a desperate female would place such an advertisement?"

"Milly," her sister murmured, her tone mildly reproachful. "We shouldn't make Mr. Brookfield feel unwelcome. We haven't even given him a chance."

So Miss Matthews could be prickly. This rose had thorns. Then he heard his words as she must have heard them, and he realized how offensive his half-formed idea of meeting the lady and her associates merely as a lark before settling down to a dreary job was.

"I'm sorry," he said. "I didn't mean it to sound that I was merely looking to amuse myself at your expense, ladies. I…I truly was impressed with your initiative, and decided I wanted to meet you."

His reply seemed to mollify her somewhat. "I see," she said, studying him. Her eyes seemed to look deep into his soul. "You're British, Mr. Brookfield?"

Nick nodded. "From Sussex, in southeastern England. But I've been in India the past decade."

"I—I see," she said again, seemingly uncertain what to do now.

Nick was increasingly aware of their audience hanging on to every word. "I—that is, I wonder if we might speak privately?" He couldn't think properly with all of them staring at him, let alone produce the right words to keep her from dismissing him out of hand.

Suspicion flashed in those changeable brown-gold

eyes. For a moment Millicent Matthews looked as if she might refuse.

Nick added the one word he could think of to change her mind, and infused it with all the appeal he could muster. "Please."

She glanced at the others, but they were apparently all waiting for her to decide, for no one said a word or twitched a muscle.

"Very well," she said at last. "We can step outside for a moment, I suppose. Sarah, will you take over the meeting? If you'll follow me, Mr. Brookfield..." She led him down the hall past the sanctuary.

Pushing open the pecan wood door, he walked outside with her, around the side of the church past a small cemetery and into a grove of venerable live oak and pecan trees behind the church. Fragments of old pecan shells crunched under their feet.

It was pleasantly cool in this sun-dappled shade, though the heat of the afternoon shimmered just beyond the influence of the leafy boughs. Insects hummed. A mockingbird flashed gray, black and white as it flitted from one tree to another. A curved stone bench curled around half of the thick trunk of one of the trees, but Millicent Matthews didn't sit down; instead, she turned to face him.

"Mr. Brookfield, before we say anything more, I feel compelled to point out that I'm merely the one who composed the advertisement. There are several other ladies to choose from, as you saw. I assure you, it's quite all right if you find you prefer another of them..."

So she had a sense of fair play and generosity. Nick liked that about her. But somehow he knew her suggestion was something he didn't even want to consider. It was incomprehensible how he could sense that already, but there it was.

"I know you will find this difficult to believe, since we've only just met, and we really don't know each other at all," he said. "I can well understand that it appears I'm making a snap judgment, and perhaps I am, but I would like the opportunity to get to know you better. I—I find you very attractive indeed, Miss Matthews, and that's the simple truth—"

He broke off, somewhat nettled as he noticed she appeared to have suddenly stopped listening. "Miss Matthews…"

"Ssssh!" Millicent hissed, suddenly holding up her hand.

Then he realized she was listening to something beyond the trees, up the road. Then he heard it, too, the pounding of hooves coming closer and a voice calling *"Miss Milly! Miss Milly!"*

"That sounds like Bobby…what can be the matter?" She jumped up, her brow furrowed, and began running toward the front of the church. Nick followed.

Just as they reached the road, a lathered horse skidded to a sliding stop in front of them and a wild-eyed youth jumped off, keeping hold of the reins. The other ladies, doubtless hearing the commotion, poured outside, too.

"Miss Milly! Miss Sarah! You gotta come home quick! There was Injuns—Comanche, I think—they attacked, and I think Uncle Josh is dead!"

Chapter Three

"Indians? Josh is dead? We have to get back there!"

Nick saw the color leach from Millicent Matthews's face until it was white as sun-bleached bones. He stepped quickly forward to catch her, but although she trembled, she stood firm. It was Sarah, her sister, who swayed and might have gone down if one of the other ladies had not moved in to hold her up.

"Sarah! Are you all right?" Milly asked, rushing forward to her sister, whom the other woman had gently assisted to the ground before starting to fan her face.

"Yes…I think so…everything went gray for a moment…" Sarah said. "I'm all right, really, Caroline. Help me up."

Still pale but obviously embarrassed at her near-swoon, she scrambled to her feet.

"We've got to get home!" Milly cried, now that her sister was standing. Her gaze darted around until it settled on a wagon whose horses were tied at the hitching post next to his mount, then back to her sister. "Sarah, come on, let's get you into the wagon—" She braced her sister with an arm around her waist.

Caroline said, "I'll help you get her into the wagon and go home with you. Dan, you run down and tell Pa and the sheriff to round up the men and come out to the Matthews ranch. And bring the doctor, just in case.... Quick, now!" she added, when it seemed as if the lad would remain standing there, mouth agape.

Then Milly seemed to remember him. "Mr. Brookfield, I'm sorry...I have to go. I'm sorry, but I won't be able to—that is, perhaps one of the other ladies..."

"Oh, but I'm coming with you," he informed her, falling into step next to her as she and the other woman helped Sarah walk.

"Really, that's awfully kind of you, but it's not your trouble. There's no telling what we're going to find when we get there," she told him, as if that was the end of the matter. Her eyes went back to her sister as the other woman clambered into the bed of the wagon and stretched an arm down to assist Sarah. "Careful, Sarah..."

"Which is exactly why I'm going," Nick said. "There's no way on earth a gentleman would allow you to ride alone into possible danger. There might be savages lying in wait."

She looked skeptical of him and impatient to be off. "Thank you, but I'm afraid you don't understand about our Comanche—"

He saw how she must see him, as a civilized foreigner with no real experience in fighting, and interrupted her with a gesture. "I have a brace of pistols in my saddlebags," he said, jerking his head toward his horse. "And I know how to use them, as well as that shotgun you have mounted on the back of your wagon seat. Miss

Matthews, I have served in Her Majesty's army, and I have been tested in battle against hordes of murderous, screaming Indians—India Indians, that is—armed and out to kill me and every other Englishman they could. Let me come with you, at least until the men from town arrive."

His words seemed to act like a dash of cold water. "A-all right," she said, and without another word turned back to the wagon. She climbed with the graceful ease of long experience onto the seat and gathered up the reins. Before he could even mount his horse, she had backed up the wagon and snapped the reins over the horses' backs.

Milly's heart caught in her throat as the wagon rounded a curve and she spotted the smoke rising in an ominous gray plume over the low mesquite- and cactus-studded hill that lay between there and home. Unconsciously she pulled up on the reins and the wagon creaked to a halt in the dusty road.

"Oh, Milly, what if it's true? What if Josh is dead? Whatever will we do?" Sarah moaned from the wagon bed behind her.

Please, God, don't let it be true, Milly prayed. *Don't let Josh be dead. Nothing else really matters, even if they burned the house.* She saw out of the corner of her eye that the Englishman had reined in his mount next to them, as had Bobby.

Braced against the side of the wagon bed, Caroline Wallace gave Sarah a one-armed hug, but she looked every bit as worried.

"We'll deal with whatever we find," she said grimly,

fighting the urge to wheel the horses around and whip them into a gallop. What *would* they do, with only a boy not old enough to shave to help them run the ranch? "And the sooner we find out what that is, the better. Here, Mr. Brookfield," she said, reaching around the slatted seat for the shotgun. "Perhaps you'd better have this at the ready."

His eyes were full of encouraging sympathy as he leaned over to accept the firearm from her. "Steady on, Miss Matthews," he murmured. "I'll be with you."

It was ridiculous to take heart from the words of a stranger, a dandified-looking Englishman who claimed to have been a soldier, but there was something very capable in his manner and comforting in his words.

"I'll go ahead, shall I, and scout out the situation?" he suggested. "See if it's safe for you ladies to come ahead?"

"And leave us here to be picked off? No, thank you," she responded tartly, gesturing toward the rocky, brush-studded hills. She could picture a Comanche brave hiding behind every boulder and bush. "We'll go together." She clucked to the horses and the buckboard lurched forward.

She couldn't stifle a groan of pure anguish when she rounded the curve and spotted the smoldering ruin that was the barn. Just then the wind shifted and blew toward the wagon, temporarily blinding her with smoke and stinging her eyes. Had the house been burned to ashes like the barn? Where was Josh? Or rather, Josh's *body,* she corrected herself, knuckling tears away from her cheeks.

Then the wind shifted capriciously again and she

saw what she hadn't dared hope for—the house was still standing. So was the bunkhouse, which stood across from it and next to the barn. Why hadn't they been burned, too? But the pasture beyond, in which some fifty head of cattle and a dozen horses had been grazing when they'd left for the meeting, was empty. There was no sign of the Comanche raiders except for a hawk's feather that must have fallen from one of the braves' hair, sticking incongruously in a rosebush by the house.

"They left Josh on t'other side a' the barn," Bobby whispered, as if fearing that speaking aloud would bring the Comanches back.

She couldn't worry about the loss of the cattle right now or how they would survive. She had to see Josh.

"Caroline, stay with Sarah, please," she said to the woman, who still crouched protectively in the bed of the buckboard by her sister.

"I say, Miss Matthews," Nicholas Brookfield said beside her, "please allow me to go first. There's no need to subject yourself to this if there's nothing to be done for the chap."

It was so tempting to accept his offer, to spare herself the sight of the old man perhaps scalped or otherwise mutilated, lying in his blood. But old Josh had been their rock ever since their father had died, and she owed him this much at least.

"No," she said, letting her eyes speak her gratitude for his offer. "But please, come with me."

Still holding the shotgun at the ready, he led the way around the barn.

At first, she thought the old man *was* dead, sprawled

there in the dirt between the side of the barn and the empty corral. He was pallid as a corpse, his shirt saturated with dark dried blood. A deep gash bisected his upper forehead, dyeing his gray hair a dark crimson. A feathered shaft was embedded in each shoulder, pinning his torso to the ground, and his left pants leg was slashed midthigh. She caught a glimpse of a long, deep laceration beneath. Not far away, a corner of the barn still burned with crackling intensity. It was a miracle flying sparks hadn't set Josh's clothes alight.

And then she saw that Josh's chest was rising and falling.

"Josh?" she called, softly at first, afraid to trust her eyes, then louder, *"Josh?"*

His answer was a groan.

She rushed past Brookfield, falling to her knees beside the fallen cowboy. "Josh, it's me, Milly. Can you hear me?" Gingerly, she touched his face, not wanting to cause him any extra pain.

Josh's eyelids fluttered and then he opened one eye, blinking as he attempted to focus his gaze. "Miss Milly…sorry…I caught them redskins stealin' cattle… tried to drive 'em off with the rifle…" He squinted at the ground on his right side and sighed. "Looks like they got that, too. St-started…they started t' take my scalp…dunno what stopped 'em from finishin'…"

"Thank God," Milly murmured. But Josh couldn't hear her. He'd passed out again.

"Bobby, go get me some water from the well," Milly called over her shoulder. "And tell Sarah and Caroline to bring soap and a couple of clean sheets to make up the bed in the spare room for Josh."

"And Bobby, bring me a couple of knives," Brookfield called out, pulling off his black frock coat and throwing it over a fencepost in the nearby corral. He rolled up his sleeves past his elbows, revealing tanned, muscular arms. "And some whiskey if you can find it. Or any kind of liquor."

Milly turned startled eyes to him and saw that he knelt in the dirt beside her, oblivious of his immaculate white shirt and black trousers. "Mr. Brookfield, what are you going to do?"

With his bare hands, he was digging into the dirt beside Josh's wounded shoulder. "Before he comes around, I'm going to cut off the arrowheads. There's no way we can pull the arrow shafts out otherwise without injuring him further."

"Are you a doctor, Mr. Brookfield?"

He shook his head without looking at her, still digging in the dirt.

"Shouldn't we wait 'til the doctor gets here to do that?"

He shook his head again. "You can't even move the man to a bed until we pull out those arrows. I've seen the regimental doctor remove a spear from an unlucky sepoy before, if that makes you feel better."

He didn't explain what a sepoy was, or if the sepoy had lived through the procedure, but she didn't have any better idea. And Dan Wallace might not find the doctor right away. They didn't dare wait.

"I suppose you're right—you'd better go ahead. But even if Josh comes around, we don't have any whiskey or any other kind of spirits. Papa didn't hold with drinking."

"It'd be to pour on the wounds mostly, though if he regains his senses I'll be giving him some to drink," the Englishman answered, with that purposeful calm he'd exhibited ever since they'd received the awful news.

Just then Bobby dashed back, a pair of knives from the kitchen clutched in one hand, a half-full bottle of whiskey in the other.

Milly's jaw dropped. "Bobby, where on earth did you get that?"

Bobby scuffed the toe of his boot in the dust and refused to meet her eyes. "Mr. Josh, he had some in the bunkhouse. He didn't drink it very often," he added in a defensive tone, "an' never 'til the day's work was done. He never would let me have any, neither. Said I wasn't a man growed yet. He said I wasn't to tell you, but I reckon I needed t' break that promise."

"That's fine, Bobby," Nicholas Brookfield said, taking the bottle from him. "Now go hold one of the knife blades in the fire for a minute."

After the boy did as he was bid and returned with the knife, its tip still glowing red.

"Now you hold the hot knife, Miss Matthews—don't let it touch anything, while you, Bobby, hold Mr. Josh by the shoulder, just so…"

Obediently, she held the knife, watching as Bobby braced one of Josh's shoulders, holding it just far enough above the ground so that the arrow shaft was visible, while Brookfield sawed at the arrow shaft until he had cut it in two, then shifted the wounded man slightly so that he was no longer lying over the arrowhead and the tip of the shaft that was still embedded in the ground. Although Josh groaned, he did not wake up.

Brookfield and Bobby switched sides.

Caroline came from the house then, lugging a bucket of water that splashed droplets out the side with each step she took. "I thought it best to set Sarah to making up the bed in your spare room…" She stopped stock-still when she caught sight of Josh. "Heaven have mercy, he's in a bad way, isn't he? I was afraid she'd faint if she saw him like this."

Milly nodded, knowing Caroline was right. She'd felt dizzy herself, just looking at all that blood, but knew fainting was a luxury she didn't have. Josh needed her to be steady right now and help Nicholas Brookfield.

The Englishman had cut the other shaft away while she spoke to Caroline and was pouring the whiskey liberally over the wounds and his hands now. "I should have told you, but I'm going to need some bandages here as well. These wounds are liable to bleed when I pull the arrow shafts out."

Milly raced into the house, but Sarah had made the bed and had only just begun to rip the other sheet into strips for bandages.

"Milly, how is he? Is he going to make it?" Sarah's face was still pale, her eyes frightened.

"I don't know, Sarah. Hurry up with the bandages, will you? We're going to need a lot of them," Milly said, and dashed back to where Brookfield and Caroline waited for her. "She doesn't have them ready yet."

The Englishman frowned. "I have a handkerchief," he said, pulling a folded square of spotless linen from his breast pocket. "But we'll need something for the other side."

She knew she could send Caroline back to the house

and hope that Sarah had some strips of cloth ready by now, but Caroline had sat down, facing away from the wounded man, and was looking a bit green herself. Brookfield looked at her expectantly.

"Wait just a moment," she said, and turning around so that her back was to Brookfield, reached up under her skirts and began ripping the flounces off her petticoat. She wondered what he must be thinking. Surely the well-brought-up young ladies of England would never have done such a thing, but then, they didn't face Comanche attacks, did they?

His cool eyes held an element of admiration when she turned around again and showed him the wadded-up flounce.

"Good thinking, Miss Matthews. Do you think you could kneel by Josh's head and stand ready to apply the bandage quickly, as soon as I pull the first shaft out? I'll move quickly on to the other one, then. Bobby, you hold his feet. He'll probably feel this to some extent, and he's apt to struggle."

Bobby nodded solemnly, so what could Milly do but agree?

Chapter Four

What a woman, Nick marveled, after they'd carried the still-unconscious old man into the spare bedroom and settled him on the fresh sheets. Not only had Milly Matthews not succumbed to a fit of the vapors while she watched him pull out the arrow shafts and the blood welled up onto the skin, but she quickly halted her sister from doing so as well. None of the English ladies of his acquaintance would have done as well as she did. His admiration for her grew apace, right along with his desire to get to know her better.

Now, of course, was not the appropriate time to express such sentiments. "We'll have to keep an eye on those bandages over the wounds, in case he continues to bleed," he told Milly. "And watch for fever." He knew he did not have to tell her that neither would be a good sign—though fever was almost inevitable. Right now, at least, only a very small amount of dried blood showed through on the white cotton.

"We'll set up watches," she said in her decisive manner. "I'll take—"

They all tensed when the sounds of pounding hooves

reached them through the open window. Nick grabbed for the shotgun, which he'd gone back outside for as soon as they'd laid the old foreman down on the bed.

"Oh, my heavens, are they back to kill us, too?" Sarah cried, shrinking into the corner.

But Milly strode over to the window and flicked aside the homemade muslin curtains. "It's the posse from town. Maybe they'll be in time to catch those thieving Comanches and get our cattle back." From the slumped set of her shoulders, though, it didn't look as if she believed it.

A minute later, the men clomped inside, spurs clanking against the plank floor, bringing with them the smells of horses and leather and sweat. Milly went into the kitchen to meet them, and he heard her telling them about Josh's injuries and how "the Englishman" had pulled the arrows out of the foreman.

All nine of them were soon tramping back into the spare bedroom to see Josh for themselves—and to satisfy their curiosity about the foreign stranger, Nick assumed.

Milly introduced each one to him. They were an assorted lot, some were tall, some short, some had weathered faces and the lean, wiry-legged build of men who spent much time in the saddle. Others were paler and slighter, like shopkeepers. A couple seemed about the same age as Nick; three were younger, boys really, and the rest had graying or thinning hair. All of them nodded cordially to Nick, and all appeared dressed to ride except for the oldest, whom he had seen climbing out of a two-wheeled covered buggy.

"And last but not least is Doctor Harkey," said Milly,

indicating the older man now bending over Josh and peering under the bandages. Doctor Harkey straightened as his name was called, and reached out a hand to Nick.

"You did well, it appears," he told Nick. "Doubt I could've done better myself, though of course only time will tell if old Josh will survive his injuries," he added, looking back at the unconscious man. "Are you a doctor?"

"Nothing like that, sir, but I'm thankful to hear you don't think I made things worse," Nick said.

"He was a soldier in India," Milly informed the doctor.

"I hate t' interrupt, but are we gonna stand around jawin' or are we gonna ride after them Comanches?" asked a beefy, florid-faced middle-aged man. "While we're talkin', those murderin' redskins 're gallopin' away with them cattle." He punctuated his words with a wide sweeping gesture toward the outside.

All the men of the posse straightened and started heading for the door.

Nick stood. "I'd like to go along, if you gentlemen don't mind. I can use their shotgun, and I have my pistols. That is, if you feel you'll be all right here, Miss Matthews."

Milly nodded, obviously surprised by his announcement.

Doctor Harkey stood up. "I'm staying here at least until the posse returns. Josh needs me more than they do."

The men of the posse looked dubiously at Nick. The beefy man found his voice first. "That's right kindly of you, stranger, but y'ain't exactly dressed fer it," he said, eyeing Nick's blood-stained black frock coat and trousers. "And we didn't bring no extra horse."

"That's my bay standing out there next to the wagon, still saddled. And this suit is probably already ruined, so it makes no difference."

"We can get him some of Josh's clothes—they're about the same size," Milly said. "Bobby, run and fetch them."

The youth, who had been standing by the door, did as he was told, gangly arms flying, boot heels thudding on the floor.

"And he could use Papa's rifle," Sarah said, springing up from her seat. "I'll go get it." She excused herself as she pushed past the men.

The beefy-faced man turned back to Nick. "We'll wait five minutes, no longer, Brookfield. And I'll warn you, we'll be ridin' hard and waitin' for no one. This ain't gonna be no canter in th' park. You fall behind, you're on your own."

"You needn't concern yourself—I can keep up," Nick informed him coolly, holding his gaze until the other man looked away first.

Five minutes later, dressed in the old foreman's denims, work shirt, boots and floppy-brimmed hat, he was galloping across the field with the rest.

"He's quite remarkable, your Mr. Brookfield," Sarah said, as they looked through the window in the spare bedroom as the riders became swallowed in the dust in the distance. She had relaxed now that the doctor arrived and old Josh was sleeping peacefully. "Why, he just took charge, didn't he? I never would have imagined someone dressed like a greenhorn could act so capable."

"And that English accent," Caroline put in with a dreamy sigh. "I reckon I could listen to him talk for hours…"

"He's not *my* Mr. Brookfield," Milly corrected her sister. She did not want to admit to anyone, just yet, how impressed she had been with the way Nicholas Brookfield had jumped right into the midst of their troubles. She would not have expected any man who'd come to town with the simple purpose of meeting a gaggle of unmarried ladies to do as he had done, doctoring a gravely wounded man, and riding with men he had never met in pursuit of the savages. And she supposed if she had nothing else to think about, the Englishman's accent *did* fall very pleasantly on ears used to Texas drawls. But right now she had to wonder how they were going to survive, so she couldn't think about such frivolous things.

"Caroline, I can take you back to town in the buckboard, if you want," she said, changing the subject. "The horses are still hitched up."

"No, thank you, not with a bunch of wild Indians in the area," the postmaster's daughter said. "Besides, I'll just wait 'til Papa comes back with the posse and ride back with him. Meanwhile, I'll make myself useful around here. Sarah, why don't we go see what we can whip up for supper? Doc Harkey, you probably missed your dinner, didn't you?"

The old physician looked up from Josh's bedside. "I did, because Maude was at that meeting with y'all. She said she'd fix it as soon as she got home…but of course no one could've foreseen what happened. Anything will be fine for me, girls. I'm not picky. Josh'll need some broth tomorrow, but I imagine he won't be taking any nourishment tonight."

"While you two are doing that," Milly said, "I'll unhitch the buckboard, then see if I can wash the blood out of Mr. Brookfield's clothes. I'm sure glad he could wear Josh's clothes. He must not know how the mesquite thorns and cactus would rip that fine cloth to shreds."

"Take a pistol outside with you," Sarah admonished, "just in case."

Milly was sure she had just nodded off beside the old cowboy's bedside when she was awakened by the sound of a cow bawling from the corral.

I must still be dreaming, because the Indians took all the cattle and most of the horses yesterday.

Then the door creaked open. The gray light of dawn—it had been midnight when she had sent the doctor to sleep in their father's bed—illuminated the dusty, rumpled figure of Nicholas Brookfield, while from the kitchen wafted the sound of her sister's voice mingling with the low voices of the other men and the smell of coffee.

"Did you…did you catch them?" she finally asked, though his weary eyes had already telegraphed the answer.

"No. We followed them until their tracks split up, each pair of horses following some of the cattle. We would've turned back sooner if the moon hadn't been full, but it was too dark to track. By that time we were considerably far from here, so we're just now getting back. But the good news is that either they missed some of the cattle and horses, or some managed to break away, because we found several along the way. So we rounded up a score or so of cattle and half a dozen horses."

Milly straightened, fully awake now. "That *is* good news. Better than I'd dared hope for." At least they wouldn't starve, although she'd hoped to sell the full herd to a cattle drover next spring. Now they might have to sell some of the horses to buy more stock. In time, more calves would be born, and the herd would grow again—if the Comanche left their ranch alone. But raiding Indians were a fact of life in this part of Texas, and probably would be for a long time to come. Until the Federal army managed to contain them in reservations or kill them, one took his chances with the Indians or moved elsewhere.

"How is he?" he asked, nodding toward the supine figure on the bed.

"He had a restless night," Milly answered, her gaze following his. "The doctor gave him some laudanum before I took over, and got some willow bark tea in him while he was lucid, for the fever, but he's been sleeping since then. He hasn't had any more bleeding."

"Thank God for that," he said, rubbing a beard-shadowed cheek.

"Yes. And you've done more than I could've possibly asked for, Mr. Brookfield," she said, giving him a grateful smile. "I smell breakfast cooking out there. Why don't you join the other men and eat, and then I'll hitch up the wagon and take you back to town. Or you could take a nap in the bunkhouse first, if you'd like. You must be exhausted."

"I'm not leaving, Miss Matthews," he informed her. "You're going to need some help around here, while your foreman convalesces."

"But...but you're not a cowboy," Milly said. "You said you had a position waiting for you in Austin. I couldn't possibly ask you to—"

"You haven't asked. I've offered. And I couldn't possibly leave two women to cope alone out here, with nothing more than a lad to help you," he said reasonably. "It wouldn't be right."

"But I could probably get someone from around here to help, until Josh is back on his feet," she said, not wanting to think about the possibility that Josh might not be able to resume his responsibilities. He wasn't out of the woods yet, and wouldn't be for a few days, Doc Harkey had said. He could still die if infection set in. "You know nothing of handling cattle and all the rest of the things a cowboy does."

"I can learn," he insisted stubbornly. "Bobby can teach me, and in time, Josh can, too. As for the men around here, it sounds as if they all have their own ranches to tend. Most of them thought you should sell out and move into town," he said. "Mr. Waters said something about making you an offer," he said.

Milly blinked. It didn't surprise her that Bill Waters saw this attack as a good time to persuade her to sell her property to him. He'd always wanted the Matthews property, because it abutted his land but had better access to Simpson Creek.

"Now, if you *want* to do that, I'd certainly understand," Nicholas went on. "But I got the idea you wanted to stay here. And in that case, you'll need me."

She stared at him while he waited calmly, watching her. Should she take him up on his offer? Could she trust him, or would he disappear as soon as he realized what a hard life he was signing up for, even temporarily? Was he just trying to impress her with his generosity, in an effort to woo her, to get her to let her guard down? Might he try to take liberties with her once she was depending on him?

"If you would feel more secure about allowing me to stay on and help you," he began, "you may dismiss what I said in the churchyard before all this happened, about getting to know you better. I know you have a lot on your mind right now besides courting, and if you only want me to serve as a cowhand, I believe you call it, and a guard to protect you and your sister, I'll understand."

"I…I don't know what to say," Milly managed at last. "What you're offering is…more than generous."

"Girl, I think you better take him up on it," a voice rasped from the bed beside them, and they both started.

"Josh, you're awake!" she cried. How long had he been listening? "How do you feel?"

"Like I been stomped on by a herd a' cattle with hooves sharp as knives," Josh said, smiling weakly. "With a little luck I reckon I'll make it, though. But it's gonna be a while afore I'm fit t'manage this here ranch an' keep young Bobby from daydreamin' the day away. This here Englishman's willin' to help you out, so I reckon you should accept an' say thank you to the good Lord fer sendin' him."

Chapter Five

Before Josh had begun speaking, Nick had watched the conflicting emotions parading across Milly's face—doubt, trust, fear, hope. Now, at the old cowboy's urging, the battle was over and trust had won—trust in old Josh's opinion, if not in Nick himself, as yet.

"Josh has never steered us wrong," she said, smiling down at the old cowboy and then back at Nick. "So I will take you up on your very kind offer, Nicholas Brookfield, at least until Josh is back on his feet."

He gave both of them a brilliant smile, then bowed. "Thank you," he said. "I'm honored. I shall endeavor to be worthy of the trust you've placed in me."

Milly looked touched, but Josh gave a chuckle that had him instantly wincing at the movement to his ribs. "Boy, that was a might pretty speech for what you just signed up for—a lot a' hard work in the dust and heat."

"I'll be very dependent on your advice, sir."

"I—I can't pay you anything for the time being," Milly said apologetically. "Just your room and board."

"My needs are simple," Nick said. "Room and board

will be plenty." He was only a third son of a noble-man, but he still wasn't exactly a pauper, so he had little need of whatever sum most cowboys were paid a month beyond their keep. He would have to write to the bank in Austin that was handling his affairs and notify them that his address would be in Simpson Creek, for now.

"I suppose you could have my father's bedroom when the doctor leaves..." Milly mused aloud.

"That won't be necessary," he replied quickly. "The bunkhouse will be fine for me."

Her forehead furrowed. "But...surely you've never slept in such humble circumstances," she protested. "I mean...in a bunk bed? I imagine you're used to much better, being from England and all."

He thought for a moment of his huge bedchamber back home in East Sussex at Greyshaw Hall, with its canopied bed and monogrammed linen sheets, and his comfortable quarters in Bombay and his native ser-vant who had seen to his every need. Yes, he had been "used to much better," but he had also experienced much worse.

"Miss Matthews, I told you I was a soldier until recently, and while on campaign I have slept on a camp cot and even on the ground. I assure you I will be fine in the bunkhouse. Besides, I cannot properly be a cowboy unless I sleep there, can I?" he asked lightly, knowing it had been innocence that had led her to offer him her father's old room.

"But—"

"Miss Milly, you can't be havin' him sleepin' in the same house with you two girls," Josh pointed out, with a meaningful nod toward the kitchen, from where the sounds of conversation and the clinking of silverware against plates still floated back to them. "Once the gossips in town got wind a' that, they'd chew your reputation to shreds."

Nick could see that in her effort to be properly hospitable, Milly hadn't thought of how it would look for him to stay in the house.

"He'd best sleep out in th' bunkhouse, where the greatest danger'll be my snorin', once I get back on my feet," Josh said with a wink.

"It's decided, then," Nick said. All at once his long night in the saddle caught up with him and before he could catch himself, he yawned.

"Good heavens, I'd forgotten how exhausted you must be, Mr. Brookfield!" Milly exclaimed. "You've been up all night! Go on out to the kitchen and get yourself some breakfast, like I said, while I take some sheets out to the bunkhouse and make up a bed for you," she said, making shooing motions.

He remained where he was for a moment. "I suppose if I'm going to work for you, Miss Milly, you had better start calling me Nick," he said, holding her gaze.

He was delighted to see he could make Milly Matthews blush—and such a charming blush it was, too, spreading upward from her lovely, slender neck to her cheeks and turning them scarlet while her eyes took on a certain sparkle. Immediately she looked away, as if she could pretend by sheer force of will that it hadn't happened.

He saw Josh watching this little scene, too, but there was no censure in the old cowboy's gaze, only amusement.

"You'd best hurry on out to the kitchen like Miss Milly said, Nick. The way those galoots out there eat, they're liable not to leave you a crumb."

Snatching up clean, folded sheets from a cedarwood chest in the hallway, Milly followed Nick. Caroline Wallace was in the kitchen, pouring coffee. She and the handful of men standing around forking scrambled eggs from their plates nodded at her or mumbled "Good morning."

Threading her way through them, she found Sarah at the cookstove, talking to Doc Harkey.

"How's Josh?" Sarah had taken the evening watch, but she was no night owl, and had gone to bed when Milly relieved her. But Milly was never at her best in the morning or at cooking, so she was grateful Sarah was up with the sun and feeding the hungry men.

"Awake. I can tell he's going to make it, 'cause he's already ornery," Milly said with a laugh.

"I'll go in and have a look at him," Doc Harkey said, and waded through the throng of men toward the back hall.

Sarah looked questioningly at the armload of sheets Milly carried.

"Mr. Brookfield has very kindly offered to stay on and help us while Josh is laid up," she said, keeping her tone low so only Sarah could hear, and nodding toward Nick. He was talking to one of the other men while spooning clumps of scrambled eggs onto his plate to join a rasher of bacon and a thick slice of bread. "I'm just going to make up a bed in the bunkhouse for him."

"I see." Sarah's knowing eyes spoke volumes and she

grinned. "Well, isn't that nice of him? You have your very own knight in shining armor."

"Yes, *we* do," Milly corrected her in a quelling tone. "It is very kind of him, though he's never done ranch chores before. But he seems to think Josh can advise him and Bobby can show him what he needs to do."

"He seems like the kind of man who can do anything he sets his mind to," Sarah commented. "All right, you go make up the bed, but once these fellows go home, you go on to bed."

"Oh, I slept a little in the chair," Milly protested. "I'll be all right."

"I'm sure it wasn't enough."

"Thanks for handling breakfast," Milly said. "How did you ever manage?"

"The eggs were from yesterday morning, the bacon from the smokehouse. I'm sure I don't know what we're going to do after that. I found a few hens roosting in the trees, and that noisy rooster, but I'm sure the barn fire killed the rest of them."

"We'll make it with God's help, and one day at a time," Milly said, determined not to give way to anxiety. Only yesterday morning Sarah had been gathering eggs, while she had been planning a meeting to marry off the women in Simpson Creek. Now she had bigger problems to worry about.

"You're right, Milly," Sarah said, squaring her shoulders. "I guess we won't be eating chicken for a while until the flock builds up again."

"Or beef," Milly said.

"We'll have to send Bobby to look in the brush. Maybe some of the pigs made it."

* * *

Weariness nagged at Milly's heels by the time she finished making up the bed in the bunkhouse and trudged back across the yard. The men who'd ridden in the posse were in the process of departing, some saddling their horses, some already mounted up and waiting for the others. Caroline was riding double with her father.

At Milly's approach, Bill Waters handed his reins to Amos Wallace and headed out to intercept her.

"Mr. Waters, I want to thank you for taking charge of the men and doing your best to find our cattle," she said, extending a hand.

"You're welcome, little lady," he said in his usual bluff, hearty manner. "I'd do anything for Dick Matthews's daughters, and that's a fact. Wish we could've caught them thievin' redskins and gotten all of the cattle and horses back, instead of just some." He shrugged. "It's a shame this has happened, it surely is," he said, gesturing at the charred remains of the barn, from which a wisp or two of smoke still rose. "Now, I think you ought to reconsider my offer to buy you out. You could find rooms in town, take jobs…or move on to some big city somewhere. Don't you see it's the only sensible thing to do now that this has happened?"

"Thanks, Mr. Waters. We'll think about it," she said, as she had so many times before, ever since Pa had died. She saw by his exasperated expression that he knew she was only being polite.

"You need to do more than just think about it. Your pa would want me to make you see reason, I know he would!"

He was getting more red in the face as he talked. A vein jumped in his forehead. Milly fought the urge to pluck the hanky he had sticking out of his pocket and wipe his brow.

"The good Lord knows I'd hoped somethin' might grow between my boy Wes and you or Sarah, once the war was over. But it didn't work out that way."

Wesley Waters was one of the Simpson Creek boys who had not returned. Milly, Sarah and Wes had been friendly, but never anything more. But Milly believed his father hadn't wanted a romance between Wes and either of the Matthews girls nearly as much as he'd wanted a means of joining the Matthews land to his.

"Just tell me, how are you two going to cope out here, with Josh laid up and only that no-account boy t'help you?" He made a wide arc with his arm, including the whole ranch.

"We'll be all right, Mr. Waters. Mr. Brookfield has very kindly offered to stay on and help us while Josh is laid up."

He blinked at her. "That foreigner? What does he know about ranchin'? Beggin' yer pardon, Miss Milly, but have you been spendin' too much time in the sun without your bonnet? And that scheme of yours of invitin' men here t'marry is just plumb foolishness. Your pa would want me to tell you that, too!"

Temper flaring, Milly went rigid. "Mr. Waters, the way you're talking, I'm not sure you ever really knew my father after all. My pa always encouraged me to pray about a problem, then use my brain to solve it."

"And this is the solution your brain cooked up?" he said, pointing an accusing finger at Nick, who had just come out onto the porch. "Bringing an outsider—a *foreigner*—to Simpson Creek?"

Nick crossed the yard in a few quick strides. From where he had been, Milly knew he could not have heard Bill Waters's words, but he'd seen the finger pointed at him, for he asked quietly, "Is there a problem, Miss Matthews?"

She could have kissed him for coming to her side just then. "No, Mr. Waters was just fretting about his need to leave and go take care of his own ranch. But I assured him we'd be fine, with you to help us."

She saw Waters try to stare Nick down, but Nick returned his gaze calmly. "I'm sure Miss Matthews appreciates your concern," he said. "And I assure you I'll do everything in my power to ensure her safety and that of her sister." He offered his hand, which Waters pretended not to see.

"I'll count on that, Brookfield," he growled. "Good day, Miss Milly," he called over his shoulder as he stalked off to his waiting horse.

Bill Waters is nothing but a patronizing hypocrite, trying to hide his greed under a cloak of concern! thought Milly.

"What did he say to you? You're shaking," Nick observed, still keeping his voice low as Waters led the way out of the yard.

Milly was still stinging at Waters's condescending words, but she didn't want to repeat what the old rancher had said about Nick. Just then, she was saved from the necessity of talking about it by the arrival of the circuit preacher's buggy rolling into the barnyard.

"Reverend Chadwick, how nice of you to visit,"

she called, reaching the buggy just as the silver-haired preacher set the brake and stepped out of his buggy.

"Miss Milly, I was in Richland Springs. I was so upset to arrive back in town this morning and hear what had happened to you," he said, embracing her, then staring with dismay at the blackened ruin of the barn. "I came straight here. I didn't stop any longer than it took to water the horses," he said.

"Reverend Chadwick, a circuit rider can't be everywhere at once. We certainly understand that," Milly protested.

"And how is Josh?"

She told the preacher about their foreman's injuries. "I'm sure he'd be pleased to see you," she said. "Come inside. But before you do, Reverend, I'd like you to meet Mr. Nicholas Brookfield, who'll be helping us out here while Josh recovers."

Chapter Six

After introductions were made, Milly mercifully excused Nick and sent him to get some sleep. He'd thought at first he'd never be able to fall into slumber on the thin ticking-covered straw mattress in the middle of the hot Texas day.

The next thing he knew, though, the creaking of the door opening woke him as Bobby clumped into the room and started rummaging in the crate at the foot of his bed.

"Oh, sorry, didn't mean t'wake you, sir," the youth apologized, straightening.

"No need to apologize," he told the youth. "I never meant to sleep so long. And you'd probably better start calling me Nick, too," he told the boy.

Bobby looked gratified but still a little uneasy. "How 'bout Mr. Nick? Uncle Josh says t' be respectful to my elders."

"Fair enough." The angle of the shadows on the wall told Nick hours had passed even before he reached for the pocket watch he had left on the upended crate that served as bedside table and saw that it was four o'clock.

He'd slept the day away! Milly, her sister and Bobby had no doubt taken on tasks he should have been doing.

"What needs to be done?"

Bobby traced a half circle with the toe of one dusty boot, apparently also uncomfortable with the idea of giving an adult orders.

"I—I dunno, s—Mr. Nick. Mebbe you best ask Miss Milly."

"All right, I'll do that."

He found Milly in the kitchen, shelling black-eyed peas into a bowl in her lap. Sarah, her back to the door, was kneading dough. The delicious odor of roasting ham wafted from the cookstove.

"Oh, hello, Nick," Milly said. "Did you have a good sleep?"

"Too good," Nick said. "I want to apologize for lying abed so long when there's so much to be done."

"Horsefeathers," Milly Matthews responded with a smile. "You must have needed it."

Her lack of censure only made him feel guiltier, somehow. "Did you get some rest, ma'am?"

She shook her head. "I'll sleep tonight."

"As I should have waited to do. I only meant to lie down for an hour. This won't happen again, Miss Milly, Miss Sarah."

"Don't be so hard on yourself, Nick," Sarah admonished, looking over her shoulder.

"Thank you, but I intend to be more of a help from now on. What should I be doing now?"

Milly's hands paused, clutching a handful of unshelled pods. "It's a couple of hours 'til supper—not enough time to get started on any rebuilding projects.... It might be a good idea if you and Bobby were to saddle up and go for a ride around the ranch so you can get an idea of how far the property extends and make a survey of what needs to be done. Oh, and you'll be passing the creek that runs just inside the northern edge. You and Bobby could take a quick dip and get cleaned up," Milly added, eyeing his cheeks and chin.

"A dip sounds good." Nick ran his fingers over the stubbly growth, imagining how scruffy he looked. He was glad he'd kept his razor in his saddlebag. He didn't want to look unkempt around this lovely woman he was trying to impress.

"Take your pistol with you," Milly called as he headed for the door. "You never know what you might meet out there in the brush."

"Do you mean Indians?"

She nodded. "Or rattlesnakes. They like to sun themselves on the rocky ledges that line one side of the creek. There's a little cave in those ledges. Sarah and I used to play there and pretend it was our cottage until we saw a snake at its entrance."

"Then I'll be sure and take my dip on the other side." He'd had enough encounters with cobras in India to have a healthy respect for poisonous snakes of any kind.

"Don't let Bobby dillydally in the creek," she admonished. "Supper's at six and Reverend Chadwick brought a big ham with him on behalf of the congregation."

"If Bobby wants to stay in the creek, I shall eat his share of the meat," he said with a wink.

* * *

Nick was as good as his word, riding into the yard with Bobby at quarter 'til the hour. By the time they'd unsaddled and turned the horses out in the corral, the grandfather clock in the parlor was chiming six times.

"Here we are, ma'am, right on schedule," Nick said, pronouncing it in the British way—"shedule" instead of "schedule." She watched him, noting the way his still-damp hair clung to his neck while he sniffed with obvious appreciation of the savory-smelling, covered iron pot she carried to the table with the aid of a thick dish towel.

"Your promptness is appreciated," she said lightly, although what she was really appreciating was the strong, freshly shaved curve of his jaw. Nick Brookfield was compelling even when tired and rumpled; when rested and freshly bathed, he was a very handsome man, indeed. She wrenched her eyes away, lest he catch her staring. "You can sit over there, across from Bobby," she said, pointing to a chair on the far side of the rect-angular, rough-hewn table that had been laid with a checkered gingham cloth.

"How about Josh? Would you like me to take him his supper and help him eat first?"

"Oh, he's already eaten," Sarah said. "He's not up to anything but a little soup yet, but he took that well at least. Maybe tomorrow he can eat a little more and even join us at the table."

Milly was moved that Nick had thought of the injured old cowboy's needs before his own. She watched now as he seated himself gracefully, then waited.

"Nick, since this is your first meal with us, would

you like to say the blessing?" You could tell a lot about a man by the way he reacted to such a request, Pa always said.

Nick hesitated, but only for a moment. "I'd be honored," he said, and bowed his head. "Lord, we'd like to thank You for this bountiful meal and the good people from the church who provided it, and the hands that prepared it. And we thank You for saving the house, and Josh, and please protect the ranch and those who live here from the Indians. Amen."

"Thank you. That was very nice, wasn't it, Milly?" Sarah asked.

"Uh-huh." Milly thought Nick sounded like a man accustomed to speaking to his Lord, but Pa had also said sometimes folks could talk the talk, even if they didn't walk the walk. "Here, Nick, take some ham," she said, handing him the platter, while she passed a large bowl of black-eyed peas flavored with diced ham to Bobby. He took a couple of slices, then passed it down to Sarah.

"We always pass the meat to Bobby last, because there'll be nothing left after he's had a chance at it," Sarah teased from her end of the table.

Bobby, who'd been watching the progress of the ham platter as it made its way down the table, just grinned.

"He's still a growing lad, aren't you, Bobby?" Nick said, smiling.

"I reckon I am," Bobby agreed. "Uncle Josh says I got hollow legs. Look, Miss Milly, I think my arms have growed some." After helping himself to a handful of biscuits, he extended an arm. The frayed cuff extended only a little past the middle of his forearm.

"*Grown* some," Milly corrected automatically, taking a knifeful of butter and passing the butter dish. "I suppose I'll have to buy some sturdy cloth at the mercantile next time I'm there and make you a couple of new ones. Josh probably needs a couple, too, though I know he'll say just to patch the elbows." She sighed. While making clothing was actually something she was good at, even better than Sarah, trying to find the cash to buy cloth or anything extra right now would be difficult. "Nick, what did you think of our land?" she said, deliberately changing the subject. She could fret about Bobby's outgrown shirts later.

"It seems good ranch country, to my novice eyes," he said, with a self-deprecating smile. "Much bigger than I thought. We didn't even get to the western boundary, or we would have been late returning."

"It's actually one of the smaller ranches in San Saba County," Milly said, but she appreciated how impressed he seemed.

"Is that right? Back in Sussex, you two would be prominent landowners. They'd have called your father 'Squire.' Most English country folk have very small plots and rent from the local noble or squire. I noticed there's fence needing repair along your boundary with Mr. Waters's land, by the way."

Before she could stop herself, another sigh escaped. "Yes, he won't repair it. He doesn't think there should be fences—'Just let the cattle run wild 'til the fall roundup, just like we always did,'" she said, deepening her voice to imitate the man. "I suspect he used to brand quite a few yearlings as his that were actually ours, before Pa put up his fence."

"Has he always been a difficult man?"

Milly shrugged. "He isn't really difficult, only set in his ways." He hadn't acted this way when Pa was alive, of course. And before the war he had cherished dreams of gaining the ranch by his son marrying Milly, or even Sarah. Milly supposed she couldn't blame the man for wanting to enlarge his property by persuading her to sell out—and only time would tell if he had been right that a woman couldn't manage a ranch.

Suppertime passed pleasantly. Nick Brookfield had perfect table manners and ate like a man with a good appetite, although not with the same fervor that Bobby displayed, as if he thought every meal would be his last. When it was over, he thanked them for the delicious meal, especially Sarah for the lightness of her biscuits, which brought a grateful warmth to her sister's eyes.

"Perhaps you should tell me what I should be doing tomorrow," he said to Milly, as Sarah began to clear away the dishes.

"I think I'll let Josh do that," she said. "Why don't you go visit with him now for a while? Bobby can see to the horses and the chickens."

"I will." He rose. "Would it be all right if sometime tomorrow I went into town? I need to pick up my valise at the boardinghouse, and let the proprietress know I won't be needing the room."

"Of course," she said. So he had taken a room at the boardinghouse before coming to meet her and the rest of the ladies, she mused. He'd intended to spend some time getting to know her. "Actually, we need sugar from the general store, if you wouldn't mind picking it up. Oh, and perhaps some tea? Don't Englishmen prefer to drink that?" At least, she thought she had enough egg money in the old crockery jar to cover those two items. She was going to have to scrimp until they had enough eggs to spare from now on.

"Coffee is fine, Miss Milly. You needn't buy anything specifically for me."

An hour later, he found Milly ensconced in a cane back rocking chair on the porch, reading from a worn leather Bible on her lap.

"What part are you reading?" he said, looking down at it. "Ah, Psalm One—'Blessed is the man who walks not in the counsel of the ungodly, nor standeth in the way of sinners, nor sitteth in the seat of the scornful,'" he quoted from memory.

Her hazel eyes widened. "Were you a preacher, as well as a soldier and occasional field surgeon?" she asked, gesturing toward the rocker next to her in an unspoken invitation to sit down.

He sat, smiling at her question. "No, but my second oldest brother is in holy orders, vicar of Westfield. They'll probably make him a bishop one day. Any Scripture I know was pounded into my thick head by Richard when I was a lad."

"And do you read the Bible now?" she asked.

He wished he could say he did. "I...I'm afraid I haven't lately."

He could see her filing the information away, but her eyes betrayed no judgment about the fact.

"And how did you find Josh? Does he need anything? Is he in pain?"

"He's not in pain, no, but he needs a goodly dose of

patience," he said, appreciating the fine curve of Milly's neck above the collar of her calico dress. "He's restless, fretting over the need to lie there and be patient while he heals. But I think he's reassured that I can help Bobby handle the 'chores'—" he gave the word the old man's drawling pronunciation, drawing a chuckle from her "—and keep this place from utter ruin until he can be up and around again. Oh, and he says there's no need to sit up with him tonight, if you'll let him borrow that little handbell of your mother's he can just ring if he needs you."

"Hmm. That sounds just like him. I'd better check on him a couple of times tonight at least. I can just picture him trying to reach the water pitcher and tearing open those wounds again. That old man would rather die than admit a weakness."

Nick chuckled. "He said you'd say that, too."

They were silent for a while. Nick appreciated the cool breeze and the deepening shadows as the fiery orange ball sank behind the purple hills off to their right.

"Nick, why did you leave India, and the army—if you don't mind my asking, that is?" she added quickly.

She must have seen the reflexive stiffening of his frame and the involuntary clenching of his jaw.

"It's getting late, and I'm keeping you from your reading," he said, rising.

"I'm sorry, that was rude of me to pry. Please forgive me for asking," she said, rising, too. Her face was dismayed.

"It's all right," he told her. "I'll tell you about it sometime. But it's a long story." He'd known the question would come, but it was too soon. He wasn't ready to shatter her illusions about him yet.

Chapter Seven

As Nick tied his bay at the hitching post outside the general store, he saw two men standing talking at the entrance, one with his hand on the door as if he meant to go inside. Nick recognized one of them as Bill Waters, the neighboring rancher who'd pressured Milly to sell out yesterday. He'd never seen the other one, the one with his hand on the door.

"Hank, I'm tellin' you, the problem's gettin' bad around here," Waters was saying, "what with them roamin' the roads beggin' fer handouts and such. Why, a friend a' mine over in Sloan found half a dozen of 'em sleepin' in his barn when he went out one mornin'. He got his shotgun and they skedaddled away like their clothes was on fire."

The other man guffawed.

"We got t'nip it in the bud, before they try movin' in around Simpson Creek. That's why I'm revivin' the Circle. Bunch of us are meetin' at my ranch tomorrow night. Can you make it?"

Nick wondered idly who the men were talking about. Beggars of some sort—out-of-work soldiers from the recent war? Certainly not the warlike Comanche. Poor Mexicans? And what was the "circle" Waters referred to?

"Excuse me," he said, when the men seemed oblivious of his desire to enter the store.

The unknown man glared at the interruption before taking his hand off the door and moving aside just enough for Nick to squeeze past. "I'll be there," the man said to Waters. "We kin blame Lincoln for this, curse his interferin' Yankee hide. I just wish I could shoot him all over again."

Nick nodded at Waters as he walked past him, but the man looked right through him.

"Good morning, Mr. Patterson," Nick said to the man behind the counter in the general store, recognizing him as one of the men of the posse. "Miss Matthews sent me for five pounds of sugar."

"That'll be thirty-five cents, please," said Mr. Patterson, measuring out the amount into a thin drawstring bag and wrapping it in brown paper.

Nick counted out the coins, glad he'd become comfortable with American currency before coming to Simpson Creek.

"Nicholas Brookfield, isn't it?" the shopkeeper asked. "How are you getting along out there? And how are the Matthews girls? And old Josh, is he recovering?"

"Nick," Nick insisted, pleased at Mr. Patterson's warm reception after the way Bill Waters had acted. He extended his hand and the other took it. "I'm well, thank you, and Miss Milly and Miss Sarah are doing fine. Josh is feeling better, though he's still in pain from his wounds, of course. I'll tell them you asked about them."

"You do that," the other said. He looked up, and raised his voice to carry to the far end of the store, where two older men were bent over a game of checkers. "Hey, Reverend—here's Nick Brookfield, that English fellow who's helping out at the Matthews ranch. Maybe he could tell you what you were wantin' t'know."

The white-haired minister who had come out to the ranch yesterday looked up, then rose and bustled over to him. "Mr. Brookfield, hello," he said, extending his hand.

"Nick," he insisted again. "I know Miss Milly and Miss Sarah would want me to thank you again for that very tasty ham."

"Oh, that was little enough. We were happy to do it," the old man said, beaming.

"What is it I may tell you, Reverend?"

"I was hoping," the preacher said, "that you might be able to suggest what else we—as a town, that is—could do for Milly and Sarah. I've known those two young ladies since they were babies, and I'm troubled about the situation they've been left in, especially after the Indian attack two days ago. I asked Milly, but I'm afraid she's determined to be self-sufficient, and I wouldn't want there to be something we could do to assist that she's ashamed to ask for."

Nick looked down for a moment, rubbing his chin. He wondered if he'd be overstepping his bounds to say what he really thought. Nothing ventured, nothing gained, he supposed. "I'd say their greatest need is for a new barn to replace the one the Comanches burned," he said.

"Would there be any men who'd be willing and able to help them build one?"

Now it was the other two men's turn to be thoughtful. "Everyone would want to help, but they're pretty busy keeping their own ranches or businesses going..."

"But we could have a barn raising and put it up in a day!" Reverend Chadwick countered, with rising excitement. "Everyone could afford one day away from their own places."

"Yeah, we haven't had a barn raisin' in a coon's age," put in the man who'd been playing checkers with the preacher, who came forward now. Nick vaguely recognized the man who'd been introduced to him as the livery stable proprietor, although he couldn't remember his name. "Let's do it! Our ladies could provide the food, and we could all make a day of it."

"You'd all come out and put up a barn for them?" Nick was frankly floored that his tentative request for labor help was meeting with such an enthusiastic response. No wonder Americans had won their independence against the mighty British army—and maintained it in another war just a score of years later, if they always seized the initiative this way.

"Sure," Patterson said with a grin. "It's hard work, but at the end of the day there'd be a barn standing there, by gum. The ladies always have a great time visiting with each other at these things, and the children run around with each other and play, then nap like puppies in the shade. Usually the day ends with some fiddlin' music and a big supper."

"But what about the lumber needed?" Nick asked.

"Miss Milly and Miss Sarah don't have much in the way of ready cash…"

"Not many do, these days," Patterson said. "You may have heard Texas was on the losing side in the recent war."

Nick figured it would be impolitic to do more than nod his acknowledgment.

"We're gonna need lumber," the livery owner went on, thinking aloud.

"Maybe Mr. Dayton could be persuaded to donate it," Reverend Chadwick suggested. "Or at least offer it at a discount."

"Hank Dayton give something away?" snorted Patterson. "That'd be something new."

Hank Dayton. Had that been the man who had just been outside, talking to Waters? Nick had to agree—he didn't seem like the generous type.

"You never know. The good Lord still works miracles," Chadwick said with a twinkle in his eye. "I'll ask him. Failing that, perhaps he would at least extend credit 'til the Matthews ladies could pay him back, or we could hold a fundraising party…"

"When are we gonna have this barn raisin'?" Patterson asked. "The ladies'll need some time to organize the food and so forth."

"Shall we say a week from Saturday? When do you think would be good for Miss Milly and Miss Sarah, Nick?"

Nick shrugged. It wasn't as if Milly and her sister had a complicated social schedule of balls and dinner parties to work around. "The sooner the better, probably. Will you be coming out to tell her about it, sir?"

"No, I'll let you bring the good news, Nick. Just let us know if that date won't be convenient."

The proprietress of the boardinghouse hadn't been surprised that he would no longer need the room, having already heard of his new, temporary job—there certainly were no secrets in a small town. She'd probably already rented out his room. He gave her a quarter for keeping his valise for him, though, prompting a surprised thanks from the woman.

He couldn't help feeling a certain pleased anticipation as he drove the buckboard back to the ranch. Milly was going to be so surprised that the ranch would soon have a proper barn again! He was glad the preacher had left it up to him to bring the news.

On impulse, he stopped the wagon on the road home when he spotted a cluster of daisylike yellow flowers with brown centers growing alongside the road and picked a bouquet-sized handful for Milly. He wondered if this was violating his offer not to press her with courting gestures during their time of hardship. Yet had she ever actually said she would hold him strictly to that? He couldn't actually remember her saying it in so many words, so surely this small cheerful bunch of flowers would cause no offense.

It didn't. After unharnessing the horse and turning him out into the corral, he found Milly in the grove of pecan trees that stood next to the house. She wore a calico dress that had seen better days and was bent over a washboard set in a bucket of water, scrubbing stains from an old shirt. Wet garments hung to dry from low branches and across bushes. In spite of the shade, she looked hot and tired. Beads of sweat pearled on her fore-head. He strode over, holding the brown paper parcel of sugar in one hand and keeping the hand holding the bouquet behind his back.

Swiping one damp hand over her forehead to push an errant lock of black hair out of her eyes, she caught sight of him and stopped. She looked as if she felt embarrassed to be caught thus, but she smiled and said, "Oh, the sugar! Thanks so much for getting that for us, Nick. Were you able to pick up your things?"

"Yes," he said, putting the sack of sugar down on the table at a safe distance from the tub of water, "and I brought you these." He brought his other hand from around his back and offered them to her. "They looked so cheerful and appealing, I wanted you to have them."

Her eyes focused on the flowers, then locked with his, and the color rose on her already-pink cheeks.

"Of course, they were just growing wild by the road," he added apologetically. "I don't know what they are. But I didn't see any roses…"

Wiping her wet hands hurriedly on her apron, she came around the table and took them from him, beaming. "They're *beautiful,* Nick! Thank you. That was so nice of you! Brown-eyed Susans, we call them. The only one I know who can keep roses alive around here is Mrs. Detwiler, and I'm pretty sure she wouldn't share hers. I think she counts and names each one," she added with a laugh. "Why don't we take them inside and put them in some water? It's almost dinnertime, and I'm ready for a break," she added, rolling her eyes toward the pile of laundry that remained. "And I happen to know Sarah made some lemonade with the last of the old sugar. She's inside cooking."

He nodded his acceptance, happy that the flowers had pleased her. "Good. I have some news from town to tell both of you."

Milly looked curious, but led the way inside.

Sarah looked up from the stove when they entered, and sent him an approving look as Milly reached for an empty Mason jar to use as a vase.

"Now, what's this news?" Milly said, gesturing for him to sit while Sarah poured lemonade into glasses.

He told them about encountering Reverend Chadwick, Mr. Patterson and the livery store owner in the general store and about the conversation which had ensued.

Milly's eyes went wide. "They want to hold a barn raising? Here?"

Sarah grinned. "Well, here *is* where one is needed," she said wryly. "Everyone else around here who needs one has one. I think it's wonderful news, Nick."

"But Sarah, we don't have any money to pay for the lumber and nails and so forth!" Milly pointed out, her voice rising. Worry furrowed her brow.

"Reverend Chadwick thought he might be able to persuade the lumber mill owner to donate the lumber for the roof and stalls, or give you a discount—"

Milly interrupted. "There's about as much chance of that as a summer blizzard in San Saba County."

"Failing that, he thought Mr. Dayton could be persuaded to extend credit until you could pay him back, or maybe the town could hold a fundraising party." Nick was thinking of another option, too, that of offering her some money to help from his own funds, but he knew she would balk at that.

"We're *not* taking charity," Milly said in a tone of finality and with a stubborn jut to her chin. "Papa never would have considered it, and he always said never to go into debt. I'm afraid we'll have to tell them we can't accept this. Not 'til we can pay for it."

"But Milly…" Sarah began, looking distressed.

Milly Matthews was as proud as a duchess, Nick thought, but before he could say anything to try to persuade her, another voice spoke from the back hall.

"Your pa never planned on leavin' you two girls alone on this ranch like he did neither," said a voice from the hallway, and all three looked up to see Josh standing there, leaning heavily on a cane, his face pale with the effort it had taken to walk from his bedroom.

Milly sprang up, crying "Josh! What are you doing out of bed?" She rushed toward him, supporting him under the arm that wasn't holding a cane.

"I told him he could have dinner with us," Sarah muttered, going to his side, too. "Josh, you promised you'd wait 'til Nick came home, or Milly and I could help you!"

"Got tired a waitin'," the old man said, as Nick gently pushed Sarah aside and began helping Josh to the nearest chair. "'Sides, I heard Miss Milly spoutin' somethin' that sounded suspiciously like false pride to me, and I thought I'd better come remind her 'Pride goeth before a fall.'"

"You think we should *allow* the town to build us something we won't be able to pay for 'til only God knows when?" Milly asked, still with spirit, but Nick heard the tiniest note of doubt creep into her voice. "We'd never live it down—Bill Waters would see to that!"

"Oh, what do you care what that feller says?" Josh retorted. "He always seems t'have the ammunition to shoot off his mouth, but when he needed your ma to help him take care a his sick wife, he was glad to let her do that, and your pa lent him his prize bull fer his heifers whenever he asked. Ever'body needs help sometime, Miss Milly. You git back on yer feet, you kin help somebody else."

Milly sighed. "I...I suppose you're right, as always, Josh. Thank you."

"Anytime," the old man said. "Is that beans and corn bread cookin' on the stove, Miss Sarah? It's 'bout time fer dinner, ain't it?"

"Yes, and the beans are flavored with the last of the ham," Sarah said. "Milly, would you please go ring the bell to call Bobby in? I think he was out there cleaning out the chicken coop."

Chapter Eight

After the noon meal, Nick and Bobby went out to repair the fence line where the Matthews ranch bordered with Waters's land. Milly busied herself with finishing the wash, while Sarah took down the clothes that had dried, then hung up the newly washed shirts, dresses and sheets as Milly finished scrubbing them.

As they worked, Sarah chattered happily. "I think I'll make pecan pies for the barn raising, Milly. We still have enough pecans from last year. You know how my pecan pies always go quickly at church suppers. Even Mrs. Detwiler praised them at the last one. It's a good thing Mama planted those pecans she brought with her from East Texas when she and Papa moved here, isn't it?" She gestured up at the trees that shaded them now, with their boughs full of ripening pecans.

"Yes," agreed Milly. "We better hope there's a good crop of them this fall because it may be one of the few things we have to eat. I can't imagine how we're going to keep the men fed without slaughtering the remaining cattle and hens—and then how will we build up the herd and the flock again? We can't serve the men beans and corn bread every single noon and night."

Sarah's expression remained serene. "'Take no thought of what ye shall eat, and what ye shall drink, for your Heavenly Father knows you have need of these things'—isn't that what the Bible says?"

"Yes, but—"

"We have a vegetable garden." Sarah pointed in the direction of the rectangular patch in the back of the house. "It wasn't too badly trampled during the attack, and I've planted some more peas and beans. Bobby and Nick can help bring in meat. Remember how Papa would hunt deer every now and then, and rabbits and doves? I'm sure Bobby would just love an excuse to go tramping around in the hills and fields instead of doing ranch chores, and I reckon your Nick is a crack shot, too, from being in the army."

"He's not 'my' Nick," Milly said automatically, but her sister just laughed.

"I think *he* thinks he is," Sarah countered. "I just happened to be looking out of the kitchen window when he brought you those flowers. You had your back to me, but I could see his expression. His heart was in his eyes, sister dear."

Milly let the chemise she'd been washing sink back into the bucket of rinse water. "Sarah, he and I've been acquainted for what, three days? He couldn't possibly know his heart *or* mind in that amount of time. Just look at me," she said, with a despairing gesture at her damp, worn dress and the loose tendrils of hair that had come undone from the knot of hair at the nape of her neck, which were now plastered to her forehead. "This is how I looked when he walked over and presented me with those flowers! Not exactly the belle of the ball, am I?"

Sarah just smiled. "It didn't seem to matter to him, from what I saw."

Milly sighed. "When I pictured a suitor courting me after I placed that ad for the Society, I pictured it so differently! I imagined parties where the applicants got to know all the ladies of the Society.... I'd planned to wear my best dresses and Mama's pearl earbobs, and have my hair done up just so.... I thought you'd be doing those things, too. And then, when an applicant and I decided we might suit one another, we would go on walks, and horseback rides, and picnics, and sitting in church together, and we'd sit on the porch and talk..."

"And then the Comanches attacked," Sarah said, her eyes warm with sympathy. "But you can still do those things, Milly. And you have Nick right here, where you can get to know him day to day, which will actually give you a lot more time with him than any of the other ladies will probably be able to have with their suitors."

Milly realized she hadn't considered that, but she wasn't ready to let go of her worry entirely yet. "But they get to prepare for their beau," Milly pointed out. "Nick came back sooner than I thought he would and saw me like *this*," she said, pointing at her face and her dress, "with my hair plastered to my forehead, with soapy water splashes on my oldest calico! I'm sure the lovely English girls he's known had milk-and-roses complexions and they surely weren't doing laundry."

"Then why didn't he marry one of them and stay in England or India?" Sarah countered calmly. "You've already forgotten he picked you out of the whole group, Milly."

"Yes, but I had one of my better dresses on then, and my hair wasn't falling down around my ears," Milly retorted, pushing another loose curl from her face with a wet hand.

"But that's the way he saw you first, and first impressions last. Enough of this fretting, Milly," Sarah said. "Nick will be gone 'til supper. As soon as we finish this laundry, we'll fill the tub and you'll have a nice bath. We'll wash your hair, put it up in papers, and you can put on a nice dress and use some of Mama's rosewater before he comes home. And tomorrow, why don't you take him into town with you—"

"What for? I already sent him for sugar."

"So you can spend time alone together," Sarah said, rolling her eyes in exasperation. "Come on, aren't you the brilliant woman who invented the Simpson Creek Society for the Promotion of Marriage? You said something about needing cloth to make Josh and Bobby new shirts, didn't you? And don't you need to check the Society's mailbox? There might be gentlemen wanting to meet the rest of us, you know."

Sarah's last sentence had been uttered as cheerfully as the rest, but it made Milly realized how self-absorbed she was being. She had started the Society for the betterment of *all* the single ladies, not just herself. Sarah deserved to find a beau just as she had.

"Why are you always so sensible?" Milly said, giving her sister a hug. "I'm sorry I'm such a complainer. And I will go into town tomorrow, with or without Nick. I'll bet that mailbox is chock-full of inquiries from bachelors."

* * *

Later, Milly hummed as she set the table for supper. She'd liked what she'd seen when she looked at herself in the cheval glass in the bedroom. The lavender-checked gingham dress showed off her slender waist and complemented her dark hair, which now curled softly around her shoulders. Better yet, the look of anxious fretfulness no longer clouded her eyes.

She *was* the founder and leader of the Simpson Creek Society for the Promotion of Marriage, and Nicholas Brookfield had picked her out from among all the other women. Now if only they were having something more exotic to eat than beans and corn bread for supper!

She heard the sound of horses trotting into the yard but forced herself to keep doing what she had been doing rather than allowing herself to run to the window. A *lady* did not allow herself to appear overeager, she reminded herself, and pretended to be busy rearranging the black-eyed Susans in their improvised vase.

She heard boot heels clomping on the porch. Nick. Would he notice she no longer looked the bedraggled laundress?

"I say, is it too late to provide something for supper?" Nick called through the window.

Milly went to the door and opened it. He was standing there, holding up a glistening stringer of ten bluegills and a sun perch or two. He grinned, clearly very pleased with himself.

"Where on earth did you find those?"

"Bobby and I had a spot of luck at the creek," he said. "We finished fixing the fence without much ado, and Bobby had stashed a couple of fishing poles and line and a trowel in that little cave. He's been taking the coffee grounds and dumping them on a patch of dirt under a big tree by the creek. He says it attracts earthworms, and sure enough, we found plenty with a little digging."

"You should see what a great fisherman Mr. Nick is. He caught twice as many as I did!" Bobby said, his look at Nick full of admiration.

"Oh, I don't know about that," Nick said modestly. "But it was great fun. Reminded of me of holidays in the Lake District, when I tagged along with my brothers when they'd go fishing. I'm sure I was a terrific nuisance, but Richard, my second eldest brother, always talked Edward, the eldest, into letting me come. There we were, just men, and our sister Violet couldn't make me come to her doll tea parties." His blue eyes sparkled.

"We could delay dinner a little to include their catch, couldn't we, Sarah?" Milly asked.

"Sure enough," Sarah agreed. "Assuming you gentlemen wouldn't mind cleaning them, of course." She went to a drawer and pulled out a pair of knives.

"Aw, Miss Sarah, I hate cleaning fish," groaned Bobby. "All those scales and guts and fish heads…"

But Nick accepted the knives and clapped Bobby on the shoulder. "Come on, lad, it's a necessary part of being a fisherman. *Ladies* should not have to deal with nasty things like fish heads, nor should they smell of fish. We'll clean them up in a trice, then go wash up while the fish are frying." He hesitated while Bobby trudged outside and Sarah returned to stirring a pot on the stove, then turned back to Milly. "If I may say so, Miss Milly, you look lovely," he said simply.

"Yes…you may say so," she said, feeling a flush of pleasure. He had noticed. "Thank you."

The fish, which Sarah had rolled in a batter of egg, corn bread and her own secret blend of spices before frying them, were devoured down to the delicate spine and rib bones.

"That was delicious. Thanks for catching them, gentlemen," Milly praised, giving Bobby an especially approving smile because it had been his idea.

Bobby beamed. "You're welcome, Miss Milly. And tomorrow night we're havin' venison," he proclaimed. "Me an' Mr. Nick are gonna go up in them hills and get that ol' buck I missed last fall when me an' Uncle Josh last went huntin'." He seemed to have no doubt that Nick's presence would guarantee success.

"You are? Uh…it would be wonderful to have some venison hanging in the smokehouse," Milly said, keeping her tone even. She didn't want to betray her disappointment that Nick would be out hunting when she had hoped to be going into town with him. It was much more important to let him provide meat that could feed the household many times than to have Nick's company for a jaunt into town she could easily do by herself, or postpone. "Well, good luck, then."

"That ol' buck is a wily one," Josh warned. "He didn't get that eight-point rack makin' foolish mistakes. You ever been huntin', Mr. Nick?"

Nick nodded. "Indeed, I have—red deer in the Scottish highlands—they're bigger than your American deer—and tigers in Bengal."

"*Tigers?*" Bobby crowed enthusiastically. "Boy howdy, Mr. Nick! Did you kill 'em?"

"One of them," Nick said. "The rajah's son got the other. A pair of them had been plaguing a village, eating their livestock, as well as one unlucky old man whom they caught out after dark on a path that led from one village to another."

"Oh dear," Milly murmured with a shudder as she imagined it. "Man-eating tigers?"

"And you weren't even afeared?" Bobby asked, his eyes glowing with hero worship. "I reckon you're 'bout the bravest man I ever did know, Mr. Nick!"

Nick looked embarrassed. "Of course I was afraid. My heart was pounding like a trip-hammer. But we couldn't let them go on killing people, could we? The honor of the Empire was at stake." He winked at Milly.

"I heard tell of a cougar like that 'round here," Josh put in. "Once they get the taste fer human flesh, they don't want to go back to jackrabbits and such…"

"Oh, please! I'll have nightmares!" Sarah murmured faintly.

"Don't you worry, Miss Sarah, that ol' cougar's long gone," Josh assured her. "And that buck sure ain't no man-eater."

"Nick, we could go tonight and camp out and everything—that would be the best way," Bobby told him eagerly. "Then we'd be right out there at dawn, ready to shoot."

"And leave these ladies unguarded at night? I don't think that would be a good idea, lad. We can leave just before first light, but not until."

Bobby's face fell. "Aw, there's not gonna be no Comanche attackin' durin' the new moon," he protested.

"B'sides, I'm here," Josh added. "I ain't sleepin' very well these nights anyways—I might as well sit up with a rifle."

Milly saw Nick hesitate, clearly loath to dismiss the old cowboy's ability to protect the sisters as he always had.

"But how quickly could you raise that rifle and shoot with your injured shoulders, Josh? For example...*right now!*" Lightning-fast, Nick drew an imaginary pistol and leveled it at Josh, and everyone watched as Josh pantomimed raising a rifle, wincing with obvious pain as he did so.

"I...I see what you mean," Josh admitted, his shoulders sagging. "I reckon I ain't quite up to it yet."

"Yes, it's temporary," Nick confirmed. "You'll be back to fighting trim before very long. But that brings up a good point, Miss Milly, Miss Sarah. You need more hands around here."

Milly's gaze flew from Josh to Nick. "More hands? Are you leaving after all, then?"

He shook his head. "No, not as long as you need me," he said. "But I think it would be wise to have someone on watch during the night, to keep an eye on the livestock, to make sure the Indians aren't creeping up on the house."

"But...but how would we pay them, even if we could feed them?" Milly asked. "Assuming there were any men available, which there aren't, Nick. Cowboys are usually unmarried men, and we started the Society because there *aren't* any of those around Simpson Creek."

Nick rubbed his chin. "I—we—didn't want it to be the first thing we told you, but when we went to repair the fence, we found the carcass of another cow."

Alarm lit both Milly's and Sarah's faces. "Could it have been an animal? We were speaking of cougars," Sarah said, with a visible effort to be calm.

"It was too neat to have been an animal," Nick said.

"But there's no tellin' if it was redskins or rustlers what killed that cow," Josh said.

"I should think if you let it be known you had positions open," Nick said, "even though for now you could pay nothing but their board, men riding through town seeking work would find their way to you. In time, they'd pay for themselves. If you had more cowhands, Bobby and I could go hunting at night, the livestock could be guarded and eventually you could enlarge your herd and pay wages."

"Well, we'd best start tonight on the guardin', not wait for any more hands," Josh said with finality. "You boys ride out after dinner and bring the herd into the corral. Like I said, I don't sleep much, so I'll sit up on the porch with the rifle. That way I kin come out and wake you so's you two can get that buck when he comes down to water. Then come mornin' I'll go sleep awhile."

Chapter Nine

He hadn't dared to expect that she would be sitting out on the porch again when he and Bobby herded the cattle into the opened corral at sunset. Yet there she was, sitting on the porch with Sarah. The women waved as Bobby jumped off his cow pony and slammed the gate shut on the lowing beasts.

"I'll put th' horses away, Mr. Nick," Bobby offered.

"Thanks, lad," he said, dismounting and handing over the bay's reins. "Next time I'll return the favor."

Sarah rose as he strode toward the porch. "Good night, Nick. I've left sandwiches for you men to take with you in the morning."

"Thank you, Miss Sarah."

He sank into the rocking chair Milly's sister had vacated. Milly resumed crocheting what looked like the beginnings of an afghan. For a few moments there was a companionable silence between them.

"I say, Miss Milly…did you want…that is, did you have something else in mind for me to do tomorrow besides hunting?"

"Oh, it was nothing important," Milly said, too quickly, and looked back at her afghan.

"Just a feeling I had from a look on your face," Nick said. A look that had flashed so quickly across those hazel orbs that he hadn't been sure he had seen it until her too-rapid denial confirmed it. "I thought perhaps you'd had some task in mind for me. Bobby and I can go track that buck any time, you know."

Milly shrugged. "No, it would be better for you to go hunting. I just thought I'd ride into town tomorrow and get cloth for those shirts I need to make...and perhaps call on Hank Dayton at the lumberyard and see what his terms would be for the lumber. I thought we could go together, but I can go on my own."

"With Comanches on the loose? I rather think not," Nick said. He flashed on an image of Milly alone, encountering savages on the road, and meeting Josh's fate or worse.

"I can't be afraid to ride into town alone the rest of my life. There might never be another Comanche raid."

But then again, there might be. "Could you still do your errands in the afternoon? Bobby and I will be back by noon, I should think, deer or no deer. The lad says it's best to hunt at sunrise, when they're seeking a place to bed down. They aren't active during the heat of the day, so I could still go into town with you—unless it's too hot for you to go then?" English ladies had never done their errands in Bombay in the afternoon, preferring to go in the morning or send their native servants in the interest of preserving their milk-and-roses complexions. And the rajah's daughter had never left the palace when the sun was beating down, sending her old *amah* to the bazaar for anything she needed.

"No, that would be fine," she said, coloring faintly. "Thank you. I can tell Bobby's tickled pink that you two are going. He thinks quite a lot of you, Nick."

And you? What do you think of me, Milly Matthews? Aloud, he said, "He's a good lad. I've actually learned quite a lot from him already."

Milly smiled. "If you get that buck, he'll be sure you hung the moon."

He laughed. "He's already planning to hang the antlers on the wall of the bunkhouse. Maybe he'll be the one to shoot it."

"Boys always need someone to look up to," she murmured.

"Yes, though I'm sure I won't replace his uncle. I can remember a crusty old sergeant major in India I felt that way about when I first arrived as a raw lieutenant fresh off the boat. I thought he knew everything about everything. He taught me a lot before…well, before he died." He wished he hadn't thought of McGowan and the massacre…. Too many good men had died in India, he thought. All for the sake of empire…

Her hazel eyes studied him in the growing darkness, as if she sensed the pain he felt at remembering James McGowan.

Clomping boot heels approaching from inside the house warned them their time alone was about to end. A moment later Josh joined them on the porch.

"Had me a nice nap, so I'm ready to go on watch now."

Nick had hoped for a longer time to talk with Milly,

but perhaps it'd be easier tomorrow during their trip into town. "Yes, well, I'd better retire if Bobby and I are going to bring down that buck," Nick said, rising. "Good night, Josh, Miss Milly."

Nick and Bobby brought no venison home to the Matthews ranch the next morning, although Nick had bagged a wild turkey that had been startled out of the underbrush near them.

"We saw that old buck, but he was too far away to hit. We'll get him the next time, Mr. Nick says," Bobby told the women, who were admiring the slain tom Nick held up by his legs.

Nick forbore mentioning that the boy had tried the impossible shot anyway, spooking the buck so that creeping up on him upwind had been impossible.

"Well, I like turkey every bit as much as venison," Milly said, and the boy brightened.

"Yes, it'll be like Thanksgiving in August," Sarah added. "Bobby, if you'll start plucking the feathers, I think I can promise turkey for supper."

"Yes, *ma'am!*"

After the noon meal, Nick said he was going to go hitch up the buckboard, but Milly said, "Oh, why don't we ride? I haven't had a chance to ride Ruby—that's that red roan mare out in the corral, Nick—and I don't want her getting lazy."

"But, Milly, all the tack burned up with the barn," Sarah pointed out.

Milly shrugged. "Who needs a saddle?" She winked at Nick. "You won't disapprove of me riding bareback, will you?"

"Disapprove of my boss? Perish the thought, though I'd be happy to let you ride my horse, saddled." Nick grinned, still dealing with the surprise of learning that his Milly was a daring horsewoman in addition to all of her other impressive qualities.

"No, thanks, I'd love the excuse to ride bareback. Fortunately, I was repairing the reins of her hackamore and it was in my room on the day of the attack, so it didn't burn up with the barn. Go ahead and saddle your bay, Nick, I'll join you as soon as I've changed my skirt."

Sarah's expression had become uneasy. "Milly, don't let Mrs. Detwiler see you," she moaned.

"Pooh, Sarah, that would be half the fun of it."

She came out to the corral minutes later, carrying the bitless bridle and wearing the divided skirt trimmed at each side with a pair of silver *conchas*. Nick had tethered the roan mare to the corral fence with a loop of rope around her neck. Now he stopped tightening his bay's girth and watched as Milly approached, noting how the riding skirt became her.

"You like it? Mother made it for me because she knew I'd have a more secure seat than if I rode side-saddle. Not to mention that it didn't reveal my...ahem!... *limbs*," she said in a conspiratorial whisper.

"You surprise me more every day, Miss Milly," he said, letting her see his admiration. "You're quite the intrepid lady."

She beamed at his compliment. "Josh taught me to ride when I was barely old enough to walk. Um...could we drop the 'Miss,' just while we're alone, Nick?"

Their gazes locked. "I would be delighted, *Milly*."

While he finished saddling his bay, she bridled the

well-mannered mare. Then Nick laced his fingers for her, providing a springboard for her left foot so she could mount.

By the time they reached the road, he'd decided her seat was as excellent as her hands.

"Does Sarah ride as well as you, Milly?" He tried to imagine an English lady cantering down the road bareback and couldn't. Texas women were full of surprises.

She shook her head. "She doesn't really like to ride very much because she had a bad fall once—from a sidesaddle. But she's a much better cook than I will ever be," she added loyally, with a self-deprecating roll of her eyes. "Her biscuits are so light they practically float away, don't you think?"

"Ah, well, one can't be good at everything, can one?" he asked lightly. If this woman learned to love him, he thought, eating less-than-perfect biscuits would be a small price to pay.

Once they reached Simpson Creek, their first stop was the post office. Caroline Wallace came running out while Milly was still dismounting.

"Oh, Milly, it's so good to see you! Still riding bareback like an Indian, I see. Mr. Brookfield, how are *you?* Is old Josh feeling better?"

Nick, tying the horses to the hitching rail, watched as Milly absorbed the other woman's conversational onslaught.

"Everything's getting back to normal, thanks, and yes, Josh is feeling much better. I can tell because he's getting ornery and trying to do too much."

Clearly unable to contain herself, the other woman

could barely wait for Milly to finish answering her question. "Milly, can you imagine, we've had *two* applications to the Society!"

"We have? That's wonderful."

"I didn't think you'd mind me looking at them," Caroline said. "I figured, what with all you've had to deal with, it might be a while before you made it to town again. They'd both like to come up from Houston to meet us," she gushed. "I don't know if they'll be here in time for the barn raising, but wouldn't that be great if they were?"

"Yes, there's nothing like putting guests in town to work right away," Milly said drily.

"It seems to have worked out well for you," Caroline teased, with a meaningful glance at Nick. "Let me tell you about the letters." She brought them out of her pocket and unfolded one. "This one sounds just perfect for Emily—he's a widower from Buffalo Bayou—but I'm calling first dibs on this other one, a fellow named Pete Collier—if I like what I see when he arrives, of course, and if he feels the same. He says he's from Galveston originally, and he owns a pharmacy, but he's been looking to relocate. And he said he knew two or three other men who might be interested, depending on what he reports back to them…"

"Oh, so he's being sent to survey the prospects, is he?" Milly said with a laugh.

Nick imagined the pride Milly must be feeling that her idea was working. Now, he only needed to make sure Milly didn't find the new gentlemen more attractive than himself!

They went across the street to the general store from

there, where Milly selected a bolt of sturdy tan broadcloth for the shirts she was going to make. "It might as well match the color of the dirt around here," she commented, politely rejecting a bolt of dark navy that the proprietor had brought down from the shelf first, "since it's going to absorb a lot of it while it's being worn..." Her voice trailed off as she stared out the window. "Oh, there's Mr. Dayton now, just going down the street," she said, looking out the window. "Mr. Patterson, will you save this bolt for me?" She dashed outside.

Nick edged toward the open door but remained within the building, wanting to unobtrusively overhear without being seen. Just as he had guessed, the man Milly was hastening toward was the same man who'd been speaking with Waters outside this store yesterday.

"Mr. Dayton, how are you? How's the family?" Milly asked, her voice friendly.

The paunchy middle-aged man stopped and shaded his eyes to peer at her. "Afternoon, Miss Matthews. Same as always."

"I hope y'all are coming to our barn raising," she said. "I haven't seen your wife in a month of Sundays, and from what I'm hearing already, the food's going to be the best this side of heaven."

"I'm sure Alice Ann will nag me into comin'," he said, looking less than pleased at the prospect. "As if I don't work hard enough all week long at the lumberyard."

Nick watched Milly's cheerful smile remain in place. "And that reminds me, I wanted to talk to you about the price of the wood for the barn. I—"

"I'll tell you right now I cain't jes' give that wood away," the man whined, his lips tightening. "The mayor's daughter's already been jawin' at me, tryin' to get me to donate it 'outa the goodness of my heart,'" he said, a sneer making his jowly features even more disagreeable.

"I completely understand, Mr. Dayton," Nick heard Milly say, still cheerful. "I was just wondering how soon you would require payment, so I could figure out if we could afford it. If we can't, of course, we'll have to wait to raise a barn when we can."

Nick saw the other man's face take on a wary look, as if he realized he might miss out on a sale altogether if he made his price too high.

"I can give you a couple weeks, ma'am, and then I'm gonna need payment in full. I got mouths t'feed, y'understand."

"Of course," she said, her voice losing none of its warmth. He marveled at her poise.

Just then he saw another man join them—Bill Waters.

"How do, Bill? Didn't know you'd be comin' inta town today," Dayton said. "Now, Miss Milly, I didn't mean t' speak too hasty," he said. "Seein' Bill here, I might could work somethin' out to help you out, under certain circumstances…"

Nick straightened. There was something in the man's tone he didn't like.

"Oh? And what circumstances would those be?" Milly's voice had cooled, but the lumberyard owner didn't seem to notice.

"Why, I'd give that wood to you as a weddin' present."

Milly sounded puzzled. "But I have no wedding

planned, Mr. Dayton. Did you mean if I married a man I met through the Society for the Promotion of Marriage?"

"Naw, I'm not talkin' about that fool business. That's jest about the featherbraindest idea any female ever came up with. Why you'd want to find a stranger to get hitched with, I don't know, since I happen to know you're standin' right next to a fine man who'd give you anythin' your little heart desired if you was to marry him."

Nick heard Milly gasp, even as his fists involuntarily tightened. So now the old man thought he could persuade Milly into marriage, if he couldn't get her to sell the ranch?

"I—I don't know what to say," she managed at last.

"Why, 'yes,' of course," the lumberman said, misunderstanding her struggle for words. "Seems to me you'd be the luckiest female in San Saba Country to get hitched t' a man like my friend Bill Waters."

Nick thought Milly might leave them without another word, but the remarks had evidently sparked her ire. "Oh, Mr. Dayton, I just know you're teasing me, isn't he, Mr. Waters? Why, Mr. Waters is older than my father was when he died! Excuse me, gentlemen, I have purchases to pick up inside." She turned back toward the store, still laughing as if she'd been told the most humorous joke ever.

"Well, maybe you ought t' see if her sister has more sense," Dayton said in a purposely carrying voice as Milly put her first booted foot on the boardwalk. "I hear that Sarah girl kin cook at least."

The two men guffawed. Nick fought the urge to go

knock both of them flat, but a display of brutish behavior would neither impress Milly nor help her in the long run.

Her composure slipped as soon as she was inside the store. Nick could see she was fighting tears. He wanted to gather her into his arms and hold her and kiss away her distress, but they weren't alone and he didn't want to embarrass her. And he wasn't even completely sure if she would welcome his comfort.

"Steady on," he said, daring to put a hand on her shoulder. Beneath his fingers, her muscles bunched in suppressed rage. "Those two are mere blowhards. I've seen their ilk before."

"Those hateful old coots," Milly whispered. "As if I'd marry Bill Waters to get free lumber for our barn!"

On the way home, he told her about the partial conversation he'd overheard between the two men when he'd entered the general store yesterday, and asked what group of people they'd been talking about.

"Probably former slaves," Milly guessed. "They were freed because of Lincoln's Emancipation Proclamation during the war, but most of them left their owners with nothing, just the clothes on their backs and no idea of how to earn a living."

"Did your father own slaves?" he asked carefully. England had abolished the trade over fifty years ago, but he'd seen plenty of racial bigotry among the British in India.

"Heavens, no," she said, then added, "he never would have, but hardly anyone else did around here either. Most slaves in Texas were in the cotton-growing areas, not on ranches. Oh, goodness, look at the time," she said, when the grandfather clock in the store chimed three. "I suppose we'd better head home…"

Chapter Ten

After breakfast Sunday morning, Milly, Sarah and Nick climbed onto the buckboard to attend church in town. Ordinarily, Josh and Bobby would have come along, but Josh still wasn't feeling up to bouncing over the rutted road, and Bobby had offered to stay home with his uncle. Milly suspected Bobby was happy to have the excuse not to attend. Bathing, wearing his good shirt and pants and sitting still for the sermon were not high on his list of favorite activities.

One could never have guessed Nick had been wearing cowboy clothes the last few days and doing menial chores like fence mending and livestock tending, she mused, trying not to steal too many sidelong glances at the Englishman beside her. He was once again the picture of a refined gentleman in his black frock coat, trousers and white shirt and tie. Thank goodness she had been able to wash the bloodstains away!

She knew she also looked well in her Sunday best dress of light blue silk-and-cotton *Merveilleux*, which had been made from a bolt of fabric sent to her mother by Aunt Tilly from New Orleans before the war. They would be the cynosure of all eyes as she walked into church beside him.

But their fine apparel wasn't what made her heart light and joyous this morning; rather, it was the memory of his pleased reaction to her invitation to attend church with her. She had told him church attendance wasn't obligatory for ranch employees—the Matthewses had no rule that cowhands must attend Sunday services if they would prefer to take their ease in the bunkhouse or elsewhere.

"Oh, but I would be most honored to escort you to church, Milly," he'd said with that enchanting accent of his and that smile that lit up his blue eyes. "I never missed Sunday services at home in Sussex or in India when I could help it, though my army duties sometimes prevented me."

"I imagine our little church in Simpson Creek will be somewhat different than what you're used to at home," she'd responded, imagining stained-glass windows of rainbow hues, walls darkened by age and a minister in formal robes.

"I imagine so," he said. "The church at Greyshaw was built in Norman times, about 1250, but it's fairly small, too, having been only the chapel of Greyshaw Castle beside it."

"Built in 1250?" she'd echoed wonderingly. "Why, that's over six centuries old!"

"Yes. My brothers and I used to joke that the vicar was every bit as ancient," Nick recalled with a grin.

"I'll bet your mother had her hands full keeping the three of you in line," she'd said.

He looked away just then, as if something she'd said

had troubled him. She didn't want to ask him about it in front of Sarah, though, and in any case, they were drawing near to the church.

Every head turned as Nick followed Milly into a pew about midway toward the front of the church, while Sarah went forward to the piano. Now he understood why Milly's sister played hymns so often on the piano at home. Here and there he recognized men he'd met at the general store, who nodded at him, or ladies who'd been present at the Society meeting the day he'd met Milly. Many of the latter waved discreetly at the Matthews ladies as they passed and smiled shyly at him. Only one older woman narrowed her eyes as he and Milly passed her pew. Could this be the infamous Mrs. Detwiler? He noticed Waters and Dayton sitting together in the front of the church, with their families spread out on either side of them. Apparently they saw no conflict in their bigotry and church attendance.

Milly's idea that the Simpson Creek church was "somewhat different" from the Greyshaw chapel had been an understatement, Nick thought as he settled himself by Milly. Yet somehow the simplicity was very appealing. A white frame building with a wooden floor, the church had no stained glass, only clear windows open because of the heat. Even so, many of the ladies wielded their fans.

The piano at which Sarah sat looked time-worn. A simple polished wooden cross graced the wall from the floor nearly to the ceiling at the front of the church. It drew the eye because of the lack of other beautiful things to compete with. Perhaps that was as it should be, Nick thought.

A man took his place at the front of the church and raised his hands for silence. "Good morning, Simpson Creek residents!" he said. "Our first hymn will be number twenty-six, 'Blest Be the Tie that Binds.'"

Fabric rustled and wooden pews creaked as everyone got to their feet and Sarah played the opening chord. Nick and Milly had taken the last two spaces in the pew, so there was only one hymnal left. Milly opened it and held it out to him. Deliberately he allowed his fingers to brush hers as he took it from her and held it so they could both see, enjoying the flush of color that rose in her cheeks and the way she cleared her throat, missing the first line of the old hymn.

After that, however, her alto voice, rich and true, blended with his tenor as they sang this song and two more before everyone sat down for the sermon.

Nick forced his mind away from the pleasant rosewater scent Milly wore. As a preacher, Reverend Chadwick lacked the resonant voice and polished speaking style Nick had always associated with men of the cloth, but sincerity shone from his shiny, perspiration-beaded face as he spoke of the Sermon on the Mount and how the townspeople should apply those truths to their living today. Nick felt blessed and encouraged half an hour later when the white-haired man closed the service in prayer.

"Oh, and before you leave," the preacher added, holding up a hand, "I want to remind everyone of the barn raising at the Matthews ranch next Saturday morning, bright and early. I'm sure you'll all want to come and help build, not to mention help out in the delicious meals that the ladies will prepare. And if anyone is able to spare any cash, Miss Priscilla Gilmore is accepting donations to help pay for the lumber." He indicated a pretty strawberry blonde, who flashed a vivacious smile.

That said, he walked down the aisle to the door to shake everyone's hands as they left.

"Your sermon was inspiring, Reverend. I'm glad I was here," Nick told him.

"And we're glad you're here, too, Mr. Brookfield, and especially pleased that you're helping Milly and Sarah," the other man said, pumping his hand with enthusiasm. "Please do come back."

In no apparent hurry to go home, people gathered in front of the church. Nick followed Milly to where her sister was chattering with a trio of ladies.

"Your piano playing was excellent, Miss Sarah," he complimented her, when there was a break in the conversation.

"Thank you. I guess all those years I tortured Milly and our parents with my practice are finally paying off," she said with a modest smile.

"Hello, Mr. Brookfield, Sarah… Oh, Milly! I just can't wait for the barn raising! It's going to be so much fun!" exclaimed the bright-eyed strawberry blonde as she dashed down the steps to join the group.

"It's nice of you to collect money for us, Prissy," Milly said. Nick thought he could detect a hint of uneasiness in Milly about the subject. "I'm not sure anyone has any to spare, but we appreciate the thought—"

"Oh, but you just have to know how to appeal to

those who can give," the other girl said with a blithe confidence. "For example, the food's going to be free, of course, but at the supper, we're going to auction off the pies and cakes. That'll bring in the money, sure enough—every one of those men has a sweet tooth. And we're posting notices about the barn raising and party to all the neighboring towns."

"Goodness, Prissy, you have been busy!" Milly praised. "Maybe we should have made *you* president of the Society for the Promotion of Marriage."

The other girl laughed. "Oh, no, I'd never have thought of your scheme in a million years! But wait, I haven't told you everything! We're going to charge a nickel a dance with any of us ladies, even for the husbands with their wives, though we'll make the husbands pay only once."

"Prissy! Are you sure Reverend Chadwick will approve of that?" Milly asked.

"Who do you think thought of it?" the other girl retorted with a wink. "He says all these men are free enough with their spare change when they come into town to buy tobacco and visit the saloon. Next Saturday they can contribute to a good cause instead."

"I've heard again from that man from Buffalo Bayou I told you about *and* the pharmacist from Galveston," Caroline Wallace announced, joining the group. "Both of them will be arriving in time for the barn raising and have been invited to meet our Society members there. I'm so excited I could squeak!"

Nick thought her excited voice already sounded a little squeaky, but he hoped the coming applicants were everything Miss Wallace wished for.

Nick's back was to the steps, but he could tell by the way the girls straightened and their smiles faded that someone disagreeable was approaching. Sure enough, when he glanced over his shoulder, he saw the sour-faced elderly woman bearing down on them. Her expression, Nick decided, looked as if she had just drunk a cup of curdled milk.

Miss Wallace and Miss Gilmore edged away.

"Good morning, Mrs. Detwiler," Sarah called out in a determinedly cheerful way. "How are you this morning?"

"Mrs. Detwiler, may I present Nicholas Brookfield, who's been helping us out at the ranch?" Milly said, glancing at Nick a little desperately.

He guessed what Milly wanted. "Mrs. Detwiler, I'm honored to make your acquaintance," he said with a bow that would have done credit to the Prince of Wales, and bestowing a smile on her that would have melted Queen Victoria at her stuffiest. "I'm told you raise the prettiest roses in the county, possibly all of Texas."

But Mrs. Detwiler was not to be charmed. "I don't know who told you that, but I hope they told you they weren't for your bouquets," she snapped, then turned. "Miss Matthews, I have a bone to pick with you."

It was hard to tell which sister she was addressing, for she glared at both. "Me?" Sarah volunteered. "Did I hit some wrong notes in the hymns this morning?"

"Not you. Your sister. Milly Matthews, I asked Reverend Chadwick to speak about this to you discreetly, but he says *he* sees nothing wrong with it, so I suppose it's up to me. I saw you yesterday, riding that horse of yours bareback like a heathen hussy. It was scandalous, that's what it was, especially in the company of a man," she said, sharing her glare with Nick. "I told your mother when you were a girl she was wrong to let you do so, but you're much too old to carry on like that now."

Nick could tell by the way Milly's chin lifted that she was holding in her anger.

"Oh? I'm sorry, I didn't see you, or I would have said hello and introduced Mr. Brookfield then, though I *thought* I saw your curtain flutter as we rode by," she said.

Nick saw the woman's face darken at the implication she had been spying on them.

"I'm sorry my bareback riding offended you," Milly went on, "but I'm afraid the saddle burned up with the barn. Mr. Brookfield did offer me his, though," she added, as if attempting to be strictly accurate.

"Well, you should have accepted it, or better yet, taken your wagon," Mrs. Detwiler told her. "I'm sure an Englishman is used to more seemly deportment than what you displayed yesterday, aren't you, Mr. Brookfield? Come now, be honest."

"I find the women of Texas, and especially Miss Milly, utterly refreshing in their conduct, madam," he told her, keeping a smile pasted on his face with some effort. "She has an excellent seat, that is, she's quite the horsewoman," he added, afraid the woman would deliberately misunderstand his words.

Stymied, Mrs. Detwiler redoubled her attack on Milly. "It's not just the fact that you're riding bareback,

Milly Matthews, but the indecorous *attire* you wore—that split skirt. I was scandalized! Your poor mother must be have been rolling in her grave."

Milly's spine became even more rigid, if that were possible. "My mother is in heaven with Jesus," she said, enunciating every word. "And she sewed that skirt for me."

Mrs. Detwiler tsk-tsked. "Well, I have done my duty and can say no more if you choose not to listen. Good day, Mr. Brookfield."

He gave her a bare nod as the woman stalked away with a rustle of black bombazine, then turned back to Milly. There was a sheen in her hazel eyes as her gaze followed Mrs. Detwiler, and her lip quivered.

"That spiteful woman!" Sarah hissed, taking Milly's hand. "Don't pay any attention to her."

"I know I said having her see me would be half the fun, and I don't care what she thinks of me, but I won't have her criticizing our mother! She was rude to her when she was alive, too." She swiped angrily at a tear that escaped down her cheek. "I'm sorry, Nick. I'm not normally such a crybaby. You've seen me cry two days in a row now!"

"Stiff upper lip, Miss Milly," Nick advised, wishing he could kiss her tears away.

She blinked at him. "How do I…"

He thought she was going to ask how on earth she was to regain her composure after the old woman's verbal attack, but then he saw that she was taking him literally, struggling to assume the expression he'd suggested. The result made her giggle, and soon all three of them were laughing.

Milly was smiling again. "It's impossible to cry when you're concentrating on keeping your upper lip straight, isn't it?"

"That's the spirit."

Chapter Eleven

The next five days passed in a flurry of preparation for the barn raising. The men spent the time outside completing the clearing of the old barn's remains and scything the yard in addition to the usual chores of caring for the livestock and providing meat for the table.

Milly and Sarah were fully occupied inside, cleaning the house from one end to the other. The barn raising and party afterward would take place outside, but the women would put last-minute touches on the food in the kitchen and nurse babies and lay small children down to nap in the bedrooms away from the heat of the day. Even if the critical Mrs. Detwiler didn't come, they wanted their home to be at its best for the rest of the women to see, a place they could be proud of.

In the evenings, Milly sewed new dresses for her and her sister, using their mother's beloved old Singer sewing machine and bolts of sprigged muslin they had found among their mother's possessions. Clearly she had set them aside to make dresses for her daughters, for pinned to the primrose yellow one with peach colored flowers was a scrap of paper with "Sarah" inscribed on it, while the vivid green one with cream colored flowers was labeled "Milly." Next to the bolts, they'd found yards of satin, wide grosgrain ribbon, buttons, lace and a couple of yards of sheer white lawn which she'd apparently bought at the same time.

Milly had sketched designs for the dresses when she'd first organized the Society for the Promotion of Marriage, thinking she'd have advance notice before they met anyone, and had gotten as far as cutting out the pattern pieces. Then Nick had appeared without warning and the Comanches attacked the same day. She'd had no time for sewing until now.

After consulting Sarah, Milly made her sister's dress a demure one with a ruffled yoke trimmed in lace and a matching ruffle at the hem. She used the grosgrain ribbon to fashion a sash at the waist and part of the lawn to make a ruffled apron with a band of the yellow muslin to form the ties.

After finishing Sarah's dress Wednesday night, she hung it from a peg on the wall and threw herself into the construction of her own, ever aware that Nick would see her in it. Her dress would have ruffles at the hem and the sleeves, as well as a lawn insert over the top of the bodice trimmed with lace, a sash of the wide grosgrain ribbon and a green-trimmed ruffled lawn apron.

"Ohh, Milly, it's beautiful," cooed Sarah, coming into the room, but she was staring at her own dress hanging on the wall. "I love it! You're so talented. But you didn't have to make my dress first," she added worriedly, seeing that Milly had only begun to stitch her own dress. "It doesn't matter what *I* wear—there won't be any beau there for me."

"Pooh, I have plenty of time to finish my dress, especially if you'll let me off the pie-making detail Friday if it's not done yet."

"It's a deal," Sarah said with a laugh. "I know you hate rolling out pie crust anyway."

"You've got that right," Milly said, relieved. "And who says there won't be a beau there for you, Sarah? What if Caroline and Emily and those two new men who are coming don't take a shine to one another, but one of them turns out to be perfect for you? You'll want to look your best."

Sarah shrugged. "I don't think there's much chance of that, but I do love parties and wearing something new."

"Well, you better try it on," Milly said, nodding toward the dress, "just in case it needs alterations."

"It fits perfectly," Sarah said a couple of minutes later, when Milly had helped her button up the back of the dress. "Don't change a thing. Oh, I nearly forgot what I came to tell you—Nick's sitting out on the porch. Josh is with him and talking his ear off, but I think he's looking for you, Milly. He looked up when I came out to bring them coffee, and he looked *so* disappointed when he saw it was only me. You've been working so hard on your sewing in the evenings, you haven't been out there at all after supper this week, you know."

The information made Milly warm inside. "You think he's looking for me? Hmm…" Would she have time to finish the dress if she went out to sit with him now, or was it better to keep sewing and make him miss her all the more?

No, she wasn't into playing coy games. She *wanted*

to spend time in Nick's company, to listen to that exotic English accent, to drown in the depths of those blue eyes when their gazes met.

"I think I have time to take a little break from my labors," she told Sarah with a wink. She could always come back after Nick bid her good-night and sew by the light of the lamp until she got too sleepy to thread the needle.

It rained at dawn on the day of the barn raising, right after the men had lowered the sides of beef onto the hot coals in the barbecue pit they had dug, but it stopped by the time they were gathered around the breakfast table.

"I don't think that rain'll hurt none," Josh opined. "It's washed away the dust, and that ain't a bad thing."

"Yes, and it's already clearing to the west," Nick said, looking out the kitchen window. "Ah, there's Mr. Dayton now with the lumber," he added as the creak of a wagon axle confirmed his words. "It appears he's brought his family with him."

Milly could already hear the six Dayton children clamoring to get down, and groaned. "Oh, dear, we're not even dressed for the party yet," she said, with a gesture at her own everyday shirt and waist. She'd thought she'd have time after breakfast to don her beautiful new green dress—completed at midnight the night before—before the first wagons started rolling in. But there would be no leisure to dress once Alice Ann Dayton crossed their threshold. Probably because of her husband's tyranny, the woman attended social events so rarely that she never stopped talking once she arrived at one, following her unfortunate listener around reciting a never-ending litany of her ailments and her noisy brood's misbehavior. They should have figured Dayton wouldn't make a second trip from town to get his family, but they hadn't expected him quite so early.

"Scoot," Sarah told her quickly, motioning Milly toward her bedroom. "I'll keep Mrs. Dayton and the children occupied while you get ready, then you can do the same for me."

"And Bobby and I'll go out and help Dayton unload his lumber," Nick said, rising.

Milly blew a kiss to her sister and made good her escape.

The wagons started arriving thick and fast about an hour later, for the men were eager to get a good start on the barn before the sun rose too high. Nick was glad they'd set up the tables and chairs under the trees the night before, for he and Bobby were kept busy assisting the drivers, unhitching the teams and turning them out in the corral. Men brought their tools—hammers, saws, shovels, brace and bits and more chairs. Their women flocked toward the ranch house, laden with picnic baskets, covered dishes and pitchers, most accompanied by excited offspring yelling at the top of their lungs. Nick kept an uneasy eye on the children lest one of them dart in front of the dancing, nervous horses he led toward the corral.

The ladies of the Society for the Promotion of Marriage arrived in one big buckboard driven by Caroline Wallace, all chattering like magpies and eyeing the clumps of men as if to see if any strangers had arrived.

Nick would have thought that Dayton, as the lumberman, would take charge of the building, but he seemed content to sit and rock on the porch and watch the women bringing dishes into the house. Instead, Mr. Patterson from the mercantile and Mr. Wallace from the post office began organizing the building of the frames.

"I've never built anything, but I'll be happy to do whatever's needed," Nick told Patterson as soon as he had unhitched the team of the last wagon to arrive.

Patterson grinned. "You reckon you're better at sawin' or hammerin'?"

Nick shrugged. "I've never done either, but let me try my hand at sawing." Another man was already sawing planks laid atop a pair of sawhorses and he figured he could watch and learn.

"Well, pick up a saw from that pile a' tools over yonder and Andy'll tell you how long to cut 'em," Patterson said, nodding toward the livery owner with the saw. As Nick walked away, Patterson cupped his hands and yelled toward the porch, "Hey, Dayton, you gonna do any work today or are you only supervisin'?"

"Seems like I done enough by loadin' up this lumber and bringin' it out here," Dayton grumbled, keeping his seat.

"St. Paul said those who do not work should not eat," Reverend Chadwick, who'd been swinging a hammer like a much younger man, retorted, with a meaningful nod at the tables under the trees. "I caught a glimpse of the bounty that we have to look forward to at midday, Hank, and I don't think you'd want to miss that."

With a put-upon air, Dayton trudged out and grudgingly picked up a hammer. But every time Nick looked up from his work, it seemed Dayton was drinking water under a tree, and once Bill Waters arrived at midmorning, the two seemed to spend more time talking in low tones to each other than accomplishing any actual work.

After a bit of instruction from Andy Calhoun, he learned how long the planks needed to be and how to saw them most efficiently and pass them over to where the frames for the sides, front and back were taking shape. Soon the whistle of his saw joined the sounds of the shovels digging holes into which the new upright beams would be lowered. Moments later the pounding of hammers rang out as men joined boards together with wooden pegs and the precious nails that had been salvaged from the wreckage of the old barn.

Nick found himself actually enjoying the physical labor and camaraderie of working as one with the men of Simpson Creek. He'd done a lot of hard work since coming to the Matthews ranch and by morning he knew his shoulders and back would ache, but he thought he had never been so content.

He enjoyed still more the occasional glimpses of Milly as it grew closer to noon. Wearing a becoming green dress he'd never seen before, she was a whirlwind, bustling to and fro from the kitchen to the tables carrying out dishes, directing other ladies and placing the additional chairs around the tables. He caught her eye once and she smiled and waved. He hoped she'd stop and talk, but she only dashed back into the kitchen. At least he could look forward to sitting with her when they stopped for the noon meal.

"Miss Milly, this is a good time to break for dinner, I think," Patterson said, coming to the porch just as Milly left the kitchen, carrying a cloth-covered bowl of biscuits fresh from the oven. "The upright beams are in place, and we've got the four frames all ready to be pegged into them this afternoon."

"Excellent," she approved. "Y'all have worked hard this morning." Milly yanked the rope connected to the cast-iron bell hanging from a post by the step and the clanging soon had men laying down their tools all across the grounds. Her eyes found Nick, who'd rolled his shirtsleeves up his arms and was now wiping his face under the floppy-brimmed hat with his handkerchief. He looked up at her then and grinned.

As the bell's clamor died away it was replaced with the sound of hoofbeats as around the bend, two men rode up on horseback.

"Sorry to be so late," announced one of them, a stocky man with graying dark hair. "We meant to make it here last night, only we took a wrong turn outta Austin, which lost us some time, then we couldn't hardly find anyone in town to direct us here." He took a look around. "I guess that's 'cause most everyone is here."

"We finally asked the saloon keeper," the other man put in, dismounting from his horse. He was a younger man, with tow-colored hair and a ready smile. "Pete

Collier's my name, from Galveston, and that there's Ed Markison, from Buffalo Bayou. We're here to meet the single ladies."

Chapter Twelve

"Wel—" began Milly, stepping down off the porch, but she didn't even get to finish the word before Caroline Wallace dashed past her and went forward to the two men.

"Welcome, gentlemen, I'm Caroline Wallace, and my brother Dan will take your horses...*won't you, Dan?*" she called to the boy, who'd already begun ambling toward the food-laden tables. "This is Milly Matthews and her sister, Sarah, and this is their ranch—"

"Ah, so it's your barn we've come to build, ladies?" Ed Markison, the older man, said gesturing toward the beginnings of the new building.

Milly, amused at the way Caroline had made sure hers was the first face Pete Collier laid eyes on, nodded. "Yes, and we're very grateful for your coming to help. We're just about to sit down and eat, and—"

"So you've come at just the right time," Caroline finished, then looked over her shoulder at the other ladies of the Society who were hovering uncertainly on the porch. "These are the rest of the ladies of the Society for the Promotion of Marriage," she said. "This is Emily

Thompson—she's a widow, just as you are a widower, Mr. Markison..." she said, and identifying each lady in turn, including Sarah, who smiled shyly and excused herself to go back into the kitchen to get another platter of food.

Nick had arrived at Milly's side in time to witness Caroline's maneuvering, and he winked at Milly. There was something in his eyes that seemed to say, *Isn't it nice that we've already found one another?* Oh, she hoped she was right about that!

"Figures these yahoos managed to get here just in time to eat," Milly heard Hank Dayton mumble to Bill Waters. She winced, fearing the newcomers had heard his churlish remark, but they seemed fully occupied gazing at the ladies.

"We're mighty pleased to make your acquaintance, ladies," Pete Collier said, bowing to all of them, but his gaze returned to Caroline. "Might it be possible to sit together while we eat, so we can begin to get to know you?"

Milly guessed Caroline wanted that, too, but to her credit, she didn't try to secure any extra privileges for herself. "Oh, but we ladies will serve while the menfolk eat. Then we'll eat while y'all get back to work."

Collier and Markison looked disappointed, and so did Nick. "I'd hoped you could sit with me," he whispered, and his voice made her all tingly inside.

"But we'll all be sitting down together at supper, when all the work is done," she said, raising her voice to include the two newcomers. "And afterward, there's to be dancing."

"I reckon we'll just have to wait for the pleasure," Markison said good-naturedly.

Reverend Chadwick stepped forward. "If the wonderful smell is any indication, the ladies have made sure dinner will be delicious," he said. "Why don't I say the blessing?"

If the good-natured groans as the men left the table were anything to go by, dinner had been a resounding success. Milly suspected many of them would have preferred to stretch out in the shade of the pecan trees and nap, but much remained to be done before a new barn would stand where the old barn had been.

"I can't remember when I've been this full. You Simpson Creek ladies are the best cooks ever gathered in one place," Nick said to her as he rose from his place at the table, where he'd been sitting between Reverend Chadwick and Mr. Patterson. "I don't believe I shall need to eat more for a week."

"Ah, but then you'll miss Josh's barbecue for supper, and that would be a shame," she said, nodding toward the barbecue pit, where sides of beef another rancher had donated were already sending their savory aroma wafting into the air. Josh, fretting at his inability to take a more active role in constructing the barn, had declared he would take charge of roasting the meat while the rest of the men worked.

"Try not to let him overdo, will you?" Nick urged softly, glancing toward the wiry old cowboy, who was getting stiffly to his feet at the moment from another table. "When he's not tending the roasting meat, he's been walking around all morning, making suggestions. I'm afraid he's tiring himself out."

"Sarah said she'd try to get him to go take a rest inside this afternoon and let her take over, but you know how stubborn he can be," she whispered back. "He hates being on the sidelines. It was either let him tend the barbecue or we'd find him up on a ladder trying to hammer the new roof."

His smile was sympathetic. "Very well, then, I'll see you later," he said, and rejoined the other men for the afternoon's work. Milly's gaze followed him, watching him help several men lift one of the frames to fasten it to the upright beams.

"The new gentlemen seem like nice fellows," Sarah said, as she gathered up a load of dirty plates to wash. She nodded toward Markison and Collier, who were taking up hammers.

"Yes, and they already seem smitten with Caroline and Emily," Milly observed, grinning as they watched the two ladies staring at the newcomers and giggling together.

"Who'd have thought Caroline was such a flirt?" Sarah remarked, laughing. "She really swooped in and took charge of that Collier fellow, didn't she?"

"Not that he minded," Milly said. "He can't take his eyes off her."

"And the widower seems very pleased with Emily, too."

Milly thought she heard a note of wistfulness in her sister's voice, and studied Sarah more closely. "Dearest, you don't…that is, you and the other ladies—Prissy,

Maude, Ada, Jane—y'all aren't feeling left out, are you?"

"Oh, no," Sarah insisted, a little too quickly. "I can't speak for them, but as for me, I—I'm very content to wait for my turn—*if* it comes. Help me get the rest of these dishes and silverware back to the kitchen, so we'll have enough for us."

Milly joined the others who were picking up stacks of dishes and covering platters of food to keep the flies off. They had to work around Waters and Dayton and three other men, who had remained at the table, talking with lowered voices, their heads all close together. They stopped talking and sat back to allow Milly and the others to pick up their dirty dishes, making Milly feel almost like she was intruding.

"We're just takin' our time digestin' that fine meal, ladies," Bill Waters said. "You don't mind, do you?"

"No," Prissy Gilmore said in her outspoken way, with a pointed look at the other men who were already hard at work. "As long as you don't mind us ladies taking over the table in a few minutes."

"Those pies were mighty fine, Miss Sarah," Bill Waters said, balancing his chair on the back two legs, his hand joined over his rounded abdomen. He pointedly ignored Milly. "Yessir, Miss Sarah would make some lucky man a fine wife. Can you imagine enjoyin' pie like this every evening?"

There were chuckles from the other men, and one of the others murmured, "Too bad I'm already hitched."

Milly could tell Sarah hated their attention by the dull flush of color. "Oh, I wouldn't bake pies for my husband every day, Mr. Waters. I wouldn't want him to get fat." She didn't look at his belly, but her meaning had been plain enough, so the other men guffawed as if she had said it.

"Guess she told you, Waters."

Milly and Sarah took their armloads of dishes and walked off without saying another word until they reached the sanctuary of the kitchen. For the moment, they were alone, but the other ladies would soon be joining them there.

"The *nerve* of those men," Milly fumed. "If I wasn't a lady, I'd tell them to go home. They came only to eat, after all. They've hardly lifted a finger to help the other men. Why, Josh has done more, keeping the spits turning, than all of them combined."

"We'll just pretend they don't exist," her sister said, laying a comforting hand on her shoulder. "But, Milly, what do you suppose they're up to? Whenever I'd bring a new platter to their part of the table, they were talking about 'the circle' and 'ridding Simpson Creek of the trash the Yankees sent us.'"

Milly stared at her, startled. Wanting to be near Nick, she'd made sure to be the one to take and refill platters and cups at his table, and hadn't heard any of this.

"I don't know what this 'circle' is, but I've heard them say nasty things about the homeless former slaves I've occasionally seen wandering the roads."

"Those men said they were going to make sure they didn't 'roost here,'" Sarah said. "And they were saying nasty things about Nick and the two new men, too— about not letting Simpson Creek be taken over by foreigners and 'Johnny-come-latelies,' and making sure they knew their place."

Milly felt a shaft of anger stab through her. "Well, they're the *only* ones who don't like Nick, then. Did you see the way the other men were talking to Nick like they'd known him all their lives? Those are the men who really represent Simpson Creek, I think. And they seemed to be making Mr. Markison and Mr. Collier welcome, too." She'd enjoyed the way the men of the town seemed to have made Nick one of their own. She'd heard them talking about plans to make the town safer in case of Indian attack, and had looked forward to asking him about it.

When they went back outside to bring in another load, their tormentors were saddling their horses.

"Good riddance," she muttered under her breath, then immediately asked forgiveness for her lack of charity and patience.

No sooner had the men disappeared, however, it seemed heaven was giving her another chance to display these virtues, for a pair of horses pulling a buckboard came lumbering around the bend and pulled to a creaking stop. It was driven by George Detwiler, Junior, who tended bar at the local saloon, and the old lady he helped down from it was none other than his mother, Mrs. Detwiler.

Lord, I said I was sorry, she protested inwardly. She'd been secretly glad this morning when her critic had failed to show up when the other ladies had arrived, and assumed this was Mrs. Detwiler's way of tacitly emphasizing her disapproval of Milly. But now here she was, and being handed down a covered dish that looked suspiciously like a cake.

Smoothing her features to hide her dismay, Milly

went forward to welcome the older woman. Where was Sarah when she needed her sister's diplomacy?

"Hello, Mrs. Detwiler," she said. "How nice of you to come. When we didn't see you this morning, we feared you might be ill—"

"You didn't care enough to send someone to check, though, did you?" the older woman retorted. "No, I couldn't very well come until my son could take an hour away from the saloon to drive me, could I? Since no one else offered to bring me," she added, with a resentful glance at the rows of parked buggies and wagons.

Milly didn't suppose she asked anyone for a ride, just waited for someone to read her mind. "I'm sorry, you're right, of course. We *should* have thought to send Nick or Bobby to fetch you." Which would have required pulling one of them away from their tasks here. "I'll see that one of them takes you home, though, whenever you're ready."

Mrs. Detwiler sniffed. "As if I'd let that young rapscallion Bobby drive me anywhere. We'd probably end up overturned in a ditch. And as for that Britisher, you called him *'Nick'*? Not 'Mr. Brookfield,' as is proper? My girl, if you behave in this fast, loose way, how do you expect to gain the favor of a real gentleman?"

Too late, Milly saw the trap she'd fallen into. "Mr. Brookfield is an employee of the ranch now, and as such, he asked that I call him by his Christian name. He calls me 'Miss Milly,' of course." *Please, God, help me keep my temper!* "But I'm glad you managed to get here, in spite of the difficulties, and how nice of you to bring… what is it, cake?"

Mrs. Detwiler sniffed. "Of course. Everyone clamors

for my chocolate cake at social events. And even if the town's duty to its widows has been forgotten, I believe I know *my* duty to support the community. I could hardly stay home at my ease when all of Simpson Creek has gathered to help you. George, dear, you may pick me up whenever you are able tonight, if I have not come home already," she told her son, who was turning the wagon in a wide circle to return back the way he had come. "My son, of course, cannot stay—not everyone is able to just drop their usual tasks for a daylong party."

Milly glanced back at where the men were muscling yet another frame to the upright beams, a strenuous job requiring teamwork. Hardly a party game.

"Come and eat," Milly said, gesturing at the food-laden table. "We ladies are about to have our dinner, now that the men have eaten and gone back to work."

Chapter Thirteen

The sun was setting, illuminating the new barn in rays of red and gold. In the next few days, Nick and Bobby would spend many hours painting it, but for now it stood in unadorned, simple splendor. The scent of newly hewn wood filled the air and mingled with the savory odor of the barbecue.

"I reckon we should pray again before we sit down to this feast. Isn't it wonderful having the ladies and gents and children all together this time?" Reverend Chadwick smiled, and standing in front of their places at the tables, everyone bowed their heads.

"Almighty God, this morning we purposed to 'rise up and build' and we thank You for blessing our efforts. Behind us stands a completed barn where this morning there were but a few ashes left from the old one. We thank You for giving our men strength and safety in this effort, and for the tasty dinner we had at noon, and the equally delicious supper we're about to partake of, courtesy of our ladies—and Josh. Amen."

There was a din of people settling into their chairs, the hum of conversation and the clinking of spoons against crockery as people passed the serving dishes piled high with barbecued beef, pinto beans cooked with bacon, hot biscuits, corn bread and slabs of butter. Amid the noise Nick turned to Milly. "So this dress is what kept you from the porch in the evenings all this week?" he asked in a low voice designed to carry only as far as her ears. "It's very becoming."

"Thank you." His compliment had her flushing with pleasure.

He had no idea how handsome he was, she thought, his skin bronzed by the sun, making his eyes seem that much bluer. Like most of the men, he'd dunked his head under the pump after the work was done to cool off, and now a loose lock of drying golden hair fell forward onto his forehead.

It would have been unladylike to confess how often her eyes had strayed to him all afternoon, watching the smooth play of his shoulder muscles under his shirt as he strained with the other men to help lift the skeletons of the barn frames with ropes. He'd climbed a ladder to help pound the rafters in place, then the roof's tin covering. Next came the boards to the sides of the barn. Agile as a cat, he'd scrambled up the frames with the others to join the higher boards and trusses in place. She'd savored his appreciative smile when she'd taken a bucket of freshly pumped cold water out to the men, and watched a mug passing from hand to hand to where he'd been straddling the ridgeline, and the muscles of his throat as he lifted the mug to swallow the water in a few quick gulps.

Had he been born with such grace?

As if reading her mind, Andy Calhoun leaned across

the table and drawled, "Nick, I thought you said you was a soldier, but you was shinnyin' up them frames like you'd been buildin' things all yore life."

Nick grinned. "I'm afraid I was the despair of my father, for as a boy I'd much rather climb a tree or help the fellow who came to repair the roof on the dower house than play cricket or chess with the sons of Lord Swarthmore."

Cricket? Dower house? What did these words mean? Milly wondered as she passed yet another steaming platter of savory barbecue. She'd have to ask him later.

"Your pa knew one a' them English lords?" the other man asked, clearly awed.

"Actually, my father was a lord himself—a viscount, actually," Nick admitted, almost as if it was something to be embarrassed about.

"Then why don't we call you 'Lord Brookfield,' or somethin' like that?"

"I'm a third son, not a lord. I'm just an 'honorable.' My oldest brother Edward inherited the title, while my middle brother Richard went into the Church. So it was the Army for me," he finished, as if that was his only logical destiny, "where my climbing skills came in handy once when the maharajah's young son managed to clamber up onto the upper reaches of an ancient banyan tree but was too scared to climb down."

Calhoun whistled. "And now you're here in Simpson Creek, Texas, buildin' a barn for Miss Milly and Miss Sarah. Ain't life interesting?"

Nick tipped his head back and laughed, a merry sound that sent tendrils of warmth curling around Milly's heart. He turned to look at Milly next to him for a moment, then back at the other man. "Indeed it is, Andy. Indeed it is."

Andy's questions seemed to break the ice for the others, and Nick could hardly get an uninterrupted bite due to all the questions he was asked. It gave Milly a warm feeling to see how completely the Englishman had come to be accepted among the townspeople. Everyone liked Nicholas Brookfield, which made her feel as if her growing love for him was not ill-judged. Everyone, she reminded herself, except those such as Waters and Dayton.

"I surely did like the idea you mentioned at noon about building a fort, Nick," Mr. Patterson, sitting up the table a couple of places, said during a momentary lull in the conversation. "I don't think it would attract the Federals here, like Waters was afraid of. I don't know when we'd all have time to work on it, but I do think it's a good idea."

There were nods of agreement from several men up and down the table.

Then Mrs. Patterson spoke to her husband on his other side, distracting him.

"Fort? What fort is he talking about?" Milly asked.

Nick looked a little uncomfortable.

"Why did Mr. Waters say it would bring the Federals?"

Nick sighed. "Possibly I've overstepped my bounds, and if I have, you need only to say so. I—I'd hoped to talk to you about it after the party. We were discussing the likelihood of another Comanche attack, since everyone thinks they might get more bold after getting away with it the last time. This time the Comanches hit only one ranch—yours—but they tell me in times past, they've raided many ranches, sometimes an entire town, burning, looting, killing, taking captives."

Milly couldn't suppress her involuntary shudder at the thought of being snatched away by savage Indians. It was said that the ones who were killed at the scene of a raid were the lucky ones. She glanced involuntarily at Josh, who was holding fort at another table about his secret barbecue sauce recipe. He was still moving stiffly, still wasn't up to taking on a cowboy's work yet.

"A fort would give people a place to take refuge when the Comanches are raiding, a place where the men could defend their families," Nick explained. "Properly placed, a lookout at a fort would be able to give warning when the Comanches were coming. We'd have a big bell up there to toll the warning. A fort might even serve as a deterrent. Who would want to attack such a community?"

"Where would you put such a thing?" Milly asked, though she had already guessed.

"Subject to your permission, of course, atop that hill behind us."

She'd been right. Milly swiveled in her seat to look behind her at the hill that overlooked the ranch, and the road from town that ran along the southeast side of it.

"A fort? On Matthews property? Made of what? Why there?"

He answered her last question first. "As a former soldier—" A shadow passed over his eyes as he said the words. "I can tell you it's a commanding position.

From that position, one could see what's coming in all directions. It's not far from town, and there's a deer trail up to the top," he went on, pointing, "that could be widened enough for wagon traffic. You and Sarah and the townspeople could take refuge there, and the men could fire at the Indians from the safety of the walls." He paused a moment, as if to let her take it in. "And as for the materials, it's a very rocky soil, isn't it? Limestone, I'm told. If all that loose rock could be gathered up, I imagine most of the fort could be made of freestone and some sort of mortar. The other men agreed that would work."

"You seem to have thought it all out," she said faintly, her mind whirling at the implications.

"Not completely, no, and as I said, I should have spoken to you first. It must seem incredibly cheeky of me to be speaking of a use for part of your land when I'm only your ranch hand."

She raised her eyes to that blue, intense gaze of his, her heart pounding. "I think you know you're becoming more than that."

He blinked. "I...I hope so, Milly. Then you're not dreadfully angry at me? Still, it would have been proper to ask you first, but at the noon meal, one of the gentlemen began talking about the likelihood of another Indian raid and the need for some sort of protection in the area...and I...I mentioned what I'd been thinking about."

"No, I'm not angry," she said. "It's a lot to consider, yes. And to discuss with Sarah, and Josh, and the rest of the town. But why did Mr. Waters think such a thing would bring the Yankees here?"

"He said if we built a defensive fortification it would look like we were planning to mount a resistance against their occupation—a rebirth of the Confederacy. And he said that would make the 'blue bellies' come down on San Saba County like a wagonload of anvils. The last thing anyone around here wants, according to him, is Federal troops occupying Simpson Creek."

Milly pursed her lips. Would building a small fort—a place that would usually stand unoccupied—bring the Yankees to her town? It seemed unlikely, but memories of the war were still raw and bitter. It might even lead to ill feelings and reprisals toward Sarah and her for allowing a fort to be built in the first place.

"But before you spend another moment worrying about it," Nick added, "I should tell you the consensus is that most of them couldn't figure out when they'd find the time to work on such a project." He sighed again. "It's not like a stone fort could be erected in a day, like a barn." His hand sought hers under the table and gave it a quick squeeze, then let hers go before anyone could notice. "Why don't we agree to talk of this later?" he suggested. "It's much too serious a topic for such a festive occasion."

For the next hour, everyone ate and talked and laughed. Even Mrs. Detwiler, seated down at the far end of Milly's table, had lost her sour expression. Sarah was keeping the old woman busy talking, no doubt asking her opinion about everything she could think of. God bless her sister for her big heart!

Then it was time for dessert. All through the meal, the children had been eyeing the plates of cookies, cakes and pies sitting on a separate, smaller table—especially

Mrs. Detwiler's chocolate cake and Sarah's pecan pies. Now several of the adults were staring at them with open interest, too.

Milly stood and rapped on her plate with her fork to get everyone's attention while Sarah came to her side.

"I'd like to thank everyone for coming," she said. "Your generosity in pitching in to build a barn for us— well, there are not words enough to tell you how appreciated that is…" She stopped then, feeling the sting of happy tears in her eyes and a thickening in her throat that made further speech difficult. "I—that is, my sister and I," she said, putting an arm around Sarah's waist to draw her closer, "we thank God for all of you and will keep you in our prayers every day. If there's ever anything we can do for you, you have but to ask. I know no one wants to hear a long speech right now, so I'll just say it again—thank you from the bottom of our hearts."

There were cheers and applause and whistles and stamps as her voice trailed off, but she held up a hand. "I'm told my friend Prissy has some instructions about the desserts…"

Prissy marched forward then, smiling broadly and waving, always pleased to be the center of attention. "I'd like to echo Milly's thanks to everyone for coming and giving of their time and effort to build a barn, and to feed those who did the building," she said. "Milly and Sarah are trying their very best to keep their papa's ranch going. But we're not done, ladies and gentlemen. That wood you've been hammering and sawing all afternoon has yet to be paid for. We don't want to build a barn, then leave Sarah and Milly with a big debt for all that wood, do we?"

"*Noooooo*," everyone chorused.

"Then we are going to have to help these girls defray the cost, aren't we?"

"*Yes…*" the diners agreed, though less enthusiastically.

"Good. I'm glad you agree. For we're about to auction off all these sweet goodies you see at the table." Everyone groaned, but Prissy went right on. "For example, who's making the first bid for this dee-licious chocolate cake, baked by our very own Mrs. Detwiler?"

Milly shared an amused glance with Nick and Sarah as the old woman preened at the attention. But bidding— led by Prissy, who was in her element as auctioneer— was brisk, and eventually Mrs. Detwiler's cake went for three dollars to a cowboy from the Waters ranch who was flush with his month's pay.

Then Sarah's pies were auctioned, one at a time. Nick gallantly started the bidding at two dollars on the first one, and kept the bids rising by adding two bits each time someone else bid. Then, once the last bidder had bid five dollars, he graciously conceded. He did this for all three of the pies she had made, and finally won the bidding on the last one. Other pies and cakes fetched lower amounts, but it all added up, and finally, the reverend purchased the cookies for two dollars and dispensed them to the children.

Prissy came forward again. "Well, we've raised sixty dollars, folks, but we still have a long way to go. You can hear our musicians tuning up over there for the dancing we've been promised," she said, nodding toward a couple of fiddlers and a man strumming a guitar. "Now, there's nothing more fun than dancing to good fiddle music, is there? But we're going to make you fellows pay for the pleasure this time—just a little. We're charging two bits a dance, except for husbands with their wives— they have to pay only once."

Groans and protests erupted, but Prissy's smile didn't dim in the least. "Quit your bellyachin', fellows. You know the ladies are worth it, and it's for a good cause. Place your coins in the bowl here on the table."

Chapter Fourteen

The moon had sunk low in the sky and all but the oldest children were asleep in or under wagon beds when one of the fiddlers announced the last dance.

"Morning's going to come all too soon, even though Reverend Chadwick's agreed to delay the service an hour. Now, we've saved the best for last—we're going to make this final one a waltz, folks."

A pleased chorus greeted this announcement. They had danced reels, schottisches, polkas and square dances—the latter entirely new to Nick, of course, with its allemande lefts and rights and do-si-dos, but he'd caught on quickly with the generous help of the partiers—but there had been no waltzes.

"So husbands, take your wives' hands, and you courtin' fellas, find a lady to dance with."

"My dance, I believe?" Nick said, crossing to where Milly had just danced an energetic reel with one of the cowboys who'd come from nearby ranches. He hadn't liked seeing the fellow claim her for the reel, but to be fair, he'd danced at least half of the other dances with

Milly. He realized she had a social duty to dance with
some of the other gentlemen present.

During these times he danced with the other ladies,
not only the ladies of the Society, but those whose husbands were not enthusiastic dancers, earning him much
gratitude.

"But I was hopin'—" the fellow started to protest.

"I'm sorry, Hap, but I did promise Mr. Brookfield the
last dance," Milly apologized. "Look—Miss Spencer
has no partner. Perhaps you should ask her."

As Hap loped away in the direction of Ada Spencer,
Milly gave Nick a smile of relief and welcome.

"I'm so glad you reserved this last dance," she whispered. "He's a nice boy, but he must have stepped on
my feet three times—and you know in a reel, partners
aren't dancing that close most of the time. I'd probably
be limping after a waltz!"

"Ah, so it's only to escape injured feet that you're glad
to see me?" Nick teased, assuming a mock-aggrieved
expression.

"Silly! You know that's not the only reason," she told
him as the musicians strummed the opening strains of
"Lorena."

Nick was glad that small-town Texas folk ignored
the custom of wearing gloves at dances, for he savored
the warmth of her smaller hand in his as much as the
glow of her eyes as they whirled gracefully around the
makeshift dirt dance floor. Other couples danced past
them—Caroline and Pete Collier, Emily Thompson and
Ed Markison, Sarah and one of the other cowboys, Mr.
and Mrs. Patterson, but he and Milly might have been
the only couple dancing. He wanted the dance to go on

forever, so he could go on holding her, moving with her, like this.

"You waltz very well," she told him, making him glad of every one of those tedious weekly dances he'd attended in Bombay. They had been held to allow the daughters of the married officers to mingle with the "griffins" as the new junior officers of the company were called, for most of those who were "old India hands" were either married themselves or, more rarely, confirmed bachelors.

"Thank you. And so do you, Milly," he said. He wondered if she had learned to waltz before the war and had danced this dance with a favorite beau. Oddly, the thought didn't trouble him. She was dancing with *him* now, and from the look in her shining hazel eyes, she was very pleased to have it so.

The other couples had dropped out by now, and they had the floor to themselves. Everyone watched them, and the fiddlers and guitar player prolonged the music. When the music faded away, there was a burst of applause.

Even in the flickering light of the hanging lanterns, he could see her blush, suddenly self-conscious, as if she had totally forgotten the rest of the world while she was dancing with him. The thought pleased him immeasurably.

Surely it was time to advance his courtship?

"I'm going to help the men hitch up their wagon horses," Nick told Milly, with a nod toward the corral, where Bobby—who'd been too young and bashful to take part in the dancing—was already doing that. "Perhaps we could spend a few minutes together on the porch once all the guests have departed?"

She blinked, and a slow smile curved her lips. "I'd like that," she said. "And now I'd better help the ladies round up their dishes and their older children."

It was over an hour before the last wagon rolled out of the yard and disappeared around the bend in the road toward town.

"Good night, Miss Milly, Miss Sarah," Josh said. "It sure was a fine party."

"Thanks in large part for your delicious barbecue," Milly said.

Sarah agreed and added, "Please, won't you share your recipe with me?"

"Mebbe," Josh said, a twinkle in his eye. "If you'll bake me another a' them pecan pies. I didn't get nothin' but one skinny piece this time. C'mon, Bobby, help this old cowboy get over to th' bunkhouse. I've stiffened up, settin' too long watchin' the dancin' and jawin' with old Mr. Preston."

"Oh, Milly, that reminds me," Sarah said, "Mrs. Preston told me they'd decided they were too old to be ranching anymore, so they're moving to San Antonio to live with their son and his family—and they're *giving* us their flock of chickens, a half-dozen pigs and twenty head of cattle!"

Nick saw Milly's mouth fall open in astonishment. "But that's wonderful! How nice of them, when they could easily sell them. I…I wish I'd known that, before they left, so I could thank them."

"That's probably why they told *me,* sister. I imagine they figured you'd insist on paying them somehow,"

Sarah said, with loving exasperation. "They told me Papa had helped them take care of the stock while Mr. Preston was laid up with a broken arm, so they wanted to do this for us."

How true, Nick thought. If the old wife had announced the gift to Milly, she *would* have tried to decline, unless she could pay for the livestock. And that would be more debt on top of the what they owed for the lumber, for there was certainly no way the money raised by the pie-and-cake auction and the dances, could have covered all the cost of the barn lumber. His Texas rose surely had stubborn streaks of pride and independence!

Milly had had no idea how much she and her sister were loved by the town, Nick thought, having watched the surprised joy in her eyes today as Simpson Creek turned out en masse to help them. Nick smiled to himself. Miss Milly Matthews was going to be one surprised lady when she went to give Dayton the money that had been raised, and tried to bargain for time to pay off the balance, for she was going to learn that a mysterious benefactor had already paid it!

Nick and Milly sat down together, not in their respective rocking chairs as usual, but this time on the porch swing. They spoke of inconsequential things until light no longer shone from within the house or the bunkhouse. Milly had kept a lantern to light her way into the house, but she had turned it down so it emitted only a faint glow between them. The only sound came from the sleepy hooting of an owl in a nearby tree and the crickets chirping in the grass.

"I enjoyed your Texas hoedown—at least that's what

Josh called it—very much, Milly," he told her, wondering how to broach the subject on his mind. "The whole day, actually. Everyone was so friendly and kind."

At least after Mr. Waters and Mr. Dayton and their cronies left, he thought, and later, the dour Mrs. Detwiler, who seemed to have it in for Milly. The crabby old woman could be avoided, but those men seemed right bad apples and Nick wished Milly and Sarah's land didn't border on Waters's.

"They like you very much, too, Nick. Everyone's been telling me how impressed they were at how hard you've been working around here, but especially today. And the ladies like your accent," she added with a giggle.

"Do they now?" he said, amused, but also touched at his acceptance by the townspeople. *Would they still like him if they knew everything about him?* "But if I stay around for very long, I might start drawling and saying 'y'all,' you know. How would you like that?"

She laughed, but suddenly she became still, as if she'd realized the deeper meaning of his words.

"I'm wondering if we might amend our agreement, Milly."

"Wh-what do you mean, exactly?"

"We agreed I was here to help while Josh is laid up, nothing more. But holding you tonight as we waltzed was like a wonderful dream, a dream I wanted to come true. I'd like to court you, Milly. I know we had agreed to postpone it until Josh had recovered, but I...I don't want to wait any longer—if you're willing, that is."

He held his breath for the endless seconds it took her to answer.

"Yes, Nick. My answer is yes. But…how do we begin?" she said, her voice sounding a little breathless.

He took a deep breath, praying he was not being too bold, but nothing in her eyes made him think so. "For one thing, we could kiss to seal the deal, rather than shaking hands."

"Ahh," she said, and tilted her face to his.

Her lips were the sweetest he'd ever tasted. And he could tell from her drawn breath that she'd never been kissed before.

Better not rush your fences, lad. Taking his lips from hers, he gazed into her face. Surely all the starlight in Texas had taken up residence in her eyes.

"Could we…I'm sorry, I'm afraid I'm being very forward, but might we do that again?" she asked, her voice tremulous.

His heart sang within him. "It would be my pleasure, dear girl," he said, and lowered his head again, intending to make this kiss deeper and much more leisurely…

Just as his eyes nearly closed, out of the corner of one eye he caught a movement in the shadows by the barn.

He jerked away from Milly and was instantly on his feet, instinctively standing in front of her.

"What is it? Nick, what's wrong? Why—"

"Quiet! Milly, get inside, now!" he commanded in a whisper, motioning for her to move quickly. To his relief, she obeyed, and he followed her.

Once inside, he reached for one of the two rifles in their horizontal racks over the coat pegs. "I saw something—someone—creep into the barn. I've got to find out who it is. You stay here."

"An Indian?" she whispered, her eyes enormous in the dark kitchen.

"I don't know," he admitted. "I didn't see more than a quick movement."

"But you can't go out there by yourself!" she cried, still keeping her voice down, but seizing his wrist with a shaking hand. "If it's a Comanche, he won't be alone! Go get Bobby—"

He blew out the lantern.

"Milly, *stay here!*" he barked. "Lock the door behind me, then grab the other rifle and have it ready. Don't make a sound!" He went back outside before she could say anything more, praying she would do as he said.

Chapter Fifteen

Milly huddled in the dark kitchen, clutching her rifle, staring out through the window at the hulking shape of the barn into which Nick had disappeared, sure he was wrong to have gone alone, sure she should run out to the bunkhouse and wake Bobby and send him to the barn to help Nick—maybe even Josh, too. She was sure that any minute now, she would hear a blood-curdling war whoop, followed by Nick's cutoff scream. Then the rest of the Comanches would erupt from the trees and attack the house…

Then she saw him walking back to the house, briskly, but his gait did not appear alarmed. She dashed to the door to let him in.

"It wasn't a Comanche," he said.

"Then who w—"

"Come, and bring the lantern. I'll show you."

Her hands still trembling, she relit the lantern and followed him out into the night once again. The lantern cast wobbling circles of light on the ground as they walked.

Once inside the barn, he took the lantern from her

and held it high, illuminating four men huddling in the corner of the rearmost stall. They were of differing ages, but similar in height and build, and alike in the darkness of their skin, the whiteness of their wide eyes and the raggedy condition of their clothes.

"Miss Millicent Matthews, may I present Elijah Brown and his brothers—Isaiah, Caleb and Micah." He pointed at each of them in turn.

All of the men pulled off their hats, three of which were tattered and floppy-brimmed, while the youngest wore a forage cap, and inclined their heads with a dignity that nevertheless betrayed their apprehension.

"We're sorry t' have give you a fright, Miss Matthews, we surely are. We was jes' lookin' fer shelter for the night, that's all, I promise you, ma'am," the one called Elijah said.

All eyes were on her, including Nick's. And as she stared back at them, she saw how thin they all were, especially the one in the middle—Caleb, had that been his name? His clothes, or what was left of them, hung from his tall frame as if he had once been almost stocky.

"But...how did you come here?" she asked.

"We been wanderin' the roads, ma'am, lookin' for work, but so far we ain't found none. We saw this barn goin' up today, and Isaiah wanted us t' offer to help in exchange fer supper, but I didn't think that was a good idea, what with all th' folks that was here. Some folks don' like havin' us 'round, y'understand." The last thing he said with an apologetic but matter-of-fact air.

"Miss Milly, might we give them something to eat?"

Nick asked. "Elijah says they haven't had anything in two days except for some pecans they found."

There was food left from the party—half a pie, a dozen or so pieces of fried chicken, a basketful of biscuits, a dish of green beans. Sarah had covered them and left them on the cast-iron stove, saying it would be their Sunday dinner, but how could Milly say no? Hope shone from the dark eyes trained on her.

"Of course," she said. "Nick, would you come back to the kitchen with me and help me carry things?"

He followed her back to the house. "Milly, I think the answer to our problem is in that barn," he said softly, once they were back in the kitchen.

She turned to him. "What problem? What are you saying?" It was late. There were four strangers, homeless former slaves, in her barn, and she didn't have time for riddles.

"You need help to run the ranch properly, these men need jobs. Why not let them stay? I imagine they'd work for their board alone, like we do, until you could afford to pay them."

She felt her mouth drop open. "I…I don't know," she said at last. "I—I'd have to think about it…and ask Sarah, and Josh…" She had no experience with other races; she'd never had occasion to even speak to a person with dark skin. Before the war, there had been few slaves in ranching country except for one or two on the bigger spreads, mostly kept as cooks and household help. Most slaves had lived in the rice- and cotton-growing plantation areas to the east and south.

She remembered the men whispering at the table today, and the conversation Nick had reported overhearing between Waters and Dayton, about how "the circle" was going to take care of the problem posed by just such men as Nick had found in the barn.

Aware that he was waiting for an answer, Milly turned back to the leftover food on the stove. "I…we'll have to see," she said. "Meanwhile, let's take this food out to them."

Was there a flash of disappointment in those blue eyes?

Milly pulled open a drawer in the cabinet and took out four tin forks from the supply of eating utensils used during spring roundups and picnics. She wasn't about to risk the loss of any of Mama's silverware. Then she felt guilty for her suspicion. She had no reason to think these men were thieves, no matter what the likes of Waters and Dayton said.

"Thank ya, ma'am," Elijah Brown said as the men eagerly took the dishes and the forks from them. "We'll be movin' on once we've et. We'll leave th' dishes and forks right here when we go. We don't wanna be no trouble."

"But it's the middle of the night," she said. "You can sleep here at least."

She thought she saw wetness in the man's liquid brown eyes, but he blinked before she could be sure. "That's right decent a' you, ma'am. Thank ya."

"I'll bring them some spare blankets from the bunk-house," Nick said, and she saw approval lighting his gaze. He followed her out. "I really think it's the perfect solution, Milly," he said, as they stopped halfway between the bunkhouse and the house.

"I'll think about it," she repeated, wishing he wouldn't

try to rush her about this. "And pray about it. I have to see what the others say. Tell those men…you can tell them not to leave in the morning until we've made our decision."

"Very well," he said, and left her, striding toward the bunkhouse without another word.

Vaguely disappointed, she went into the house. Why couldn't he tell her he understood her hesitation? Hadn't he just kissed her? Hadn't they just agreed to begin courting?

In the morning, over breakfast, she told Sarah, Josh and Bobby about their visitors, and Nick's idea, while Nick ate his eggs and biscuits and said nothing.

"Well, what do you think?" she said into the thoughtful silence.

Sarah shrugged. "I don't know, Milly…. Whatever you decide is all right with me."

Milly shot her sister an exasperated look before turning to the old cowboy. "Josh, what do *you* think? Is it a good idea?"

Josh leaned back in his chair. "Well…we could give it a try. Tell 'em they could stay on a trial basis, see how it works out. We *do* need help around here, like Nick says. I ain't never worked around them folks, though…" He grinned crookedly and chuckled. "Might be worth it just to put a stick in Bill Waters's spokes."

Milly sighed. It was all very well for Josh to be gleeful about aggravating their cantankerous neighbor, but she and Sarah would bear the brunt of any reaction, not Josh.

She was going to get no real help in making the decision, she saw, other than the feeling she had gotten while lying awake praying until nearly dawn this morning.

If you do this for the least of these My brethren, you do it for Me.

She sighed. She needed to decide, so they could all get on with getting ready for church. "All right, Nick, I suppose we can—" she began, but shut her mouth again as the sound of hoofbeats reached her ears.

It was Waters and a trio of his ranch hands, she saw from the window, and by the time she got to the door, they had stopped in front of the house, sending a cloud of dust flying through the air. The men were all armed, with rifles tied to the backs of their saddles and pairs of pistols in their belt holsters.

"What can I do for you, Mr. Waters?" she said, hearing someone coming to stand behind her and knowing without looking that it was Nick. "We were just getting ready for church."

"Sorry to disturb you, Miss Milly, but we're out lookin' for that band a' ex-slaves that's been robbin' folks blind around these parts. I found 'em roastin' a steer on my property, bold as you please, and I wanted to make sure they weren't botherin' you, too."

By an effort of will, Milly kept her eyes from straying to the barn behind the men, lest she give away the four men's presence. If what Waters said was true, the men in the barn had lied to her about being hungry. But they hadn't looked at the food like men who'd just eaten beef steaks. *Please, God, don't let them come out of the barn right now or even peek out.* "No, they haven't bothered us," she said with perfect honesty.

"That's good. Well, you go on to church, then, but

if you happen to see 'em on the road, you tell them to git outta San Saba County, or there's white men who'll teach 'em a lesson they might not live to regret, them and anyone fool enough to shelter 'em." He touched the brim of his hat automatically, the gesture of respect mocking after the threat he'd just uttered.

Chilled to the bone despite the heat of the sun, Milly stepped back inside without a word while the riders wheeled and galloped away.

"I'm sorry," she said, as soon as she'd closed the door. "I'm afraid they can't stay after all. You'd better tell them to move on."

He looked thunderstruck. "You're going to let that… that blowhard tell you what to do?"

She flinched at the incredulity in his voice. She'd hoped he wouldn't question what she said. "You heard Waters," she said, her hand outstretched in a plea for his understanding. "Surely you can understand I—we— have no choice. Those men might be in danger if they stay, and we can't chance having trouble here. Why, they might even burn the ranch down."

Josh and Bobby and Sarah were silent, watching as Milly pled for his understanding.

"Or they might understand that it's your choice to employ whom you please, Miss Milly," Nick said evenly, while his eyes flashed blue sparks of ire. "People like Waters are cowards, and they thrive only as long as they can intimidate others into doing what they say."

It was a challenge, and she knew it, but as much as she wanted to quench the anger in his gaze, she couldn't give in. A part of her was angry that he'd placed her in this position and made her choose. Her heart ached in realization that saying no would probably toll the death knell over what had been beginning between them.

"You're right, it *is* my choice to employ whom I please, Nick, and I'm telling you I can't risk what you're asking me to do. You're a foreigner here, and you weren't here to see the hatred and violence that ran rampant here between the men like Waters and the men who disagreed with them about slavery and such."

His eyes were hard as flint. "I've seen bigotry before, Miss Matthews. There was plenty of it in India, coming from the British and aimed at the very people whose country they'd taken over. They called the sepoys—the Hindu and Moslem Indians who served in the army— 'blackies' and treated them with contempt, even though they couldn't have held on to their comfortable life of privilege without them. I've seen the Indians themselves and their mistreatment of the 'untouchables,' the lowest caste, and I tell you I can't stomach it. But as you've reminded me, it's your decision to make."

There was nothing she could say to quench the contempt in his eyes, she thought, blinking against the sting of tears. "I'm sorry," she said again. "Does that mean you won't stay either?" She held her breath, afraid of his answer.

It was an eternity before he answered, and when he did he didn't look at her. "I've made a promise to you, and I'll keep it," he said at last. "I'll stay until Josh is able to work again. Then perhaps I'd better go back to Austin and take that job at the embassy, if it's still open."

She realized that he was telling her that anything

would be better than this, for he'd already expressed his distaste for that tedious position.

"Very well," she said.

"I'll tell them," he said, and left the house, letting the door slam behind him and leaving his breakfast half-eaten on the table.

When it was time to leave for church, there was no sign of him.

Chapter Sixteen

Josh stated he felt well enough to attend church, and whistled from the back of the wagon all the way there. Bobby, as usual, tried to wiggle his way out of going, but his uncle insisted that if he was going, Bobby was going, too. So the boy finally clambered aboard, his cowlick firmly wetted down and wearing his Sunday clothes.

Milly was grateful that their presence kept Sarah from speaking to her about the confrontation with Nick. Her feelings were too raw, too uncertain to talk about it. She already dreaded the end of the service, when someone was sure to ask her why her handsome British "cowboy" hadn't come to church with her this time.

She felt like a wooden puppet as she entered the church, greeted others, sat down with her sister, Josh and Bobby and sang the hymns. She was just going through the motions.

Nicholas Brookfield had nothing but contempt for her now, and as soon as Josh was completely back on his feet, he would leave. He thought her a coward for not being willing to employ the four homeless men because of Waters's threats.

But you just don't understand the risk, she argued with him in her mind. *I'm responsible for the welfare of my sister and the employees I already have, Josh and Bobby. How can I continue to feed them if the Matthews ranch is nothing but a smoking ruin? Where would Josh, as old as he is, get a new job? Where would Sarah and I live, in a tent?*

"My message today," began Reverend Chadwick, "is taken from the sixth chapter of Micah, verse eight, 'What doth the Lord require of thee, but to do justly, and to love mercy, and to walk humbly with thy God?'"

Inwardly, she groaned. How could refusing to give those men jobs be "doing justly"? Employing them would be showing mercy, but what if it caused them to come to harm at the hands of the mysterious "circle"? Surely it was better to let them move on to somewhere where their lives would be safer?

Even if she wanted to change her mind, though, those men were already gone—she knew this because she had peeked inside the barn while Bobby was hitching up the wagon. There was no sign of them, though the dishes and forks were neatly stacked in a corner of the stall on top of the folded blankets.

I'll show mercy next time, Lord, I promise, and act justly, I promise. I'm sorry I did the wrong thing this time. But how am I to make this right with Nick? Is it too late for that, too?

"Don't worry, it's all going to work out," Sarah whispered to her, as they stood to sing the final hymn.

Milly gave Sarah a grateful look. She was always so

perceptive. Milly had pretended to pay attention to the sermon, but her sister had sensed the presence of the turmoil within her.

Now she had to run the gauntlet between the church door and their wagon. *Please, Lord, don't let anyone ask me about Nick...*

"Now, where's that handsome gentleman I saw you waltzing with just last night, Milly Matthews?" Mrs. Patterson cooed. "My, he is a good-looking man! And I just *love* the way he talks, don't you?" She aimed the remark not at Milly but at Mrs. Detwiler, to whom she had been speaking when Milly and her sister drew near.

"I...uh..." What should she say?

"Evidently *foreigners* think it's all right to lie abed on the Lord's Day after a party," Mrs. Detwiler sniffed. "As for the way he talks, why, I don't know what's wrong with plain *American* speaking. It was good enough for me when my George walked this earth."

"We let Mr. Brookfield get some extra rest today," Sarah said, stealthily squeezing Milly's elbow. "It seemed only fair, since he was up on top of those rafters as much or more than any other man there. I noticed several of the men were missing this morning."

"Yes, my husband, for one," Mrs. Patterson said. "He's so stiff and sore this morning he could hardly get out of bed. I reckon he did too much, trying to keep up with the younger men like Mr. Brookfield. I told him the Lord would understand if he didn't come to church this morning."

Mrs. Detwiler was neatly caught. She could hardly

continue to criticize Nick for not being there if Mrs. Patterson's husband had stayed home, too.

"Good seeing you ladies," Milly said. "We must be getting home to start dinner."

But they were unable to make it to the wagon without encountering Caroline Wallace and Emily Thompson, who were accompanied by their two new beaus from the coast and looking happy as butterflies in a field full of bluebonnets. Fortunately, they were so wrapped up in their own joy that they accepted the same excuse Sarah had given the other two women at face value.

"Pete, Mr. Markison, Emily and I are going to have a picnic on Simpson Creek this afternoon," Caroline burbled. "Why don't you and Nick join us?"

"Oh, and you, too, Sarah, naturally," Emily added quickly.

Milly saw Caroline flush with embarrassment at her inadvertent gaffe.

"Oh, thanks, but after all the excitement yesterday I think I'd just like to rest," Sarah said imperturbably.

"Me, too, I'm afraid," Milly said. "Thanks for asking us. Another time, perhaps."

"We'll count on it."

After that, they made their escape to the wagon, where Josh and Bobby were already waiting.

"I'm sorry Caroline left you out of the invitation," Milly said, as she steered the horses back out onto the road. "She never seemed so giddy and thoughtless before."

Sarah patted Milly's hand and smiled. "She's not thoughtless, Milly, just excited. I'm pleased for her that it's going well so far. I wasn't feeling left out, I promise you."

Milly sighed and clucked to the horses to urge them into a trot. "You're a much better person than I am, Sarah." Although she, too, was pleased for the other ladies, her heart had ached that she couldn't accept their invitation—she wouldn't have had an escort either.

When they drew up at the ranch, she spotted Nick up on a ladder already slapping paint on the barn.

"Where did you get that?" she asked, pointing to the bucket from which he was brushing white paint onto the raw timber.

Nick had turned around when the wagon pulled into the yard, but now he turned back to his work. "Mr. Patterson brought it when they came yesterday. I thought he'd mentioned it."

"No. How thoughtful of him," Milly said, wishing Nick would turn around again, disappointed that he evidently hadn't gotten over his anger at her while she'd been gone to church. But she was a fool to have hoped he would, she told herself. "We'll call you when dinner's ready," she said, trying to sound bright and cheerful.

"I'm not hungry," came his curt reply.

Milly exchanged a look with Sarah.

"Well, come down from there and have some lemonade at least, and rest this afternoon," Sarah urged. "It's going to be too hot to be out here painting this afternoon. You'll have a sunstroke."

Nick turned half-around, then. "Thank you, Miss Sarah, but after a decade in India, I'm used to the heat." He might have been speaking to a stranger, he was so polite. "You needn't worry."

"But it's Sunday!" Milly protested, before she could stop herself. But she was once more speaking to his back.

"This needs to be done, Miss Milly," he said, plying his brush. "It would be a shame to let termites or rain damage such a new building."

"I'll be right out to help you, soon's I eat, Mr. Nick!" Bobby called, full of eagerness to help his hero and oblivious to the tension stretching between the man on the ladder and the woman on the ground.

"Let him go, Milly," Sarah whispered. "He'll come in when he's ready."

But he did not come in until supper, ate silently and quickly, then excused himself to go to the bunkhouse, muttering something about a headache.

"It ain't surprisin' he's got a sore head, bein' out in the sun all day like that," Josh commented, looking after him with shrewd eyes.

Nick had just asked her to partner him in the Virginia reel. In the illogical way of dreams, the Englishman showed no sign that he remembered their earlier dis-
_____ ment. He wore the gray dress uniform of a Con-
_____ ate officer, complete with a saber dangling from
_____ sh around his waist. He laughed as he bowed to her from the line of gentlemen that faced the ladies while the fiddler played the introductory notes of the tune.

"Miss Milly, Miss Milly!" Bobby's urgent shout pierced the pecan wood door and the fragile bubble of her fantasy.

What on earth? Another Comanche attack? But no war whoops pierced the stillness outside. Throwing a wrapper around her nightgown, Milly dashed to the door of her bedroom, rubbing the sleep out of her eyes as she went.

Bobby stood there clutching a lantern, the light transforming his worried face into that of a nightmare creature.

"What is it, Bobby? Is Josh w—"

"Naw, it's not my uncle, it's Mr. Nick. He's sick, Miss Milly, and shaking so hard I'm afraid he's gonna fall outta bed. And he's talkin' outta his head. Uncle Josh says you better come."

While he'd been speaking, Sarah's door had opened across from hers and Milly saw her sister standing there, taking in every word. "You go ahead, Milly," she said. "I'll get out some willow bark and start brewing a tea and bring it out to the bunkhouse as soon as it's ready."

Pausing just long enough to throw her shawl over her wrapper, Milly dashed after the boy, running to keep up with his long-legged stride. What could have struck Nick down so quickly? He'd worked too hard out in the heat all day, of course—could this be sunstroke, striking so many hours later?

Josh already managed to light a couple of lanterns in the bunkhouse, banishing the shadows to the far corners of the room and underneath the bunks. He'd been bent over one of the cots, but when he straightened and turned at the sound of the door banging open, his weathered, worn face was as apprehensive as Bobby's had been.

"Miss Milly, he wuz sound asleep when me 'n' Bobby came in t' bed down, but a few minutes ago he woke us up complainin' about the cold, and beggin' fer blankets." Josh said, shaking his head in amazement at a body needing blankets on a July night. "We piled every bit a' covering we could find in here on him, but it didn't seem to warm him at all. Then he was shoutin' about a tiger about t' spring on him, an' mumblin' some outlandish foreign gibberish." He took a step backward, sagging into the chair behind him, and Milly could see the cot on which Nick lay.

Even before she reached his bedside, Milly saw the sheet over Nick fluttering from his trembling beneath it, and heard a rhythmic clicking. She thought it was the legs of the bed shaking against the floor planks, but then she realized it was it was Nick's chattering teeth. His face was pale and his skin bumpy with gooseflesh.

"Nick!"

His eyes were slitted open and seemed to track the sound, but there was no recognition in them. "Ambika…" he said, and mumbled some unintelligible phrase.

Ambika? What—or who—was Ambika? Was he speaking some tongue he'd learned in India?

"Sarah's coming with some willow bark tea," she murmured over her shoulder to the old man and the boy. "Hang on, Nick." *Oh, Sarah, hurry!* She collapsed onto her knees next to the bed. *God, save him! Don't let him die!*

Chapter Seventeen

She appeared to him in his dream—Ambika, youngest daughter of the rajah. Her name meant Goddess of the Moon. She was the most beautiful woman he had ever seen, with her thick, lustrous, raven-black hair like a river of silk. Aptly named, she could be mysterious as the moon, too, favoring him with one of her rare smiles and letting him see the gleam of her fathomless dark eyes in one moment, pouting and veiling herself the next in the filmy, iridescent fabrics trimmed with pearls and sparkling gems. She wore anklets and bracelets with tiny golden bells, so her walk was as musical as her voice.

She'd promised him much with her eyes, and even knowing it could never work, he'd fallen in love with her. But now, in his dream, she was watching his ceremony of disgrace, just as she had on that day. He thought he heard her laughing at him, and not even her veils could muffle the acid scorn in it. *"No wonder they call you Mad Nick..."*

Mad Nick.

Millicent Matthews was there in his dream, too,

but she was not laughing. Instead, she stood opposite Ambika, with the assembled ranks of the Bombay Light Cavalry between them. Compassion and sorrow etched her face. She seemed to be reaching out to him, stretching her arm as one did to a drowning man, but even though he extended his arm to her, he could never seem to make contact. He was being swept away, not by water, but by rows and rows of uniformed soldiers, mercilessly pushing him onward.

Maybe someday he'd stop dreaming of a woman who, in the end, had only caused him pain.

As she watched, he stopped shivering and the pallor of his face was gradually replaced with flushing. She reached out a hand to touch his forehead and yanked it back, alarmed at the intensity of the sudden heat. He was burning up! Where was Sarah with that tea?

"We got t' take them blankets off him, Miss Milly, so he kin cool off, afore he gets so hot he has a fit," Josh told her, and she yanked the coverings away until Nick was once again covered only by a sheet.

"Fetch me some water, Bobby!" she said, and when he ran back in with a bucket from the well she drenched the bandana hanging on his bedpost and sponged Nick's sweaty face. He yelped in alarm at the first cool, wet touch of the cloth, then sank back, eyes closed, still shivering as he submitted to her ministrations. She sponged his face, then uncovered one arm at a time, then the other, wiping them down with the cool wet cloth as she had seen her mother do when Sarah had come down with a fever as a child.

Sarah arrived an eternity later, carrying a cupful of

the tea, and with Bobby helping to raise him up, they managed to ladle the tea into him, spoonful by spoonful. Eyes screwed shut, he grimaced at the taste, but in some recess of his heated brain, he must have known they were trying to help him, for he allowed them to continue until he had taken the entire cupful.

"Bobby, you'd better ride for the doctor," she said. The boy nodded wordlessly and pulled on his boots.

Nick raised his head off the pillow and muttered something that sounded like *"Kwine...ih v'lees..."*

"What, Nick? What are you saying?" Milly asked. More Indian words?

But he said nothing more, his head falling back on the pillow once again. While she waited, she prayed silently. *Please, Lord, save him! You sent him to help us, didn't You? So You wouldn't let him die of a fever when we need him so badly, would You?*

Then she realized how bossy her prayer sounded. Surely it was wrong to talk to the Almighty like that.

Lord, I'm sorry for speaking to You that way. I'm just so afraid for him! Please save him, I beg of You! If he dies, I don't even know how to notify his family... But Your will be done...

Across the bed she saw Sarah, her eyes closed, her lips moving. She was petitioning Heaven, too.

An hour passed, and as she watched, ever so gradually the dry hotness of his skin became damp, then wet. Great pearls of sweat rose on his forehead and dripped down his cheeks. When she touched him, he felt cooler, though still overwarm, and she saw that the sheets on top and beneath him were drenched with sweat.

"We've got to change these sheets or he'll get chilled

again," Milly muttered. "Sarah, could you please get some dry sheets from the house?"

As soon as her sister returned, with Josh insisting on helping despite his stifled grunts of pain, they turned the unconscious man on his side, first to one side of the bed, pulling out the drenched sheet beneath him and replacing it with a fresh dry one and repeating the process until he was once more surrounded by clean, dry sheets. He never woke. When he was once more lying on his back, Milly stared, hypnotized by the regularity of his chest rising and falling beneath the covering.

By now, Josh was snoring in his bunk. Sarah's head nodded forward as she fell into slumber, then jerked herself upright, blinking as she struggled to regain full alertness.

"Sarah, go back to the house," Milly told her, gently touching her sister's shoulder. "I'll send Josh if I need anything."

Sarah shook her head. "I couldn't sleep," she insisted, her words belying the yawn that escaped from her right afterward.

"Well, at least curl up on one of those empty bunks over there," Milly said with a wry smile. "You almost fell out of the chair just then."

Sitting in a cane back chair by Nick's bed, Milly had nodded off herself when, some time later, she woke to hear his voice calling her name.

"Yes, Nick?" she said, leaning toward him and feeling his forehead. Once again, it was hot and clammy to her touch. His eyes were open, and he shivered, but there was a spark of recognition in his red-rimmed blue eyes.

"*Lareea*. Need *kwine*…quinine," he corrected himself, jaws clenching in an obvious attempt to keep his teeth from chattering again. "My v'lees."

She didn't understand the first word, or the last, but finally comprehended quinine. "Quinine? You need quinine for what's ailing you?" Where was she to get that?

"In my v'lees," he said again. "Under…th' bed…"

Kneeling, she felt underneath the bed, her hand coming in contact with something solid and made of leather, and pulled it out by the handle. It was the leather grip he had brought with him from the boarding house. Ah, he'd been saying *valise!*

"In…s-side," he said, motioning for her to open it. "Bottle…quinine. Drops…put a few drops in water…"

She did so, finding a small amber bottle with a stopper atop some papers. She grabbed a cup that was sitting on his bedside and poured a glass of water, then carefully tipped the bottle to allow a few drops of the quinine to mix with the water before swirling it around. He drank it down as if his life depended on how fast he could swallow, and for all she knew, it did. Then she almost giggled at the awful face he made as he drank the last sip.

"Nasty, dr-dreadful stuff…bitter…"

The effort of drinking the quinine water seemed to exhaust what little energy he had left, and he sank back on the pillows, his eyes closing once more in sleep.

* * *

"Milly, it's morning," Sarah's whisper and her gentle touch on her arm, roused Milly from sleep in the chair by Nick's bed.

Milly jerked herself upright, conscious of needles of pain from her stiff neck. Startled that she had fallen asleep when she'd meant to keep vigil, she immediately turned to look at Nick. The Englishman still slept, one arm atop the sheet, the sound of his breathing regular and unlabored. His color looked all right, though a little pale, but just to reassure herself, she reached out a hand and touched his forehead. His skin was dry and warm, but not overly so.

Outside in the yard, the rooster announced the rising of the sun.

"Why don't you go back to bed in the house for a while?" Sarah said, still whispering. "You can't have slept very well, all scrunched over like that."

Milly stretched, yawning, pushing an errant strand of hair from her braid out of her face, and reached a hand back to knead her stiff neck. She looked at Sarah, then back to Nick, hesitating.

"Josh is awake, and he can watch over him for a while. I'll check on him every little bit. Go on, now."

Milly looked around. "Where's Bobby? Didn't he ever come back from the doctor's?" The boy's bunk was empty.

"Doc Harkey's at a ranch between here and San Saba, delivering a baby. Bobby left a message to come when he could. He's out spreading hay for the horses."

Surrendering, Milly started for the door.

"Th-thank you, ladies…"

They whirled to see that Nick was awake, his eyes open.

"I'm sorry, we didn't mean to wake you," Milly said, going back to the bedside. "How are you?"

"Weak as a cat, I'm afraid…but it would have been worse without your help," he said, his voice raspy. "The quinine's…only thing that helps."

"Do you know what caused your fever?"

He nodded, eyes closing with the effort, then opening again. "Malaria…"

"Malaria? Malaria caused your fever?" Milly said, catching sight of the alarm that flooded her sister's face.

Nick had evidently seen it and interpreted Sarah's expression, too. "Not…not c-catching," he said. "It's…a souvenir of my…time in India…returns every now and then t' remind me. Not…often… The quinine helps… shorten the attack somewhat… But it's not over…there'll be more…"

"So how can we help you recover? What do you need?" Milly asked.

"W-water…" Nick's eyelids drooped, as if the few words he'd said had exhausted him.

She poured a fresh cup of water from the pitcher; then with Sarah helping to prop him up, Milly helped him sip it. He drank thirstily until the cup was empty.

"Th-thanks," he said again. "Sleep now…"

He was asleep as soon as Sarah lowered his head to the pillow.

It was three days before the cycle of chills, fevers and sleeping, followed by lucid intervals, was over and

Nick, assisted by Bobby, felt well enough to leave the confines of the bunkhouse for a chair on the porch, where Milly waited in one of the rocking chairs.

He felt a great deal better now that Bobby had brought him hot water and assisted him to wash and shave, but his legs felt about as strong as pudding. He hated to have Milly see him this way, pale and leaning on the boy. What a bad bargain she must think she had made, depending on him for help with the ranch!

And how beautiful she looked in her simple calico everyday dress, her face lit from the sunlight on her right, her dark hair gleaming with reddish highlights.

"Thanks, lad," he said, as he sank into the rocking chair. "I'm much obliged to you."

"Aw, 'tweren't nothin', Mr. Nick…" the boy mumbled.

"Nonsense. I wasn't fit for the company of a lady before you helped me clean up," Nick insisted, and the boy smiled shyly.

"You're welcome. I—I'd better get on with my chores. Holler when yer ready to go back to bed, or you need anything," Bobby said, clumping down the steps. He strode back across the yard to the corral.

"Would you like some coffee?" she said, indicating the pot and cup on the low table between them.

"Indeed, I would," Nick said, savoring the excuse to just sit there and watch her as she poured the steaming brew into the cup, then handed it to him before pouring a cup for herself.

He closed his eyes in bliss as he swallowed. "Ah… that's wonderful stuff. I'm getting quite fond of your

Texas coffee, Miss Milly. It's making me forget all about tea."

"It's Arbuckle's brand," she said. "It's new this year—the first coffee that comes pre-roasted. It's actually made by Yankees, but we drink it anyway," she murmured with a wry smile. "Each bag comes with a peppermint stick—Bobby always begs for that."

Nick cleared his throat. "I…I'm sorry you had to see me like that, Milly—when I was delirious with the fever, I mean. These malarial attacks don't happen often. In fact, it hasn't happened for so long I didn't recognize the signals and thought I was only overtired from the heat. If I'd recognized it, I'd have drank some quinine water and perhaps have succeeded in heading it off."

She looked surprised. "Becoming ill is nothing to apologize for, Nick. I…we…just felt sorry for you, and wished we could do something to make it go away more quickly."

He winced inwardly. Sorry for him was not at all the way he wanted her to feel.

"You said you got this malaria in India," she went on. "What causes it? Why don't we have it here?"

He shrugged. "I don't think even physicians know exactly. But it seems to be prevalent in marshy areas, so I should think it's too dry here for that."

She nodded her understanding, then took a deep breath. "Nick, I…I just want to say I'm sorry for the quarrel that we had Sunday, about the ex-slaves. You were right, and I was wrong. I was being a coward."

He looked down at his hands for a moment, then back up at her. "It's all right. I was wrong, trying to impose my wishes on you. You know best what the realities are here after all."

"It's good of you to say, but no, I was totally at fault. I realized it, sitting in church. I let my fear of confronting men like Bill Waters make me afraid to do the right thing. And we *do* need help around here."

"Yes, my falling sick rather proved that point, didn't it?"

Milly sighed. "Of course it did. I...I don't suppose it would be possible to find those men and bring them back?" she asked, with a tentative smile.

He felt the grin spreading over his face. "When I sent them on their way, I told them about the cave over by the creek, and the fish they could catch there with the poles we left in the cave. With any luck they're still there. Bobby could go out there and tell them you're willing to offer them jobs."

Chapter Eighteen

Bobby returned with the men riding in the back of the wagon, all smiling broadly. Once it had pulled to a stop between the barn and the house, they clambered out, the other three waiting while Elijah approached, hat in hand, to where she still sat on the porch with Nick. Sarah came out to join them, wiping her hands on her apron, and behind her hobbled Josh.

"Miss Milly, Bobby told us 'bout you offerin' us jobs as hands, and I want to say for all of us, we're right grateful. We're gonna show you how grateful by workin' hard for you, ma'am. You just have to tell us what you want, and me 'n' my brothers, we'll do the best we kin for you and your sister. We ain't never ezactly been cowboys, but we've tended livestock. We'll learn quick, I promise you."

Milly smiled at Elijah and his brothers beyond him. "Welcome to our ranch. This is my sister, Sarah," she said, nodding at her. "And our foreman, Josh. You already know Nick Brookfield. It's we who should be grateful that you were willing to come back. I—I'm sorry I sent you away the other night. I—"

But Elijah held up a hand. "'Scuse me for interruptin', Miss Milly, but you don't have t'apologize. We understand givin' a job to folks like us ain't somethin' you do lightly, an' bless you for givin' us a chance." His eyes were understanding and kind.

"Thank you," she murmured, feeling she'd just experienced a profound moment of grace. "Josh and Nick will be giving you your orders, showing you the ropes and providing you with tools. You'll sleep in the bunkhouse," she said, pointing to it. "You'll eat…" Milly stopped to consider. The kitchen table was a little small to accommodate four more men. "I think we'll need to move the table onto the side porch, and combine it with the one in the bunkhouse. That'll work until the weather gets cold, at least."

Elijah looked a little uncomfortable at this. "Miss Milly, you don't need to do that," he said. "Me an' my brothers, we could pick up a pot o' beans or whatever in the kitchen and take it out to the bunkhouse. It ain't fittin' for us to eat at the same table as our boss."

There was a muted chorus of agreement from his brothers.

"Nonsense," she said. "Our other hands don't eat in the bunkhouse, so neither will you. Perhaps someday this ranch will be a bigger operation and the hands will have to eat in the bunkhouse, but right now that's hardly the case."

"But ma'am…"

Sarah, behind her, spoke up. "I'm the cook, and I agree, much less work for me that way. And none of you other men object, do you?" Her gaze took in Josh, Bobby and Nick.

Bobby looked surprised to be asked, but shook his head with the other two men.

"Thank ya, ma'am. We ain't met with such kindness since…since I don' know when," Elijah said, his eyes suspiciously wet before he looked down again.

But all the thanks Milly needed was the warm glow of approval in Nick's blue gaze.

"Then that settles it. Why don't you get settled in the bunkhouse. Josh, would you be able to show them where the sheets and blankets are? Bobby, please help me move the tables onto the side porch."

"And what am I to do, Milly?" Nick said, rising.

"Your job is to sit right there and rest," she told him. "Tomorrow will be time enough for you to start earning your keep again," she added with a wink.

Over dinner, they learned more of the four brothers. Once again Elijah, as eldest brother, served as the spokesperson. They ranged in age from twenty-five to nineteen. All of them had been slaves on a large cotton plantation in eastern Texas, but none had been aware that they'd been set free by Lincoln's Emancipation Proclamation until General Gordon Granger brought the news to Texas in June. None of the men were married. Elijah had had a wife, but she had died in childbirth. Isaiah had been sweet on a girl, but she'd been sold away from the plantation and after that the two younger brothers, Caleb and Micah, had been reluctant to set their affections on any of the female slaves on the plantation.

"I told 'em there'd be time enough for that later, once we're settled down, with jobs and a place to live and such," Elijah said, with an air of wisdom far beyond his years.

They were curious about the history of the Matthews ranch, too. Josh was clearly in his element while telling the story of the Comanche attack that had nearly cost him his life—which led naturally enough into Nick telling them about his plan for building a stone fort up on the hill.

"Sure, we'll help you build that," Elijah said. "Sounds like a good idea, case them Injuns come raidin' again." He ran a hand over his head full of tight black curls. "I don't fancy *my* scalp decoratin' no Comanche spear."

"We'll work on that only when we have time to spare from our other chores," Nick told them. "One of the local families is donating their stock to the ranch, and they're bringing them tomorrow, so we'll need to get them settled in."

"Mr. Nick, mind if I ask you where you come from, sir?" It was Isaiah, speaking up for the first time. "I ain't never heard nobody speak like you do. Are you from some furrin' country?"

Nick's brow furrowed for a moment in confusion, and Milly was about to explain that Isaiah meant *foreign,* but he must have figured it out then, for he explained he was from Britain, by way of India, a country on the other side of the globe. The man's eyes grew wide. "I bet you got some stories to tell, Mr. Nick."

Nick laughed. "Indeed, I do. I imagine we'll find time to swap yarns, as Josh puts it."

"Then how'd you end up here, Mr. Nick?" Caleb asked.

"You two stop bein' so nosy," Elijah said. "I 'pologize

for my brothers, Mr. Nick. I reckon we've been so busy findin' our way in the world, I ain't properly taken the time to teach 'em manners, like mindin' their own business. Please forgive 'em for askin'."

"I don't mind," Nick assured him. "But it's rather a long story," he said, glancing at Milly. "Perhaps we'd better tell it another time."

It had been a good day, Nick mused at sunset the next day as he washed up at the pump before supper. He'd gone to bed right after supper the night before, still weak from the effects of the fevers, but today he felt much stronger and he'd been able to properly pull his weight.

The Prestons had come as planned, bringing the cattle, pigs and chickens, and now six new pigs contentedly wallowed in the pen Bobby had built for them while Nick was ill. There had been a few minor skirmishes between the old hens and the new, but the pecking order had been rearranged, and Milly and Sarah were already discussing how many eggs to leave the hens to set upon, and how many to use for cooking or selling.

The twenty head of cattle were rangy longhorns, like the ones already at the ranch, but in addition there was a vigorous young bull, which would more than replace the old one the Indians had slaughtered.

Even over the sloshing of the water, Nick could hear the cattle lowing as they explored their new enclosure. He thought of the stockier breeds of cattle back in England, and wondered what kind of cattle they might produce if they were bred with the hardy Texas cattle.

Perhaps Edward could be persuaded to ship him some from England, he thought. Ah, but he was getting ahead of himself, wasn't he?

"Mr. Matthews must be pleased as punch to see this," Josh said, staring out at the corral and the pasture beyond as he joined Nick at the pump. "Why, this is like the glory days before the war."

"You believe those in heaven can see what's going on on earth?" Nick asked, smiling. "So do I." He hoped that Milly and Sarah's father was happy he had come into their lives.

"'Course I do," Josh said. "I don't think we stop carin' 'bout the ones we loved when we go through them pearly gates." He rubbed his bristly chin. "You know, with a little luck, it won't be but a couple of years before we can send Matthews cattle along with some trail drive to Kansas, mebbe even head up the drive ourselves." He looked wistful at the thought.

"Sounds like you'd like to be a part of that," Nick observed.

Josh whistled. "Trail drives are hard on a young man, and I sure ain't young no more," he mused, rubbing his lower back. "Between the river crossin's, the Injuns, the rustlers and the stampedes, not to mention snakes, it's a dangerous trip, and that's a fact. But Bobby would be jest the right age by then."

Both men watched as the lowering sun illuminated the figure of one of their new hands as he threw out flakes of hay for the horses in the corral.

"That was a good thing you done, persuadin' Miss Milly to give them men a chance," Josh said. "Didn't want to pressure Miss Milly to set her mind a certain way because a' what *I* believed. But I reckon now that those men are free, they need work same as a stove-up ol' cowboy like me does. Mind you, not ever'body in Simpson Creek's gonna think so."

His words confirmed Nick's suspicions. "You think there will be trouble from men like Waters?"

Josh rubbed his chin again. "Oh, Sheriff Poteet will probably discourage any *real* mischief from those fellas in that 'Circle'—" his face wrinkled with contempt as he said the name "—but there might be some unpleasantness. Some folks jes' ain't happy 'less they kin hold someone else down. And it's likely the Circle knows about it already."

Nick was surprised. "But how?"

"Mr. and Mrs. Preston seen 'em when they was here, and they probably mentioned it t'somebody, innocently enough, and that person told somebody, who told somebody…" His hand made circles to indicate the speed at which gossip traveled. "And the Waters hands might see the Browns out mending fence and tendin' cattle…"

"I…I see."

"I'm just tellin' you so you kin keep your eyes open, that's all."

"Should I—should we—discuss it with Miss Milly, do you think?"

"Naw, I wouldn't go worryin' her," Josh said. "Just be watchin'. And while I'm handin' out free advice, young man," he added with a grin, "it's my opinion you oughta git busy courtin' Miss Milly in earnest."

Nick was startled at the older man's frankness. "What makes you say so?"

"I've been knowin' that young lady since she was

knee-high to a horned toad and I saw the way she fretted over you when you were sick. Any fool kin see she loves you, Nick, so I'd get crackin' if I were you."

Without another word, Josh walked into the house. Nick stared after him. Clearly, the old cowboy approved of him or he'd never have urged Nick to step up his courtship. What Josh had just said had sounded more warm and fatherly than any of Nick's real father's infrequent attempts at conversations. The fourth Viscount Greyshaw had been distant as the clouds, decreeing that his third son should go into the army simply because he already had an heir and a second son in the Church. The army had suited Nick very well until recently, but he had often wondered how his father would have reacted if Nick had had other ideas. He already knew that if his father had been alive when Nick had been stripped of his colors and drummed out of the army, he would have disowned him.

His brother Edward hadn't done so, of course, but Nick suspected he was relieved, nonetheless, that his disgraced younger brother had decided to put an ocean between them rather than return to England. One shouldn't have to be embarrassed by a family connection to Mad Nick Brookfield. It was bad enough that his mother, after giving her husband three sons and a daughter, had become legendary for her indiscretions.

Nick shook his head as if to clear it. What was done was done. Mad Nick had been left behind in Bombay. He was Nicholas Brookfield, and he was going to take Josh's advice about stepping up his courtship of Milly.

Chapter Nineteen

"Good morning," Milly said to the postmaster sorting mail behind the counter. "Is Caroline around?"

Amos Wallace looked up, but the normally friendly man didn't smile at her as he usually did and return her greeting. "She's in the back office. Caroline!" he called over his shoulder. Then he went back to his sorting, almost as if Milly was a stranger.

Caroline emerged from the office before Milly could think much about his demeanor. "Come on back, Milly," she said, beckoning and opening the swinging half door. "I was hoping you'd come in today."

Milly followed her into the small office and sat in the chair next to the roll-top desk. "Why? Are there any new letters from prospective suitors?"

"Yes, three!" Caroline grinned, pulling them out of a pigeonhole. "And they all sound like good candidates. Shall we convene a meeting of the Society?"

"Wonderful! Let's see, today's Friday...how about Monday for our meeting?"

"That's when the Ladies Aid Society meets," Caroline reminded her.

Milly felt a guilty twinge as she realized she hadn't even thought about the Ladies Aid Society since the Indian attack, but quickly dismissed it. She'd had quite a lot to contend with since Josh was laid up.

"All right, Tuesday, then. Help me pass the word."

"As president, you should take these and give them a preliminary look," Caroline said, handing the letters to Milly.

Milly put them in her reticule, intending to study them later.

"How are things going with Mr. Collier?" Milly asked, and was delighted to see her friend blush.

"Pete's coming for supper tonight!" Caroline's voice fairly squeaked with excitement. "Ma and Pa met him at the barn raising, of course, but this will be the first time he's had supper at our house. I'm going to cook chicken and dumplings and black-eyed peas and peach pie, all my specialties. Ma's going to help me a little," she admitted. "I have trouble getting it all done at the same time."

"That's the way, show him what a good cook you are," Milly approved. "I've always heard that's the way to a man's heart."

"And how's that handsome Englishman of yours?" Caroline countered with a grin.

"Better now, but we had quite a scare," Milly said, and told her about Nick's attack of malaria.

"How frightening," Caroline commented. "And this could happen again?"

Milly nodded. "I'll know what to do next time, though. Apparently taking quinine shortens the attack. This time it caught him unaware, though, and he was delirious and couldn't tell us what he needed." Then she remembered the delicious news that she'd come to share with Caroline before going on her other errands.

"You look like the proverbial cat that swallowed the canary," Caroline said, studying her. "I take it it has nothing to do with the subject of nursing a man with a fever."

"Nick asked me to dinner at the hotel this Saturday night," she said. "He made a reservation—or as he said it, 'I've bespoken dinner at seven, if that's agreeable to you, Miss Milly,'" she said, imitating his accent as best she could. She couldn't stifle a giggle. "I couldn't bear to tell him no one's probably ever needed a reservation for supper in the entire history of the hotel."

"Oh, how sweet," Caroline gushed. "Well, it certainly seems as if he'd like to move things along—"

Just then Mr. Wallace entered the office. "Caroline, if you're going to take off the last part of the afternoon, I need you to get back to work," he said, his voice uncharacteristically brisk. His gaze avoided Milly.

Now Milly was sure something was wrong. Usually Mr. Wallace had plenty of time to crack a joke with her, to ask her how the ranch was doing. Now he wouldn't even look at her.

Caroline jumped up. "Sure, Pa, Milly and I were just talking," she said. "What do you need me to do?"

"Your ma needs you to run down to the mercantile and fetch some sugar," he said.

"Sure, Pa. Milly, I guess I'll see you later…"

Milly rose, too. "Actually, I have something to buy there, too," she said. "So I'll walk with you. Have a good day, Mr. Wallace," she called, but he'd already gone back to sorting the mail and offered her no reply.

"Caroline, what's wrong?" she asked, as soon as they'd crossed the street and were heading toward the mercantile. "Did I come at a bad time?" Suddenly, she guessed what her friend was going to say and she felt sick at heart.

Caroline sighed and looked down at her feet, her feet slowing. "Papa's heard about the new hands you hired for the ranch."

"I…I see…" Milly said. Josh had been right—the news had gotten around. "Does he think I should have turned them away?" she said, guiltily aware it was exactly what she had done at first. "Caroline, the ranch needs cowhands, and there hasn't been anyone else passing through, looking for work—especially since I can't pay anything but board right now. I—I didn't realize your father felt that way."

Caroline's eyes were startled. "It's not that—you know we never had any slaves, before the war. It's just that he knows how men like Waters feel about it…"

"Caroline, your father's not a member of the Circle, is he?"

Her friend looked confused. "Circle?"

"That group Waters and Dayton are part of, that wants to keep any of the former slaves from settling anywhere in San Saba County."

"No, I'm sure he's not. He just doesn't want any trouble…"

"And I'm sure my new cowhands won't cause any trouble," Milly said, a trifle stiffly. "They just want a home and honest work."

"Please don't be angry with *me,* Milly," Caroline said, putting a hand on her friend's shoulder. "I don't feel that way. In time, he'll see it's no problem, but don't be surprised if other folks act like he did."

Once inside the store, Caroline immediately bought the sugar she'd been sent for and left, while Milly went to the back to where the bolts of fabric were kept. She needed to buy enough denim to make shirts for the four brothers, for she'd learned that the ragged, threadbare ones they wore were the only ones they possessed.

Mr. Patterson, when he was measuring the cloth and wrapping it up for her, acted the same way toward her Mr. Wallace had—brisk, businesslike, treating her as if she was a stranger.

"What's wrong, Mr. Patterson?" she asked, once he'd handed her her wrapped package. Was she to be treated this way by everyone in town? "Is it our account? We should be able to pay it by the end of the month." She knew it wasn't their bill that made him so taciturn, but she wanted to hear what he would say.

"Nothing's wrong. End of the month will be fine, Miss Milly," he said, but he wouldn't meet her gaze either.

"Do you disapprove of the new ranch hands I hired, Mr. Patterson?"

His grip tightened on the pencil he was using to figure the cost of the fabric. "None a' my business, Miss Milly."

"But you *do* disapprove. Yet you never owned slaves either."

His eyes met hers for the first time. "It has nothing to do with that. It's just that ex-slaves living here will probably lead to more of them coming, and then an office of the Freedmen's Bureau here, sooner or later, and Yankee carpetbaggers to run it. They'll say they're here to make sure the former slaves are treated fairly, but these Freedmen Bureau fellows are scoundrels, Miss Milly. Opportunists. Swindlers. We don't need that in Simpson Creek."

"All that will happen because I hired some help?" she questioned, her tone ironic.

His gaze softened, and he was once more the kind man she'd known all her life. "It could. You just be careful, Miss Milly."

She thought at first he was warning her about her new employees, and she was about to insist she could trust them, when he went on.

"You be careful around men like your neighbor and his cronies. They aren't pleased about those men living out on your ranch."

After the last two encounters, she wasn't looking forward to speaking to Mr. Dayton about what they owed for the barn lumber, but it couldn't be helped. She didn't like owing any money to anyone, even Mr. Patterson, but owing a large sum to a surly man like Dayton was especially onerous.

How they were going to come up with the money to pay the balance, she had no idea. In time the ranch would once more be self-sufficient, making money from the sale of cattle, horses, chickens and eggs, but for now they were cash-poor.

Lord, You've promised to meet our needs. Help me to figure out a way to earn some money, she prayed as she trudged along the dusty street between the mercantile and the lumberyard.

Her mind not on her steps, she dropped the hem of her skirt which she'd been holding out of the dust, then nearly tripped as her booted foot caught and partially tore a flounce. Ah, well, it wouldn't be a difficult repair…

I can sew. And mend.

Suddenly she reversed her steps and nearly ran back into the mercantile and up to the counter where she found Mr. Patterson was dusting the shelves.

"Mr. Patterson, I have an idea for making some money," she said, "if you're willing to allow me just a little more on the ranch account."

He looked up, waiting, his expression a bit wary.

"Would you be interested in selling ready-made dresses in your store? I hear a lot of mercantiles are doing that now, not just selling the fabric to make them. I could make them up in a variety of sizes. Oh, and if you're willing, I could leave a card with my rates for alterations and mending, and a basket. Folks could leave clothing that needs mending here, and I could pick it up, mend it and bring it back for them to pick up."

The mercantile proprietor took off his glasses and dusted them on his shirt before answering. "We could try it, I suppose, and see how it goes…. I won't charge you for the fabric now, but take the cost out of the profit when they sell. But you'd have to pay me back eventually if they didn't sell," he added, his brow furrowing.

Even his doubt couldn't quash the flow of confidence she was feeling. "They'll sell," she told him. "Ever since Mrs. Ferguson's eyesight failed, there's been no town seamstress. I just wish I'd thought of this sooner! Very well, I'll take that bolt of blue-figured calico and that green gloria cloth. I'll have these ready within the week, I promise."

Now when she walked to the lumberyard, her feet seemed to have wings. Surely selling dresses would enable her to pay off the debt for the lumber a lot sooner.

She found Hank Dayton in the lumberyard, planing the sides of a stack of planks.

"Good morning, Mr. Dayton," she said, though it was nearer to noon. "I've come to find out what we owe you after the amount raised at the barn raising was taken out." She was going to offer him one or two of the steers, if he was willing to take them in lieu of cash.

He wiped his sweaty brow with a rumpled, yellowed bandana, then stuffed it back into his pocket. "Nothing," he said, then spat into the wood shavings as if the answer left a bad taste in his mouth.

She blinked. "Nothing? How can that be? I know how much was raised that night, and from the price you quoted me, we must owe you about a hundred dollars at least."

He narrowed his eyes at her. "You gone deaf, Miss Milly? Must be all that sweet-talkin' that British fella's been doin' to you, when you ain't doin' things like hirin' those shiftless beggars I heard about. You don't owe me nothin'. Not one red cent." From the scowl on his face she decided he found the fact vastly disappointing.

"But how can that be?" she demanded, ignoring his jabs about Nick and the new hands. Not for a moment would she believe this man had just decided to wipe the debt off his books out of the goodness of his heart.

"Look, you got any questions, you talk to that foreigner about it," he snarled. "Meanwhile, I got work t' do."

He was as good as telling her to leave, but she stood her ground. "Are you saying Mr. Brookfield settled the balance of our debt?"

"Yep," he said, using the plane with such savagery that it seemed he wanted to shave the wood down to paper. "Your fancy 'cowboy' came in and paid what you owe. Said I wasn't to tell you how it was paid—only I thought you oughta know. Around here we got a word for women who let men they ain't married to pay their debts."

She actually felt the blood drain from her face as the meaning of his ugly words sank in. And then it rushed back, filling her cheeks with heat.

"How dare you say such a thing, you sneaking sidewinder?" she said, taking refuge in one of her father's old phrases. "He meant to be kind and generous, and you want to make it sound horrible! Well, you just hand me the money he gave you and I'll give it back to him, and we'll pay you with a couple of the new steers the Prestons gave us. You can sell them or butcher them, I don't care. Will that make us even?"

"Now, I cain't do that, Miss Milly," he said with a smirk. "I got bills t'pay, too. That money's already spent, y'see."

Her hands fisted at her sides in frustration. "I see, all right. Good afternoon, Mr. Dayton."

Chapter Twenty

She found Nick up on the hill with the four new cowboys. Driving the wagon up the narrow track to the top, Milly was amazed to see they'd already laid out a perimeter for the stone fort and had gathered a pile of rocks of various sizes as high as her shoulder. Right now they were taking a break in the shade formed by an outcropping of limestone, passing around a couple of canteens of water.

"This is amazing!" she marveled, forgetting for a moment her encounter with Dayton.

Nick grinned up at her. "It's a good start, isn't it? I think it's getting too hot to do more today, but if we can use the wagon, it'll be easier to gather up the rocks the next time we can work on it."

"Sarah just asked me to tell you dinner's ready. She didn't figure you could hear the bell up here. You can ride down in the wagon bed."

While the four brothers went ahead to the pump to wash up, Nick helped her unhitch the horses and turn them out in the corral. She used the moments alone with him to tell him what Dayton had said.

Nick's blue eyes blazed with fury by the time she finished the account. His hands clenched into fists just as hers had. "The blackguard! I believe I'll pay him a call this afternoon and make him pay for his blasted cheek! Texas doesn't allow dueling, does it?"

"No..." she said, though she knew there were lawless towns farther west where quarrels were commonly settled with guns.

"Pity. I'll have to settle for giving him a proper drubbing, then."

She put up a hand. "No, you mustn't do that. Don't you see, it'll only make things worse. Then he'd have to retaliate. As it is, no one with any sense will believe his nasty insinuations. Anyone who would doesn't have the brains God gave a goose."

Her words caused his lips to curve into a half smile. "I'm so sorry, Milly. I never meant for what I did to help to cause you any embarrassment. I...I suppose it *could* look like..." He reddened. "Like an inappropriate gift."

"Only to the evil-minded. Just ignore Dayton and his sort," she pleaded. "We won't need to do more business with him anytime soon. I *do* want to thank you for what you did, Nick—for paying off the balance," she said. "It was more than generous of you."

"You're welcome," he said. His eyes retained some of their storminess. He gave a deep sigh. "I wanted to be an anonymous benefactor. Blast the man!"

Then Milly caught sight of Sarah beckoning from the side porch. "I think we're holding up dinner. We'd better go wash. But not a word about what Dayton said, please, Nick. I don't want to upset Sarah, too." She would tell

Sarah later about the way Mr. Wallace and Mr. Patterson had acted toward her, though, in case Sarah went into town and was treated likewise.

"Very well, if you'll promise not to tell her about my paying off the lumber bill—at least in front of me. I didn't do it to be thanked, you see."

She stared up at him, hardly able to believe how unselfishly *good* he was.

Over the meal, she told Sarah and the others about her idea of selling ready-made dresses at the mercantile.

"What a great idea, Milly," Sarah praised. "I've heard lots of ladies at church wish they had your skill with a needle and your eye for decorative touches."

"I'll start on them right after the shirts I'm going to make for you men," she said, then told them about the denim she'd purchased for that purpose.

"Is it Christmas?" Micah wondered out loud. "Sure looks like summer out there to me, but I ain't never had new clothes 'less it was Christmas."

Everyone chuckled.

Sarah's eyes had gone thoughtful. "I wonder if I could interest Mr. Patterson in selling my pies, too? What do you think, Milly?"

"I don't see why not," Milly replied. "Maybe the hotel restaurant would buy them, too."

Nick raised his glass of cold tea. "I'd like to propose a toast," he said. "To the Matthews sisters—entrepreneurs extraordinaire!"

"That was delicious!" Milly said, putting down her knife and fork after taking the last bite of tender roast beef. "Sarah's a great cook, but it's nice to eat supper elsewhere for a change…especially when I'm with only you."

Nick studied her across the restaurant table. Milly Matthews looked delicious tonight, too, in an entirely different sort of way. She wore a dress of some rose-colored silky fabric and a lacy shawl around her shoulders. She'd put her hair up, allowing him to appreciate the graceful length of her neck. A cross pendant dangled from a simple, delicate gold chain. A faint hint of rose-water wafted from her skin, a more appealing scent than any of the exotic musky perfumes he'd ever smelled in India.

He wanted to kiss her tonight. Surely the sparkle in her eyes ever since they'd left the ranch together indicated that she wouldn't take that amiss? He'd head out of town on the road back to the ranch, then stop the wagon and kiss her.

"Would you folks care for dessert?" the waiter asked, breaking into his thoughts.

"Oh, no, I couldn't…" Milly murmured.

"That's a shame, ma'am, 'cause the cook made a Boston cream pie that looks absolutely delightful."

Milly groaned. "It's tempting…"

"The lady will have a piece. And we'd like coffee," Nick said. The waiter had been perfect, there when he was needed, friendly without being obsequious, a distinct contrast to the hotel proprietor, who'd pretended not to hear when Milly had called "Good evening" to him as they'd walked through the lobby toward the restaurant. Apparently he'd heard about the ranch's new employees, too.

"Mmm, you really must try this," Milly said, holding

a forkful out to him after the waiter had come and gone again.

It was sweet, but not nearly as sweet as looking into those mercurial green-gold eyes and watching her rosebud lips open involuntarily as she fed him the morsel of pie. Did she know how irresistible she was?

"Nick…" Milly began, as if she had something on her mind.

"Yes?" he murmured, unable and unwilling to remove his gaze from her eyes and mouth.

"Nick, what is 'Ambika'?"

He couldn't have been any more astonished if Milly had asked why he'd been called Mad Nick.

"How…how do you know that name?" he asked, when he could find his voice.

Something in his face must have told her the word had unpleasant memories attached to it, for she said, "So it's not a *what,* it's a *who?* I'm sorry…it's just that you called that name, over and over again, when you were delirious with fever. I wrote it down—at least, the way it sounded to me…I'm sure I misspelled it—so I could ask you about it some time. I—I was just curious, that's all. You don't have to tell me if you'd rather not."

Of course he'd rather not. He'd rather the name had never intruded into this romantic dinner. Her eyes, which had reflected the candle's dancing light, were anxious now. Troubled.

He could lie, he knew. Make up some innocuous story about Ambika, say she was the colonel's children's *amah,* or something like that. The real Ambika would remain thousands of miles and oceans away.

But he couldn't lie to this woman he had begun to

love. He was planning to kiss her tonight and perhaps even begin to talk about their wedding.

He could answer her questions, tell her the truth… just not all the truth.

"Ambika was the youngest daughter of the maharajah—the prince, that is—of the Bombay area."

"And you knew her? You were friends?"

"We were acquainted, yes. Though one could hardly say a princess could be a friend of a lowly British captain. Her father was allied with the major general, and so the rajah often brought his family to joint social events." *Please, Milly, leave it at that.*

"Was she…very beautiful?"

Beautiful didn't begin to describe Ambika's sultry, sloe-eyed appearance.

He shrugged, as if Ambika's looks had held no importance to him. "I suppose you could say so, yes. A lot of the lads in my company fancied themselves in love with her."

"What about you?" Her changeable hazel eyes were merely curious, not probing or accusatory, yet he knew the truth could wreck their growing feelings for one another. And he could not do that.

He laughed. "I? Well…I was taken with her for a time, I suppose…she was pleasant to look at and all that…and enjoyed talking to young officers…. But I never for a moment thought…that is to say, she was a princess, destined for an arranged marriage with some rajah somewhere, whoever her father decided he needed an alliance with…" He shrugged, trying to imply that's all there was to it, an infatuation that was soon over.

"You called out her name, Nick. Several times."

As much as he willed himself to, he could not continue to look Milly in the eye. He shrugged again. "I dream of India, sometimes…and of people I knew there. The dreams I have when the malaria fevers come… Milly, they're weird, outlandish. I suppose I was remembering her…but last night I dreamed of the major general," he said, as if Ambika was just another person his dreams dredged up from his soldiering time. "It was the oddest thing," he said with a chuckle that sounded forced even to him. "In my dream, he was working alongside Elijah, Isaiah, Caleb and Micah, building the fort on the hill…"

Just as he'd hoped, she was distracted. "Yes, dreams can be strange—"

"As I live and breathe, it's Mad Nick Brookfield!" said a voice coming from across the room where an archway separated the hotel lobby from the restaurant.

It couldn't be.

Nick looked up, praying he had imagined the voice calling his name, a voice he'd thought never to hear again.

Of course he had not imagined it. Captain Blakely Harvey stood in the entranceway, transfixed, a smile curving beneath his bushy mustache. As their eyes met, Harvey started forward, eyes alight, extending a hand. "It *is* you, isn't it?"

Nick wished the man would suddenly be miraculously transported to the steppes of Russia, but when it didn't happen, there was nothing for it but to rise and greet him.

"Harvey, whatever are you doing here?" he asked. Harvey wasn't in uniform.

"I could ask you the same," the other man retorted. "And in fact I will. I came to Texas to visit my dear uncle the ambassador. I expected to see you there, naturally. But when I arrived, you were nowhere in evidence. I asked the old man about it, only to learn you had never taken up your post in Austin, but had instead sent him some crazy message about visiting the countryside before you settled down to your duty. And now I understand why," he said, his gaze sliding in an oily fashion over Milly. "In fact, your rusticating in this dusty little town makes perfect sense now."

Out of the corner of his eye, Nick saw Milly dart a glance at him. Doubtless she was wondering why he didn't have the good manners to introduce them.

"Fair lady, I will introduce myself since Nick apparently isn't about to," the other man said, giving a low bow. "I am Blakely Harvey, late of Her Majesty's Bombay Light Cavalry, just as Nick is."

Milly darted an uncertain glance at Nick, then looked up at Harvey. "I'm Milly Matthews, sir. How…how nice that you've come to visit Nick. You two must have many memories in common."

"Don't we, indeed?" Harvey said with a chuckle. "I look forward to reminiscing with him while I'm here."

Nick had had enough of this charade. He stood. "Miss Matthews and I were just leaving, Harvey. And you may as well tell your uncle I will not be assuming my post, and I apologize for not writing him to that effect sooner. Now that you know that, you may as well leave Simpson Creek."

Harvey's eyes dueled with his for a long moment.

"Leave this delightful hamlet on the same day I've arrived? My dear boy, how inhospitable of you! Why, you must know I've gone to no end of discomfort to reach here, taking the stage as far as I could before hiring a hack—though the miserable bony thing that conveyed me the rest of the way here could hardly be called such, or even horseflesh," he said. "No, I'm afraid I will need to rusticate myself for a few days, to recover from the journey. Surely there's some amusement to be had in this charming little town, perhaps other beautiful ladies to meet, Nick, old boy?"

"There's hard work 'to be had' here, but since you were always averse to that, I know you'd be too bored to remain," Nick said, taking a step forward so that there were only inches between them. The other man was shorter, so Nick had to look down to lock eyes with Harvey, but he did so now. The other man looked away first.

"And if you're really fortunate," Nick went on, "you might meet up with our neighboring Comanches. Their hospitality rivals even that of the Punjabis," he added, referring to the fierce tribesmen of the region northeast of Bombay. "Good evening, Harvey. Nice seeing you again."

Chapter Twenty-One

Milly held her tongue until the wagon passed the last house in town; then, as if she could hold back her curiosity no more, she broke the uncomfortable silence.

"Nick, why were you so unfriendly to that man? You two were in the army together. I mean, I suppose he *was* a little forward toward me, but..." Her voice trailed off.

He said nothing, trying to figure out what to tell her without telling her too much, until at last she sighed and ventured, "You don't have to tell me. It's none of my business."

He didn't want Milly, *his Milly,* transformed into this timid woman. "I'm sorry," he said at last. "Blakely Harvey and I were never friends. He's a double-dealing scoundrel and a womanizer, and I didn't like him even breathing the same air as you. I only hope he'll take the hint and depart in the morning." He didn't really think he could be so lucky, though.

"I...I see..." she murmured. "May I ask why he called you Mad Nick?"

He stared between the horse's ears ahead of him,

wondering what to tell her. There was no way he could answer her question with complete honesty—he'd rather be struck dead by a bolt of lightning, here and now.

"Oh, I suppose it was because I was a 'neck-or-nothing' rider when I was a griff—a newcomer to India—and because I'd take any dare, risk any gamble, both on campaign and during the silly games we played to stave off boredom…" That much was true, but it wasn't the madness that had finally made the nickname irredeemably his.

"Oh. I could tell you didn't like it, when he called you that."

That, my lovely Milly, is the understatement of the century. He could hear the puzzlement in her voice. Perhaps she thought he wasn't a good sport, that he was overreacting to good-natured teasing. He'd a thousand times rather she think that than know the truth.

"Well, we needn't speak of him again," she said, as if that settled the matter completely. "It certainly was a delicious supper, Nick. I had no idea the cook at the hotel could produce a meal like that. Thank you for taking me."

She was trying, Nick thought, but there was no way to bring back the light, intimate atmosphere that had been present at their table in the restaurant, when Nick had been thinking of kissing her tonight. He knew the time wasn't right now. Seeing Harvey, with his smirk, appear out of his nightmares had poisoned the air too much.

There would be other nights, he thought. He loved Milly no less now that he did before Harvey had materialized at the hotel, and he wanted a future with her just as much as ever. Maybe more.

He could see the hill in front of the ranch as a hulking shape in the distance.

"I'll have to be careful not to go on too much about that roast beef in front of Sarah," Milly mused aloud, clearly trying to fill the silence, "or she might think I don't appreciate her cooking... Nick, was that a gunshot? There...there it is again! And do you smell smoke?"

Then there was a volley of gunfire, and the wind brought the smell of smoke unmistakably to their nostrils.

The horse had been ambling along at a slow trot, but now he started and whinnied in alarm, even as Nick reached back and grabbed the rifle that was kept in the wagon. He flapped the reins over the horse's rump to hasten him along. "Get on there!"

"Oh, dear God..." Milly cried, clutching him as the horse lurched into a gallop. "It must be Comanches again! Sarah! Nick, hurry! If they've hurt her..."

It was fortunate the road was level, for the horse slowed his pace only slightly as they careened around the bend.

Nick saw several things at once—horses with riders disappearing around the next curve in the road, Josh and Bobby, illuminated by flames forming a ring around the trees, firing at the riders, while Sarah, a shawl clutched around her, screamed from the porch.

And he saw the ring of fire around the trees, and the four new hands, who had formed a bucket brigade from the pump to the circle of fire.

Nick tossed the reins to Milly, then jumped down

from the wagon, and ran into the barn to where the shovel was kept. The fire wasn't high, but it had been a typical hot, dry summer, and in moments the fire could spread and engulf the grass, and then the trees. In a minute he was back, frantically beating at the fire with the shovel and digging at the loose dusty ground and throwing dirt on it, while the other men threw buckets of water. Josh and Bobby had given up firing at the departed riders and appeared at his side, carrying buckets, which they'd filled with the loose dirt they'd scooped up in the corral.

Between them, they subdued the fire in a few minutes. Milly came out to join them, Sarah at her side, each of them clutching lanterns, and silently they all assessed the damage.

The grass inside the ring was singed, as were some of the lower leaves on the trees, but blessedly, the trees had not caught on fire, nor had the fire spread to the house nearby.

"Who was it?" Milly demanded. "Not Comanches."

"No," Josh agreed. "Them fellas wore white hoods over their faces. I was sleepin' sound, but Isaiah was on watch and heard 'em ride up. They were real organized, Miss Milly, 'cause one a them threw a rock inta a window of th' house, while the others poured somethin' out of a jug in a ring 'round them trees and then set the torches they were carryin' to it. We snatched up our guns, and while that fire was flamin' up, they ran their horses round the bunkhouse, yippin' like wild Injuns while we shot at 'em. 'Bout the time you drove up, they must've had enough, 'cause they took off."

Nick hadn't noticed the damaged window, but now he looked up and saw it was the parlor window that had been broken.

"Here's the rock," Sarah said, producing it from a pocket in her wrapper. "And the message that was tied onto it," she added, handing a crumpled piece of paper to Nick.

Milly held up the lantern so they could read the scrawled message:

SAN SABA COUNTY FOR WHITES ONLY! YOU HAVE BEEN WARNED!

"What's it say, Miss Milly?" asked Elijah. "We…we never had any book learnin'."

Milly's eyes were full of unshed tears as she faced the oldest Brown brother. "I—I don't want to say such awful words. This is the work of that Circle. I guess a circle of fire is some kind of symbol."

Elijah's voice was respectful but insistent. "I reckon we better know the whole truth, ma'am."

Her voice shaking, her body visibly trembling, she read the ugly message as Sarah came to stand by her side. Nick put his arm around Milly.

The four brothers eyed one another, their faces both alarmed and angry.

Milly and Sarah exchanged glances full of silent understanding. "I…I'll understand if you want to leave, and we'll find a way to pay you something for what you've done so far, Elijah. But if you're willing, we want you to stay. Papa didn't raise us to bow down to bullies."

"Especially bullies who won't even show their faces," Sarah added, and both women turned to Elijah.

"You're runnin' a risk, Miss Milly, Miss Sarah," he said, his face sober. "But I reckon you know that. We could keep runnin', but before long we have to make a stand, I figure, 'cause we got a right to exist and earn an honest livin'. As long as you're willing, it might as well be here."

"We are. I only wish we'd have been a little quicker getting home," Milly said. "I'd like to have pulled that hood right off that coward Bill Waters."

Sarah shuddered. "I'm just thankful you got home when you did, so Nick was able to help put out the fire before it did any real damage to the pecan trees. Thank God the wind was out of the west so the house didn't catch."

"We're blessed," Milly agreed. "Thank You, Lord."

"Amen," chorused the four brothers.

Nick added a prayer of thankfulness in his heart, combined with a request for continued protection.

"Yes. And thank you, Isaiah, for being on watch," Sarah said, and he nodded.

"Should I ride back to town for the constable—I mean, the sheriff?" Nick asked. He thought he might also pay a late visit to Blakely Harvey. No doubt he was staying at the hotel. Perhaps he could be a little more persuasive about the benefits of Harvey leaving Simpson Creek early next morning.

"Not tonight," Milly said with a sigh. "There's nothing he could do tonight, anyway. We can leave a little early in the morning for church and pay him a visit—if you think it's even safe to leave the ranch, Nick."

But Josh answered before he could. "I reckon it'll be safe enough here—bullies like to strike in the dark, not in broad daylight. We'll stay and guard it. Don't be too surprised if Sheriff Poteet don't get all het up about the fire, though. He 'n' Waters've been amigos for years."

Nick saw Milly's eyes widen with dismay and felt an aching sympathy for her. First the Comanches, and now the two sisters faced not only social disapproval but the threat of violence because they had dared to employ four ex-slaves. Surely the shoulders he now held an arm around were too fragile to handle all this! He wanted to take her away from all this, to some place where these threats could never reach.

"No one on this ranch should go anywhere—on the ranch or off it—alone," he said instead. On a Texas ranch, it probably went without saying that no one should go anywhere without being armed.

"Sounds like liquored-up cowboys jest out indulgin' in tomfoolery," the sheriff drawled the next day, when they stopped in to see him on the way to church.

Milly felt a spark of irritation at his casual dismissal. "Drunken cowboys don't ride around with hoods over their faces, carrying torches," she retorted. "Would you have called it tomfoolery if the wind had shifted and our house had caught fire? As it is, we nearly lost our pecan trees and had to put out a grass fire."

"But the house didn't catch fire," Sheriff Poteet said in that same maddeningly condescending tone, as if she'd been silly to bring up the possibility.

Nick had been a solid presence at her back since she entered the sheriff's office. Now he touched her shoulder lightly and stepped forward. "Any further such 'tomfoolery' will be met with appropriate force, Sheriff.

The Matthews ranch will be defended. If you hear of anyone who was involved in last night's incident, Mr. Poteet, perhaps you ought to warn them of that."

Milly saw the sheriff's eyes narrow in his weathered face as his gaze shifted to Nick. "Ain't you takin' a bit much on yourself, Brookfield? Last I heard, you were jest workin' for Miss Milly and Miss Sarah."

"I can assure you, Mr. Brookfield speaks for me in this matter, Sheriff," Milly said.

Poteet ignored her. "Miss Milly and Miss Sarah have brought some of this on themselves, and that's a fact."

"Indeed, sir?" There was a wealth of contempt in the two icy words Nick uttered.

"Yep, they surely have. You're a foreigner, and I don't expect you t'understand these things, but no one approves of those shiftless beggars she's given shelter to. I'd say those fellows in the hoods were only expressing the feelings of the community."

"Those shiftless beggars, as you call them, were honest men looking for work," Milly said. "I was in need of help on the ranch. My problem and theirs were solved when I gave them jobs. Now it remains to be seen if you're going to do *your* job, Sheriff, which is to uphold the law."

Poteet leaned forward, his small eyes cold in his middle-aged face. "Your papa must be rollin' in his grave t' hear you talkin' like a blue-belly Yankee."

The injustice of his remark took away her breath and left a seething anger in its place, so much so that she didn't dare speak. Didn't the Bible say in the book of Romans that Christians should be subject to the higher powers, and render them respect? But how could she respect a lawman who wouldn't uphold the law?

Nick stepped forward. "This conversation is over. If you won't be responsible for the safety of the Matthews ladies and their ranch and its other inhabitants, I will be."

Chapter Twenty-Two

Visiting the sheriff—and telling Sarah, who had been waiting in the wagon outside, about it—had been hard for Milly, but walking into church and finding Blakely Harvey sitting in the back row next to Ada Spencer nearly put Milly over the edge.

Milly saw Nick tense beside her at the sight of the man, and guessed he would have liked to turn on his heel and walk back out, but he took Milly's arm as if nothing were wrong and headed toward their usual pew. He gave no acknowledgment of Harvey's smirking nod, but Milly could see Ada waving animatedly at her, obviously pleased as punch with the new acquaintance she had made. Milly forced a smile onto her face and waved back. If they'd been earlier, she knew Ada would have beckoned her over to introduce Harvey, but since they had arrived just as church was about to begin, Milly and Nick took their places quickly, while Sarah hurried forward to sit at the piano.

"Of all the blasted cheek," Nick muttered, his voice pitched low so as to reach only Milly's ears.

Milly sent him a sympathetic glance as she sang the

first line of the hymn. There would be no escaping Ada and her new friend after the service, of course—and no way to warn Sarah that Nick's fellow Englishman was not cut from the same cloth as Nick.

Sure enough, Ada, with Blakely Harvey in tow, practically ran up to Milly before she and Nick had even descended the church steps.

"Milly, can you imagine? What are the odds that I'd meet *another* Englishman, just walking along our streets, taking his constitutional?"

Just as she said these words, Mrs. Detwiler passed by. She gave the foursome a hard stare. As she stalked by, she muttered, "Blasted foreigners are taking over this town. You'd think they never heard of the Revolutionary War!"

In spite of himself, Nick began to chuckle, and Harvey joined in. For a moment Milly had hopes the scene would be carried off without open hostility.

"Why, Mr. Brookfield, Mr. Harvey says he knows you!" Ada exclaimed. "Did you know he was here in town?"

Nick gave a rigid nod at Harvey, who hadn't lost his smirk, before replying to the excited Ada. "Yes, we discovered his presence at the hotel restaurant last night."

The spareness of his reply ought to have given Ada a hint, but just then Harvey squeezed her arm and bestowed on the dazzled woman a smile of distracting charm.

"And I just know you're tickled that he's here to visit, aren't you?" Ada gushed. "It'll be wonderful for you, won't it, having another Englishman here in town, and not only that, but he tells me you and he were in the army together!"

"Ah, but alas, since he can't stay very long, it'll be a transient pleasure," Nick murmured.

"Well, I'm already trying to change his mind about *that*," Ada admitted with a coy wink. "Simpson Creek is a wonderful place to live, isn't it, Milly? Wouldn't it be nice for your Nick if there was another Englishman living here?"

Milly could see Ada thought she had a good chance of persuading Harvey to stay.

"Ah, but what would I *do* here, dear lady?" Harvey said with a fond smile that virtually begged for Ada to find him a reason to stay. "I'm a diplomat, not a cowboy, and my uncle, the ambassador in Austin, declares he would be lost without me. I merely came to catch up on old times with M—with Nick, here."

He had so nearly said Mad Nick, and not by mistake. Milly knew he was toying with Nick like a cat does with a mouse trapped between its paws. Only Nick was no mouse, she thought with rising irritation.

"Sarah, hello! Let me present my new friend to you, who's also Nick's old friend," Ada bubbled, as Sarah joined them. And so Milly and Nick had to hear the whole story over again and to watch in silence as Harvey trained his dazzling smile on her sister.

And Sarah agreed that it was wonderful that Nick had a fellow countryman here, and how pleased she was to meet him.

"Mr. Harvey, you must—" Sarah began.

Milly knew her sister, so she knew what Sarah was about to say—"come have dinner with us, for I know you'll want to spend more time with Nick. Bring Ada, too, of course"—and she knew she had to act quickly and decisively.

Standing next to her sister, Milly moved her foot discreetly and quickly, and under the cover of their long skirts, brought it down on Sarah's foot—not sharply or painfully, just firmly, so that Sarah could not mistake it as an accident.

Sarah faltered.

"Must what, Miss Sarah?" prompted Harvey. He may have been aware some message had just been conveyed between the two sisters, though he couldn't know how, for they weren't looking at each other and their hands weren't touching.

"Ah…continue to enjoy your time here in Simpson Creek," Sarah finished, a slight flush appearing on her cheeks. "Hadn't we better be getting home, Milly? I've got to get dinner in the oven. Nice to meet you, Mr. Harvey. We'll see you later, Ada," she said, and headed toward the wagon without another word.

"She's right, we do need to be getting home," Milly said. "Ada, don't forget about the meeting on Tuesday afternoon at the church."

"I won't. Blakely, why don't you come for dinner at my house. Ma and Pa would be thrilled to meet you," Ada said. "They didn't come to church today because Pa's rheumatism was acting up."

"I'd be delighted, Miss Ada," Harvey said, giving her a courtly bow. "Nick, old boy, why don't you join me for supper again tonight at the hotel? We can catch up on old times then," said Harvey.

Milly saw Nick hesitate, then nod. "That would be most…agreeable," he said, and it was as if the word agreeable was a polite euphemism for something else. "Shall we say seven o'clock?"

"Perfect. Very well, then. Miss Milly, Miss Sarah, it was a pleasure meeting you. I'm sure our paths will cross again while I'm here."

"Nick, why did you agree to meet with him?" Milly asked, after they had left the church and Nick had explained to Sarah that Harvey was not someone whose acquaintance she should cultivate.

"I'm hoping to persuade the cur to leave town without further ado," Nick said darkly, and from the way he clenched the reins, Milly was rather afraid he meant to use his fists, if necessary. Blakely Harvey must be a villain, indeed.

As it happened, however, Nick returned from town before Milly had even left the porch to retire for the night.

"How was your supper with Mr. Harvey?" she called, as he dismounted his horse. From the tension on his face, it didn't appear to have gone well, but she couldn't see any scrapes or bruises to indicate Nick had had to resort to fisticuffs.

Even in the deepening twilight, she could see his face darken. "It didn't happen. He failed to appear. The hotel proprietor said he returned to the hotel in late afternoon, then left again a short while later."

"Do you think he's avoiding you?"

"Possibly. Perhaps the wisest thing he's ever done," Nick said, but she could see he was frustrated.

"Well, come inside when you've unsaddled your horse and I'll fix you something to eat, then," Milly said.

"Wait, there's something else," he said, when she would have turned and gone inside. "This was sticking in the dirt at the bend in the road," he said, pulling something out of his pocket and holding it out to her.

It was a crude doll made of straw tied to a straight stick by means of some twine. The doll's body had been painted black.

"There was straw stacked around the stick like a pyre," Nick said. And there had evidently been a circle of fire lit around it, then stamped out. "I was meant to find it, I think."

They stared at each other.

Milly looked around the group of women Tuesday when the Spinsters' Club—as everyone in town insisted on calling it, rather than by its proper name—reconvened. She couldn't help but wonder if any of the ladies' fathers or brothers were part of the Circle that had left the threatening symbol near her house Sunday night. None of them mentioned Milly's new cowhands, or seemed as if they were uncomfortable in Milly's presence, but perhaps they didn't know of their relatives' participation in the hateful group.

She had to stop being so paranoid, she told herself. The group had formed for the purpose of finding husbands, and she needed to concentrate on running the meeting.

"These candidates sound very promising," Milly announced. "I'm going to pass around the three letters so you can all read them. There's a rancher from Bastrop, a bootmaker from Grange and a physician from Brazos County. Only one of them, the rancher, enclosed his picture…"

There was a pleased sigh as Prissy Gilmore, sitting beside Milly, received the picture and studied it. "Why, he's a handsome fellow and no mistake. I'll bet those eyes are blue as bluebonnets, too…"

"None of the others sent pictures," mused Sarah. "I wonder what that means?"

Caroline shrugged. "It worked out well enough without a picture for you, Milly, and for me and Emily."

"Maybe the men can't afford to have them taken," Jane Jeffries suggested in her tentative way.

"Or they're not only not handsome, but are fat, bald and homely!" chuckled Maude Harkey, a little nervously.

"You know, that man could have had that picture taken years ago," pointed out Caroline Wallace. "He might be considerably older now."

"Perhaps some men just don't want to be judged by a picture," Milly suggested.

"That might not even be *his* picture," opined Ada Spencer, pointing to the daguerreotype of the rancher. "We only have his word for it, after all." A smug smile spread over her face. "I'm glad I found Blakely on my own."

"Oooh!" crowed Prissy. "So things are going well with you two, then?"

Ada blushed and grinned. "So far, yes. He has such refined manners! And that accent! Why, he could charm the doves out of the trees when he talks!" Her blush deepened.

Ada wouldn't think so highly of her visiting Englishman if she'd heard Nick's opinion of him. Ought she to try to warn Ada? She doubted the woman would listen.

"But what will you do when he goes back to Austin? He's only visiting, isn't he?" Maude Harkey asked.

"We'll see," Ada said mysteriously. "He went out riding with Bill Waters the other day to see some ranch land that was for sale. He's thinking about buying up quite a bit of land and becoming a cattle baron, he says."

Milly could barely stifle a groan. Even with as little as she knew about Harvey, she didn't relish the idea of having him around permanently—and especially not as a friend of Bill Waters. Even if Nick hadn't said anything negative about the other Englishman, there had been something about Harvey that was too slick, too polished to be real. She hadn't liked his overbold manner, or the way his gaze wandered where it shouldn't. She hoped Ada wasn't being too trusting in the Englishman's company.

Milly gently steered the club back to its agenda.

"Ladies, if we might go back to the subject of what we're going to do about the men who wrote these letters—would we like to pick one of us to start writing each of them, or should we invite them to Simpson Creek to meet us all at some social event?"

"Why don't we do both?" suggested Jane Jeffries. "One of us could write to each of the men and tell him a little about us, and invite him to whatever event we plan—with the understanding that he'd be free to pick any of us once we've all met—those who don't have anyone yet, I mean."

"Let's see, how many of us haven't met anyone yet?" Prissy said. "Jane, Maude, Sarah, Hannah, Bess, Polly, Faith and me. Are we not to count you, Ada?"

Ada shook her head. "You can leave me out. I'm sure I've found *my* Prince Charming," she said.

Milly was equally sure she hadn't. She *had* to warn her, she decided, before the other woman lost more than her heart.

Maude said, "Let's draw straws, and the short straw holders don't write the letters—though they might be the ones picked when the men actually come, right?"

"True," Prissy agreed, and went to find the church broom to pull some straws. When the drawing was over, Sarah was one of the winners.

"Slowly but surely, we're putting the Spinsters' Club out of business," crowed Maude.

"Not really," Bess Lassiter said. "My sister's going to be eighteen this fall, and she says she wants to participate, too."

"And my cousin's coming to live with us from San Antonio," Faith Bennett put in. "Her fiancé died at Palmito Hill," she said, referring to the last pitched battle of the war, which had taken place on Texas soil. "And while she's not in a mood to think about courting again just yet, I know she will be one day."

"And my friend over in Lampasas heard what we

were doing and wants to come for a visit so she can take part," put in Hannah Kennedy.

"Our success is perpetuating the club," Prissy remarked, as each of the three winners blindly selected a letter. Sarah picked the letter written by the doctor.

"Well, we have yet to celebrate our first wedding," Milly pointed out, "but it seems likely we will be soon."

Which of them would be married first? Would it be her?

"I have a suggestion," Prissy said. "We wouldn't have to plan anything on our own if we invite them to the Founders' Day Celebration."

"Perfect!" Maude cried. "It's not 'til October, which is far enough away that we can expect at least one reply letter from each, and possibly more, and each will have time to travel here."

"And it should have cooled off a little by then," Jane added, fanning herself. The intense heat was typical for August in Texas.

"And there are activities all day, from the speeches in the morning, the box lunches at noon, games in the afternoon and the square dance at night," Sarah said. "Sounds perfect to me."

"Founders' Day it is, then," Milly concluded. She knew Nick would be glad to see them come out, for he had accompanied them on the road for their safety. "Ladies, we are adjourned." She turned to Sarah. "Wait for me by the wagon with Nick, will you?" Milly whispered, as the ladies dispersed. "Ada, may I speak to you?"

"Oh, Milly, can it wait 'til another time?" Ada said,

already halfway to the door. "Blakely's coming to take me on a ride. And here he is now," Ada said, as the door to the social hall opened from the outside. Harvey stood there, smiling in his smirking way.

Chapter Twenty-Three

"You saw Harvey go in?" Milly asked Nick, when she and her sister came out to the wagon. She'd already told Sarah what Nick had said about the man.

He nodded. Yes, he'd seen the blasted scoundrel go in and come out with Miss Spencer, wearing a doting, besotted expression on his face as if he were half-blind with love. Only Nick knew the expression was as false as anything else about Harvey.

"Did you two speak? Did he apologize for not showing up for your supper together?" she asked, as Nick reined the horse in a wide circle to head the wagon back down the road toward home.

He shook his head. "I left my calling card at the hotel Sunday night, so he cannot claim to have forgotten entirely about our engagement, and he's made no attempt to come to me to apologize. Anyone at the hotel could have told him my direction. So when he walked by me on his way into the church, I gave him the cut direct."

Milly's brow furrowed, and he realized she must not have understood the British term. "Sorry, my

Englishness is showing, I fear. I meant I ignored him. He seemed content to do the same to me."

Then Milly told him about Harvey's riding around with Waters to look at property, which had him stifling the urge to disparage the man's parentage aloud. What kind of game was Harvey playing? Was he trying to torment Nick by making him think he would settle here, or would he actually do so? Having him living anywhere near would be like having a cobra in the room, but not being able to see it, never aware when it would strike.

"Nick, I tried to speak to Ada alone back there," Milly said, breaking into his worried thoughts, "to warn her, but she rushed off with Harvey instead. Should I keep trying?"

"Are you good friends?" he asked.

Milly was thoughtful. "Not like Caroline and I are. More like acquaintances, I'd say. We've known one another ever since we first learned our ABCs in school, but then Mama died at the beginning of the war, and we were busy helping Papa, and she's been taking care of her parents…"

"She probably won't listen to you," Nick said, aware he sounded cynical, but it was the truth, from his experience.

"I've got to try, don't you think?" she said, her hazel eyes troubled. "She's clearly head-over-heels about him. If Harvey's as much of a snake-in-the-grass as you say…"

"Oh, he is," Nick said, "every bit of it." *And more.* "You can only try, but often people hear only what they want to hear. So what did you ladies discuss at your meeting?" he asked, wanting to distract Milly from her worries.

He listened while Milly and Sarah chattered about the men who'd written letters and how three of the ladies had been selected to write back and invite them to come for Founders' Day. Nick was glad to hear that Sarah was one of the ones picked and that she, too, was pleased about the prospect in her quiet, unassuming way. Sarah deserved to be happy, too, he thought. He only hoped the man to whom she would write was worthy of her.

"That meeting went on way longer than I would have thought it was going to," Sarah fretted after glancing up at the sun's position. "Goodness, our men must be thinking we've taken off and left them to starve!"

"Oh, I think Josh could warm up last night's beans and make some biscuits, if he had to," Milly commented drily. "He wasn't born eating your cooking, you know. Once we get done with dinner, though, I'm going to start working on a dress for the mercantile."

"The new men seemed real pleased with their shirts," Sarah said. "Bobby said they couldn't stop looking at their reflections in the bunkhouse mirror, as if they thought they were wearing royal robes."

"Maybe they never had any clothing before that wasn't someone else's castoffs," Milly mused aloud.

Nick could tell she was gratified by the new cowhands' appreciation, and his heart warmed again with love for her.

When the wagon reached the turnoff that led to San Saba, however, they encountered a mounted troop of blue-coated soldiers about to turn in the direction of the county seat.

Seeing the long blue line of cavalry, Nick felt a moment's nostalgia. Once he had ridden at the head of a troop like that, all smartly dressed in the uniform of Her Majesty's Bombay Light Cavalry. Now, if he could encounter them again, it would be he who was given the cut direct.

Out of the corner of his eye, he saw Milly stiffen. He supposed her suspicion was natural, given that blue coats had been a symbol of the enemy even earlier this same year. It would take time, Nick supposed, for Texans and other Southerners to feel part of the Union again. His own country had had its civil wars, the Wars of the Roses and between Cavaliers and Roundheads, but that had been long ago.

"Afternoon," said the commanding officer at the head of the double line of mounted troops, touching his brimmed hat with a gloved hand. "I'm Major McConley of the Fourth Cavalry."

"I'm Nicholas Brookfield, and this is Miss Milly Matthews and Miss Sarah Matthews. May we be of any assistance?" He felt the heat of Milly's glare as soon as the words were out of his mouth.

The major shook his head. "Thank you, no, we're out on patrol. We've had reports of Quanah Parker and his braves raiding over by Chappell. You had any trouble with Comanches?"

Briefly, Nick told him about the raid that had taken place the day he arrived, and about the carcass they'd found after that.

"No problem since then, eh?"

None caused by Indians, Nick wanted to say, wishing the soldiers could do something about the threats made by the Circle, but he knew Milly wouldn't want him to give these Federals any reason to linger.

"Keep your eyes peeled meanwhile," Major McConley advised. "I'm sure they'll be raiding every chance they get now to build up their food stores before they move to the Staked Plains for the winter." With a final salute, he motioned the troop forward, and they rode past toward San Saba.

It was sobering to remember that whatever their problems were with white troublemakers, the potential still existed for an attack by Indians that could be far worse.

Milly let her breath out in a great whoosh. "I thought sure he was going to ask who was building a fort up there and why," she said, nodding at the hill in the distance where they had begun their fortress.

Nick doubted the major could have noticed the low rectangle of rock from the road, and even if he had, it might not have occurred to him what the building was to be. Nick thought it was even possible that the major might have approved of the citizenry doing what they could to protect themselves. He couldn't be sure, though—perhaps Milly's suspicions were based on Texan experience with the occupying troops.

Milly's mention of the barely begun fort, coupled with the major's words, made Nick thoughtful. They had wanted to build their fort on the ideal high ground, but so far all they had been able to accomplish was to establish a rocky perimeter. Their duties of tending the livestock and keeping the fences mended, as well as the difficulty of working under a hot summer sun that rivaled Bombay for intensity, had kept them from accomplishing very much. There was still so much more work to do before it would be tall enough to keep anyone safe within it. At the barn raising, several men had been interested but so far no one had shown up to help build it. It might be due to their disapproval of the four ex-slaves, or perhaps the men thought a fort overlooking Matthews land might not help them in town all that much. Perhaps it was merely that everyone was busy with their own affairs. Nick had no way of knowing for sure.

At the present rate, though, with just the six able-bodied men on the ranch working on it, it might be a year before the walls were high enough to protect anyone. It wasn't just a matter of building four high, stout stone walls. They needed parapets near the top of the walls where men could fire at attackers through slits in the walls as he'd seen in medieval castles in England. But they couldn't assume the Comanches would wait until the fort was done before they attacked again.

When they reached the ranch, the news was even more sobering. Over dinner, Elijah announced that Caleb had been shot at just as he succeeded in untying a calf he'd found lying helpless on its side, its legs tied together. The young man hadn't been hit, or seen who had fired at him, but the shot had come from the area where Waters's ranch bordered with both the Matthews ranch and the road. He had returned fire in that direction, then jumped on his horse, hightailing it back to the ranch.

"The calf was obviously tied up and left there for you to find," Nick speculated, "so someone could get a shot off at whoever found it. I'm thinking they were counting on it being one of you brothers, rather than Bobby or I."

"I think so, too," Elijah growled. "And I don't like it. There's somethin' else they've been doin' and we didn't tell you about it—didn't want to worry you, Miss Milly, Miss Sarah—but now I reckon we better."

"Oh?"

Elijah nodded. "Three-four times now, we found nooses hangin' where we'd be sure t'see 'em. Little ones, like doll-sized, and big ones. Hangin' from tree limbs, mostly…but we found one right in the barn."

Sarah gasped in horror.

Milly clutched at Nick's arm. "So you think it was one of the Circle, trying to terrorize the Browns into leaving?" Sarah asked Nick.

"Yes, and I think they'd seen me leaving with you ladies on the way to town."

"But we can't prove it was someone from the Circle shooting at Caleb, can we?" asked Milly, frustrated. "If the shot came from where Waters's land borders with ours *and* the road, it could have been anyone—even a Comanche—shooting from the road. At least that's what Waters and his Circle cronies will say—that Caleb was too scared to see where the shot had come from."

"I wasn't scared. I was mad, Miss Milly," Caleb said. "I wanted to hit whoever the buzzard was who shot at me."

"And end up being hanged as a murderer?" Isaiah asked. "They'd claim you shot an innocent man who hadn't fired his gun, and you know it."

Caleb was silent.

"Well, I'm tired of living like this," Milly said with

some heat. "The Comanches have always been a danger around here from time to time, but with the new threat posed by the Circle, I feel like none of us are safe away from the house and that when we go to town, we leave the ranch more vulnerable," Milly said. "I'm beginning to feel like we're prisoners on the ranch, especially you fellows," she said, nodding toward the four brothers. "I'd like for it to be safe for you to go to town if you wanted to without people acting nasty toward you, or worse."

Elijah nodded. "Yeah, Miss Milly, it's like we're still not free, no matter what Mr. Lincoln said, God rest his soul."

Nick could only agree. He wanted peace, not only for the sake of those living on the ranch and in the town, but so he could court Milly and move toward marriage.

"Let's all ponder the problem this afternoon, then put our heads together after supper and see if we can come up with some solutions."

Take that, and that, and that, Milly thought, slicing through the chalk line she'd traced on the length of cloth.

"Easy, there," murmured a familiar English voice from the doorway of her sewing room. "Who are you slicing up?"

Milly whirled around and straightened, seeing Nick leaning against the doorway with negligent grace, holding a glass of cold lemonade in each hand.

She felt herself flushing in embarrassment that he had so accurately guessed her thoughts. "Bill Waters, Blakely Harvey and the Comanches, alternately," she confessed. "Not very Christian of me, is it?"

"It's very *human* to be angry at those who are trying to hurt you," he said, handing her a glass. "Especially those who are supposedly civilized and should know better. Anyway, I was thirsty and thought you might be, too."

"Thank you," Milly said, raising her glass in salute before drinking down a cool, refreshing sip. "Did you come to discuss strategy?" How handsome he was, smiling at her from the doorway, his teeth flashing white in his suntanned face, his eyes sparkling with a compelling blue warmth. Did he have any idea how he affected her?

"No," he said. "Strategy can keep 'til after supper, as we said. I came for this." In three short strides he closed the distance between them and drew her near. And then he was kissing her, with a sweetness combined with that same fierce intensity that she had been using to slice through the cloth only a minute ago. He kissed her as if Sarah wasn't just down the hall in the kitchen, white to her elbows with flour. His kiss was warm and tender and full of promise, and for a long moment she wanted him never to stop. But at last he did, and let go of her, but he gazed down at her as if she was the most beautiful woman in the world.

"W-why did you do that, just now?" was all she could think to say, and then wished she hadn't opened her mouth and said something so idiotic. Perhaps if she'd had the sense to remain silent and had gone into his arms again instead, he would have given her more of those wonderful kisses.

"Because, my dear Milly, because we both needed it,"

he said in that completely English way of his. "Because we've been so busy, not only with the tasks of everyday living, but with big problems. A man who's in love with his lady would naturally want to kiss her, but each time, a problem reared its ugly head."

"You are?"

His brow crinkled in puzzlement—or maybe he was just teasing her, to get her to say it. "I am what?"

"A man in love with his lady? With me?"

He smiled that slow, dazzling smile that set her heart to pounding. "I am, indeed, Milly Matthews. I'm in love with a lady who uses her imagination to solve a problem—a group of unmarried ladies who have no men to marry, I mean—a lady who stands her ground, who doesn't resort to the vapors when faced with danger. Yet she feels guilty for pretending a piece of cloth is her worst enemy as she slices through it. I just thought that lovely woman should know how I feel, and I decided to come take the time to tell her so."

"Ohh…" she said, completely unable to say more. "Oh, Nick. I love you, too. I—I just feel guilty that I've involved you in something much more than what you bargained for. You didn't ask to be confronted with murderous savages—red or white."

"No," he admitted. "I came to Simpson Creek on a lark. But having found you, Milly, I'm not about to let you go, or let problems, big or small, frighten me away. We'll solve the problems, Milly, I know we will, with God's help. And then I want to marry you and raise children just as spirited as their mother."

He spoke with such sincerity that she knew he meant
it, and would see his hope become reality.

"And with the quiet strength of their father," she said.
"Let's kiss on it, shall we?"

Chapter Twenty-Four

"The way I see it, Waters and the rest of his associates are counting on that trapped feeling Milly mentioned at dinner," Nick said to the solemn group gathered around the table after supper. "They're treating you like a hawk does a hare, swooping over it often enough that it doesn't feel safe in its refuge or out of it, so at last it becomes too anxious to stay. It flees, which leaves it vulnerable to the hawk. In this case there is one hawk using another to help it—between the Comanches and the Circle, we don't feel completely safe on the ranch or off of it, am I right?"

Slowly, everyone nodded.

"There are people who could be allies in town, but the hawks have isolated you from them, so you feel reluctant to go to them for help for fear they'll refuse, and they feel some distrust of you, too. If we can break that isolation somehow, if we could prove we are more valuable to the town than any of these men in the Circle, we would have allies who would come to our aid, and the Circle wouldn't feel free to attack. And the town could become safer from the Comanches. But it will mean postponing something we've started here at the ranch, at least for now."

"What?" Milly asked for all of them.

He explained.

Milly sighed after he finished. "I suppose you're right," she said. "But how are we to get them to agree to this?"

"Here's how I propose to do it," Nick began. "First, we have to think of a way to speak to as many people as we can at one time. When is almost everyone gathered together all at once?"

"At church," Milly and Sarah said in unison.

Nick smiled as if he were a teacher and they were clever pupils. "Do you think Reverend Chadwick would support our plan?"

"Sure, he'd back our plan, all right," Josh agreed. "He don't like folks treatin' other folks badly, no matter what the reason is."

"The success of the plan," Nick went on, "depends on us getting to Reverend Chadwick and soliciting his support secretly, so that the Circle is taken by surprise. Do you think he would let us use the church to hold our meeting directly after Sunday's service?"

"Yes, I think he would," Milly said. "But how do you propose we ask him, without tipping our hand, so to speak?"

"I'd suggest sending Bobby to town in the morning, ostensibly to buy some item at the mercantile you might need, but in reality his main purpose will be to deliver a letter to Reverend Chadwick, outlining our reasons for having this meeting right after church, and not announcing 'til the end. We'll ask him to give Bobby an answer either immediately, or if he wants to pray and think about it, we could send Bobby back next morning. No one's likely to bother Bobby riding to and fro."

The youth grinned from ear to ear at being selected for such an important mission.

"It could work," Milly murmured, her elbow propped on the table, her fingers rubbing her chin.

"If we must, we can mention meeting that cavalry detachment on the road, and what the major said about the Comanche raids likely increasing before winter. That tacitly reminds the townspeople you have the option of involving the cavalry to help against the Circle, if they won't help, without actually saying so. But I think we should avoid that if we can."

"And if they will help, you think that will break the power of the Circle?" Sarah asked.

"Yes, especially if the Brown brothers would be willing to assist," he said, turning to them. "And may I say, I for one wouldn't blame you if you chose not to participate," Nick said, his gaze directed at Elijah, Isaiah, Caleb and Micah.

When he had finished explaining this part of the plan, the brothers each looked at one another. Then, slowly, they nodded.

"It'll make the Circle's fool notions about them look downright silly," Josh said.

"Exactly," Nick agreed. "Especially if the men of the Circle are taken by surprise and react without time to think."

Josh cackled with glee. "You mean, if they shoot off their mouths? Bill Waters is good at that."

Nick nodded, smiling at the older man's enthusiasm.

"It will show the town who's for the town's good and who's out only for their own good."

"I'll write the letter," Milly said, rising and going to the parlor, where she found a pen, ink and paper in their father's old desk.

Reverend Chadwick, however, didn't send an answer back with Bobby. He came himself, driving his buggy into the yard at noon with Bobby leading the way on his horse.

"Reverend, you're just in time for dinner," Sarah called, wiping her hands on her apron while Milly was still staring from the doorway.

"Good! I was hoping a hungry man could find a bite to eat after that hot, dusty ride. You got some sweet tea, too?" Reverend Chadwick asked as he climbed down from the buggy.

"Of course."

"Sarah, Milly, I had no idea you were faced with such dilemmas," he said, striding toward the porch, raising a hand in greeting to Nick and Josh, who'd heard his arrival and come out of the barn and bunkhouse. "Oh, I heard bits and pieces of that ugly nonsense Bill Waters and Dayton and their friends have been spouting, of course—people don't always lower their voices quickly enough when I come in the room," he added with a wink. "But I hadn't realized things had come to such a pass that your men were being shot at. It's a terrible business, terrible," he added, as Milly ushered him to a seat at the table, and Sarah handed him a glass of cold tea. "I suppose some of the good people of Simpson Creek have allowed themselves to become persuaded of the silly fables men like Waters tell about folks like your four new cowboys," he said, speaking frankly since the Brown brothers were just now riding in from the north pasture and couldn't hear him. "If we don't put a stop to it, the town will only be further and further divided, and then how could we fight off the Comanches? Besides, I don't want men like Waters gaining the whip hand over this town. Mayor Gilmore's getting along in years, and when he steps down, I don't want Bill Waters taking his place if I can help it."

Five days later, Reverend Chadwick lowered the hands he had raised in benediction. "And now, before we go our separate ways," he announced, "I have been asked to call a meeting of the townspeople."

As a hum of speculative conversation rose in the pews around them, Milly's gaze locked with Nick's. Taking his hand, she gave it a little surreptitious squeeze and felt his reassuring squeeze in return. The moment was at hand.

"Who asked for this meeting? I don't know anything about a meeting," Prissy's father called toward the pulpit, confusion creasing his features and causing the ends of his bushy mustache to twitch.

"I haven't heard anything about it either," Bill Waters declared from the back, rising.

"The Matthews sisters and Nick Brookfield have requested it, and having heard what they wish to discuss with all of you, I support it," Reverend Chadwick said with quiet dignity. "I suggest we pray once more and ask the Lord to bless this meeting and that His will be done," he added, and bowed his head, praying aloud for exactly that.

Bill Waters hadn't sat back down while the reverend was praying, and now Dayton stood, too. When Milly had arrived at church she'd been dismayed to see that Blakely Harvey was once more sitting by Ada; now he looked as if he was about to get to his feet, too—as were several other men sitting in the back rows.

"I'm not interested in hearing anything those three would have to say," Waters shouted.

"Ain't no law can make us stay, is there?" Dayton demanded.

Reverend Chadwick unclasped his hands, palm upward. "Of course not," he said in his mild, resonant voice, "but I think you'll find the subject matter particularly of interest to you. So I'd encourage you to remain, gentlemen."

Muttering and eyeing one another, Waters and Dayton and the rest sat back down.

"The Matthews sisters have chosen Mr. Brookfield as their spokesman," Chadwick went on. "Nick, would you come to the front, please?"

"A blasted foreigner's going to speechify at us?" one of Waters's cronies protested, and received an indignant look from Harvey.

Milly watched proudly as head high, his posture ramrod-straight, Nick strode toward the pulpit. He was so brave—he had not taken the easy way out, either with her or with the town, and now her heart swelled with even more love for him.

Nick cleared his throat. His gaze touched hers briefly, then he looked out over the congregation. "It's been my pleasure to have gotten to know many of you since I came to Simpson Creek a short few weeks ago, and I thank you for your welcome," Nick said. "Most of you will remember that the day I arrived was quite a dramatic one, a day in which the Misses Matthews's foreman nearly lost his life in a Comanche raid. I'm told some of you have suffered similar attacks in the past, and even lost family members. We were blessed that no one was killed this time." He paused and let his gaze roam the pews. "So I know you will understand that the choice I'm about to put in front of you could be a matter of life and death."

He had their attention now, even that of Waters's bunch, who had relaxed since the Englishman didn't seem about to accuse them of anything.

"At the barn raising, some of us men talked about building a fort atop the hill overlooking the ranch. As a sentinel post, it's a perfect place to build it, but my thoughts have changed on it somewhat."

"What are you saying?"

"Yeah, spit it out, Englishman!"

"I think that should be the second fort, the lookout fort. The first fort should be erected right here in Simpson Creek."

Now a hum of conversation rose again, and after a moment, Reverend Chadwick raised his hands for quiet.

"Comanche raids usually come without much warning, correct? And I'm told that the raids are expected to grow more frequent in the fall as the Indians steal what they need before they travel to their winter quarters."

How clever of Nick to cite the informed opinion of the

cavalry major without identifying him, Milly thought, because many of the townspeople were predisposed to discount any opinion coming from a bluecoat.

"Many of you, I think, have wondered how it would be possible for you to reach the safety of the fort atop the hill if a band of braves suddenly appeared—and you're quite right—you might not have time. However, you *could* make it to a fort right here in Simpson Creek. Therefore, I am proposing we build a fort in town, and because we believe so deeply in this project, the men of the Matthews ranch will start work as soon as the site is chosen, and we'll work right alongside everyone else—or alone. We'll be there either way, because we value the town of Simpson Creek and want safety for its citizens." He paused to let his words sink in, and during this time Milly looked around her. Faces were thoughtful, heads were nodding. She could hear them reminding each other how some communities had "forted up" in abandoned garrisons during the war when the Comanches had roamed the state almost unopposed.

Nick has them, she thought.

"I did say 'the men of the Matthews ranch,' did you notice? I meant *all* of us—Josh, Bobby, me—and our four new hands, Elijah, Isaiah, Micah and Caleb Brown."

Silence cloaked the room as everyone looked at everyone else—and then all gazes were trained on Waters, Dayton and the others of the Circle to see what their reaction would be.

They were silent, impassive, their arms crossed, as if by remaining immobile they could stop what was coming.

"I think it's only fair when a person is being talked about that he be present, don't you?" Nick went on. "Gentlemen, will you come in?"

The door that led from the pastor's study to the sanctuary opened, and out walked Elijah, Isaiah, Caleb and Micah Brown, eyes wary but heads held high. They had gone in there through the outside entrance during the service, Milly knew, and had been waiting there ever since.

Several people gasped aloud.

"How dare you?" shouted Waters, eyes bulging, his face red with fury. "We don't let those people in our *church!*"

Reverend Chadwick, who had been standing to the side of the front pew, raised an arm now. "These men are here with my permission, and I warn you, I'll take any insults or harm offered them as a personal affront. This is a church, and a church is sacred ground."

Glaring, with his hands on his hips, Walters drawled, "I got a question for Miss Milly."

Milly stood, wondering what he had in mind, and faced the older man. "I'm listening, Mr. Waters."

"You 'n' Miss Sarah, you pay them boys up there?" He pointed a stubby, age-spotted finger at them. "Real money, that is?"

Milly felt hot anger knot her stomach. She knew what Waters was about now.

"No. At the present time, we can't afford to." *Like many of you, the war left us cash-poor,* she wanted to say, but Waters had made it personal, and she would not take refuge in an easy excuse, however reasonable it was. "They get room and board. But as the ranch begins to prosper again, we plan to—"

"My cowhands make twenty dollars a month," Waters shot back. "And now you're proposing to have them labor to build the town a fort—hard work for men just getting room an' board, I'd say. How's that different from them bein' slaves? My pa had a few slaves once. That's all we 'paid' them, too—room an' board."

Milly felt her face flush. "I don't pay Nick anything either," she argued. "Or—"

Waters interrupted with a suggestive snicker.

Milly's hands clenched at her side, but she knew she had to retain her dignity to keep the high ground. "And Josh or Bobby haven't been paid either, ever since the war began. You wouldn't call them slaves, would you?"

"Reverend, may I say something?"

It was Elijah who had spoken. Everyone stared. Waters ground his teeth as if enraged by Elijah's effrontery.

"The difference between us and slaves is we *want* to be workin' for Miss Milly and Miss Sarah," Elijah said. "And we're *willin'* to help y'all folks with buildin' that fort—if you're willin' to have us help."

Elijah stepped back into line with his brothers, and Nick once again took hold of the pulpit and began to speak. "But the problem with having these four strong young men building a fort for everyone's safety is that because of the bigotry and prejudice of a few, these young men who are willing to work hard to make Simpson Creek a safer place to live might not be safe themselves—on the road to and from town, or while they're here building. And everyone here knows I'm speaking of the Circle."

Chapter Twenty-Five

Bill Waters jumped to his feet, shaking his fist. "You've got a lot of gall, Englishman, coming here and accusing us of anything!"

"I'm not accusing you of just 'anything,' Mr. Waters. I'm accusing you and your associates in the Circle of hiding under white hoods and attempting to terrorize these men who only want to live and work like the rest of us. You've set fires and left hangman's nooses where these men would find them. When that didn't work, you attempted murder—"

Waters was the picture of outraged innocence. "Attempted murder? I don't know what you're talking about."

Milly left her pew and dashed up to the pulpit before she even realized she was moving. "You know exactly, Bill Walters, but I'll tell those who don't—I'm speaking of the bullet that was fired at Caleb Brown when he was in the southeastern part of our land last Tuesday. Fortunately, your assassin failed."

The hum in the room became an excited buzz.

"You're a liar, Milly Matthews. Becoming an old maid has addled your brain," snapped Waters.

"Careful," warned Nick, his soft voice a lash. "You're speaking to a lady."

Waters smirked and crossed his arms over his barrel chest. "All right, I'll put it more politely. Miss Matthews, you've been lied to by that boy and you've imagined all the rest. Perhaps you've been overly influenced by that foreigner next to you."

"Brookfield, you don't know what it's like, dealin' with people like them," Dayton snarled, pointing at the brothers, his face flushed. "You lily-white English only know folks as white as you. You never had a passel a' helpless fools let loose on you after a war."

Nick's blue eyes blazed in his sun-bronzed face. "It's true, we freed our slaves some time ago, and without a war." He stood his ground at the pulpit while the hum of conversation rose to a wasplike buzz, then died down as the congregation waited to hear what else would be said. "And as for lily-white…can you mean *me?*" he asked, and rolled up his sleeves, revealing forearms as tanned as any Texas rancher's there.

Several ladies and men chuckled. His humor had brought them back to him, Milly thought.

"Yes, I'm English, and I wasn't here during your Civil War. But the British Empire extends all over the world, and in India, I assure you, white Englishmen were distinctly in the minority—a few thousand in a vast country of brown-skinned people. Yet for the most part, we respected them and worked alongside them, helping bring modern civilization into that country."

Milly, who'd been sitting sidewise so she could see

both Nick and the reactions of the Circle, saw Blakely Harvey step into the aisle now.

"Oh, yes, Nicholas Brookfield *respected* the Indians—if *respect* is what you'd like to call his ah…*liaison* with the rajah's lovely daughter, the Princess Ambika," he said, his voice silky. "But the army called it inappropriate and 'conduct unbecoming an officer' and he was drummed out of the regiment in utter disgrace. That's how he came to be in Texas, good people. I daresay he wasn't welcome back home in England. And you'd consider letting him advise you what you should do?"

Milly saw Nick's face drain of color and his gaze fly to her. He flinched as if the words had been a physical blow.

So he hadn't trusted her enough to tell her the truth about Ambika, the woman whose name he had called in his delirium. *"We were acquainted, yes…I was taken with her for a time…"*

Yet Harvey was saying his relationship with the Indian woman had been much more. A shameful amount more. If Nick lied to her about this, what else had he lied about?

Could she love him now?

Love rejoices in the truth. Love bears all things, believes all things, hopes all things, endures all things.

Milly looked Nick in the eye and mouthed the words, *I love you.*

There would be time to hear his side of things, time to hear the complete story, but right now, the important thing was to stand with this man who loved her. And she believed in his love, whatever he had done.

She saw Nick straighten. "There is more to this story than what Mr. Harvey insinuates, of course. But the person who has a right to hear it first is the woman I love, Miss Millicent Matthews, and I pledge here and now that she will."

Silence gripped the church.

Reverend Chadwick stepped forward and let his gaze roam about the church. "Let he who is without sin among you cast the first stone."

Milly saw men, and even some women, drop their gazes and stare down at their feet.

Nick cleared his throat. "Mr. Harvey called you 'good people,' and he's right about that, at least. You are good people. And we're asking, good people, for you to let Elijah, Isaiah, Caleb and Micah Brown work alongside us *in safety* to build that fort for the common good of us all, earning their right to be as respected as any of you. Which means telling the men of the Circle that you won't tolerate, silently or openly, their hatred and violence."

There was utter silence as Nick stood there with Milly next to him, as each person in the church eyed his neighbor, then Waters and Dayton and the other men who stood with them at the back of the church, then looked back at Nick and Milly—and at Reverend Chadwick as he came back to the pulpit to join them.

"Well, what do you say?" the pastor asked. "Are you the 'good people' that Nick, here, called you?"

Mr. Patterson stood up. "I don't know about the rest of you folks, but I went to war, and I've had enough of killin' except to defend myself and my family. I vote yes—let's build the fort, and the more folk that want to pitch in—" he gestured at the four brothers up front "—the quicker we'll have us a fort."

Mr. Wallace stood up now. "Haven't we lost enough in this war? I lost my son. Waters, you lost yours, too. Why, Miss Milly had to organize a group of ladies just to bring more young men to this town! Ain't you hated enough for a lifetime without hatin' anybody else? I vote yes, too."

"Anyone wants to make life safer from them Comanches, I'm all for that," the town's milliner announced.

One by one, townspeople stood and aligned themselves with Nick and Milly.

Then Mrs. Detwiler rose ponderously to her feet, and Milly had to stifle a groan. Would the old woman say something awful that turned the town against Nick again? *Please, God...*

But when Mrs. Detwiler began to speak, Milly thought she could indeed believe in miracles.

"Bill Waters, you gonna hold on to your stiff-necked ways 'til the Comanches stampede through here again?" the old woman demanded. "Not me!"

That seemed to be the final straw for Waters, who raised his arm and made a disgusted, dismissive gesture with his hand. He turned on his heels and walked out and the others of the Circle stomped out after him. Harvey went as well, leaving Ada looking stricken.

Mrs. Detwiler gave a sniff of satisfaction, while Milly tried to make up her mind whether to laugh or cry happy tears.

Then the old woman pointed at Sheriff Poteet, who'd been sitting midway back, his arms stretched out over the back of the pew. "Sheriff, did you know about any a' these goings-on?" she demanded.

He dropped his arms and sat up straight. "Ma'am?"

"You heard me, young man."

Milly had to stifle a smile, for Poteet was only perhaps a decade younger than Mrs. Detwiler.

"Well…" He drew out the syllable as far as it could go. "Miss Milly did come to me a few days ago about that fire some yahoos lit around her pecan tree…and she did say they was wearin' hoods over their heads, but shucks, ma'am, that didn't give me no proof who they were…"

"And you didn't even investigate, did you? Same as when someone stole some a' my prize roses, or the pie I had cooling on my windowsill. You just couldn't be bothered. From now on you better shape up, Sheriff Poteet, 'cause this town pays your salary. Otherwise we're liable to vote that foreigner in as our new sheriff— he's shown a lot more gumption than you."

"That won't be necessary, Mrs. Detwiler," the sheriff said, meek as a lamb.

The old woman harrumphed at that, as if not fully convinced. "And furthermore, I'm one to put my money where my mouth is. You know that big old field in the back of my house? Mr. Detwiler bought us a big piece of land behind our house, planning to build homes for our children one day. But he was always too busy being the parson, and the Lord took him home before he ever got the chance. Bein' as it's near the center of town, I'm thinking that lot would be a good place to build a fort—if y'all agree."

Reverend Chadwick started to clap, and in seconds, everyone was clapping and cheering their approval.

When the applause finally died down, Mrs. Detwiler's face was pink with pleasure. Milly couldn't recall seeing her smile.

Nick bowed from the pulpit. "Bravo, Mrs. Detwiler. Your generosity will inspire all of us. I propose we name it Fort Detwiler."

Again, there was thunderous applause.

Mrs. Detwiler beamed. "Generous? Not me—I just want to be closest to the fort, that's all. I'm an old woman, and I can't run so fast."

Everyone laughed.

"It's not necessary to name it after me, young man, but thank you for the thought. And now I reckon we'd all better get home for our dinners and rest up, 'cos bright and early Monday morning, I expect to see all you menfolk hard at work with these young men—" she pointed at the Brown brothers "—building that fort."

After the meeting was brought to a close with another prayer from Reverend Chadwick, Milly, her heart in her throat, approached Mrs. Detwiler to thank her for what she'd done. To her astonishment, the old woman hugged her, and begged Milly's forgiveness for the way she'd treated her ever since Milly had thought up her scheme to bring bachelors to town for the unmarried girls.

"I was just pure jealous at your daring, don't you see, Milly? I never had such spunk in my whole life, and I was coveting yours. Now I've got to admit I'm proud to know you. And don't worry, you and your young man will work out any problems about the past. None of us come to our spouses straight from heaven, you know. None of us is perfect," she said.

"Thank you," Milly said, and burst into the tears she'd been trying so hard to hold back. Nick handed her his handkerchief.

Then Sarah came forward and invited Mrs. Detwiler to come home with them for supper.

"Thank you," she said, "but two of my sons are coming in from Deer Creek this afternoon. In fact, they're probably already at the house wonderin' why I'm not home from church yet. But I'll take a rain check, sweet girl."

Chapter Twenty-Six

No one spoke of Blakely Harvey's embarrassing revelation on the way back to the ranch. Everyone but Milly and Nick seemed eager to fill the silence. The Brown brothers voiced relief at the town's willingness to work with them and reject the Circle. Sarah chattered about Mrs. Detwiler's amazing turnaround as if oblivious to Milly's distracted quiet.

Milly had told him she loved him while he stood alone in front of the church, giving him a flash of hope that her love for him had not died in the instant that Harvey had coldly attempted to destroy his reputation. Perhaps in that moment her generous heart had overridden her self-respect and motivated her to support him in case of public censure. But now that she had time to think, she might not be so quick to ally herself with a man who was, despite his high moral pronouncements, nothing but a liar after all.

"I'll unhitch the horses," Nick said aloud as they pulled up in front of the barn. He was not surprised when Milly lingered with him rather than following Sarah into the kitchen to help put dinner on the table as she usually did. The other men went into the bunkhouse.

Once the wagon horses were in the corral, by tacit agreement she followed him into the cool dimness of the barn. He turned to face her with the same feeling a man must have when turning to face a firing squad.

"Do you…do you hate me, Milly? Do you want me to leave?" *Or merely abandon any pretense that I am worthy of you?*

She blinked at him. "*Hate* you? No, of course I don't hate you. How could I hate you? Didn't you see me mouth the words 'I love you'?"

He held up his hands, palms upward. "Yes, of course I did, and I thought perhaps it was a noble gesture, not abandoning me publicly in front of the wolves—the Circle, that is—and the townsfolk. I thought once we were alone, you might tell me that you've reconsidered how you feel, now that you know what I've done—"

She flew at him now until she was practically toe-to-toe with him, her face upturned, her eyes blazing. "You British idiot! You thought I was being *noble?* Is that what a proper English lady would do? Well, Texas women are different! We don't give up so easily on someone we love. I came in here to hear the truth from you, not some silly self-sacrificing *nonsense!*"

She was magnificent when she was angry, but he didn't want to chance making her angrier still by telling her so.

"I love you, Nicholas Brookfield, and that's not going to change," she went on. "But now I believe you have something to tell me—or so you promised back there in church."

He nodded and gestured toward a pair of old chairs. "Why don't we sit down?"

He waited while she settled herself, took a deep breath, then said, "Yes, it's true that I had feelings that were inappropriate for the maharajah's daughter Ambika. It will not excuse me to say that she collected the hearts of naive British officers like some women collect jewelry, or that she had claimed Blakely Harvey's affections before she turned her efforts toward me. Nor is my shame any the less though I can say we never... that is to say, didn't actually..." He broke off, his face flushing. "Oh, Milly, none of this is proper to say to you..."

She leaned forward, her eyes full of compassion. "I believe I understand."

"We were alone together in her bedroom when we were interrupted by the intrusion of a servant girl who came in to clean the room, not knowing I was there with the princess. Princess Ambika flew into a rage, striking the poor terrified girl again and again."

His eyes closed as he relived the incident in his mind, remembering how the silky, enthralling woman had been transformed in an instant into a screaming, brutal virago. "She would have killed the poor girl then and there had I not intervened, restraining her and telling her I could not allow anyone, even a princess, to beat a helpless servant. Then she turned on me, screaming and telling me to be gone and take the worthless girl with me. I left the palace, vowing never to return except in the course of duty, and never alone. I saw that the servant girl was given employment in the army compound in the household of a colonel's wife. But the colonel's wife reported she soon disappeared. I assumed the girl had returned to her village, but then she was found murdered. A knife left by the body bore the royal insignia."

He heard Milly gasp, and felt her hand on his shoulder, felt its warmth even through his shirt. He took it for a moment, squeezed it to show he was grateful for her touch, then rose to his feet, unable to sit still any longer.

"I thought living with my guilt was awful enough, but Ambika was not finished with her revenge. No one shames a maharajah's daughter, it seems, and escapes unscathed—though of course my guilt in knowing I'd had a part in the servant girl's death hardly qualifies as unscathed."

Milly had risen behind him. "Ambika is the one who got you thrown out of the regiment," she guessed.

"Yes, her father called my commanding officer to the palace and berated him for allowing an officer to attempt to despoil his daughter—as if that were possible!" He gave a bitter laugh. "The maharajah was demanding my head—quite literally."

Again, he heard her gasp. "Hadn't you told him the truth?"

"Of course, but try to see it as he must have—after all, the maharajah could command thousands to attack, and the army had been through the massacre at Calcutta some years before. What was one stupid fool of a captain more or less?"

"But in the end, that's not what happened."

"No. Obviously, I stand before you with my head very much attached to my shoulders. In the end, the general made a very brave decision not to let a maharajah decide the fate of one of Her Majesty's soldiers, and settled for drumming me out of the regiment in disgrace. I was forbidden to tell the truth to anyone, for my own safety and the preservation of relations between the British government and the maharajah. But Blakely Harvey, back in Ambika's good graces, spread the story of my foolishness among my fellow officers. For the most part, they thought me an idiot allowing the fate of a serving girl to matter. That's when the nickname 'Mad Nick' took on a life of its own. Harvey's gossip wasn't traced back to him, though. He paid no price for it."

"No wonder you despise him," she breathed.

"God forgive me, yes. And to have him show up here…" He shrugged. "Just to be on the safe side, for they didn't trust the maharajah not to have me permanently silenced, the general hustled me out of Bombay in the dead of night and put me on a ship."

He fell silent, drained by the confession.

"Is that it? Is there anything else I need to know?" Milly asked.

"What more could there be?" he asked, genuinely confused.

"I just want there to be complete honesty between us," she said simply. "The subject of your family came up once, and you looked distinctly uncomfortable, Nick. I…I didn't want to pry, but I think it's better I know everything that could affect us in the future."

"Oh. Well, I suppose it does explain why I was such a fool with the maharajah's daughter," he said, realizing it just that moment. "I suppose I never thought about it.… My mother was a lovely woman who decided after my sister, her fourth child, was born that she had been dutiful to the viscount, my father, long enough. She threw over the traces, as it were, and became something of a scandal. She finally left my father. He divorced her, and I never saw her again before she died."

"How old were you when she left?" she asked quietly.

"Fourteen. Father was never quite the same after that. He'd always been a bit distant, the proper Victorian noble who believed children should be seen and not heard, but after that, he may as well have lived on the moon."

He didn't realize he was shaking with suppressed tears until she circled around him and took him into her arms.

"I love you," she said, after a while. "Broken places and all. We may argue from time to time, but I will never, never cause you not to trust me or doubt my love."

He stared at her. "You're more than I could ever deserve," he said at last.

"None of that," Milly insisted, putting a finger to his lips. "You were wonderful today," Milly told him. "And so brave—like a general leading his troops into battle."

"I had you fooled, then," he said wryly. "I was shaking in my boots—for me and the Browns," he told her. "I wasn't sure if the Circle fellows would pull out guns or if the townspeople would tar and feather me. But they came through for us, didn't they?"

"Especially Mrs. Detwiler!" she said, shaking her

head in wonderment. She still couldn't believe it. The old woman who'd reminded her of a dragon was now a friend.

"Simpson Creek's going to be a different place, thanks to you," she murmured. "I feel so much safer."

He sighed. "My dear Milly, you give me too much credit. The Comanches are still out there, and they could still attack here at the ranch. I promise you, though, we'll have a fort on top of the hill next year, but until then…"

She loved hearing him speak of next year, as if he assumed he'd be there with her for all the years to come. They'd be married by then, she thought. They hadn't spoken of a date yet, but she knew they would.

"I've told you before the Comanches have always been a possible threat," she said calmly. "Until you build that fort, we'll do what we always do—pray for the Lord's protection."

"Your faith is strengthening mine, Milly Matthews," he said, gazing into her eyes. "It's just one more reason I love you."

The compliment and his declaration swelled her heart with joy. "And your goodness is making me a better person, Nicholas Brookfield. I would not have been brave enough to hire the Browns on my own, or to take on the whole town as you did today. So we will help each other grow in faith, I think. What's that verse in the Proverbs—'Iron sharpens iron'? And then it goes on to speak of one friend sharpening another?"

He smiled. "We were friends first, Milly, and I always hoped the woman I married would be my best friend, too. I can hardly believe I'm daring to ask this after what happened today, but will you marry me?"

"Yes. Oh yes, I will marry you!"

Cupping her chin, he kissed her, tenderly and thoroughly.

"When?" she asked, as he lifted his lips from hers.

He was thoughtful. "As soon as the fort is finished? Will that give you enough time?"

Milly nodded, already thinking of the wedding dress she would sew.

"I should write and invite my brothers and sister to come. Richard, the vicar—he'll adore you. He'll tell you you're much too good for me," he said, a fond smile curving his lips. "I imagine he never expected me to marry a woman who lived her faith like you do."

"Perhaps he could take part in the wedding ceremony. I imagine Reverend Chadwick wouldn't mind."

Chapter Twenty-Seven

The rest of August and September flew by. Every morning, as soon as the chores were done, the men would ride into town to work on the fort. They always left two of the men home with Milly and Sarah for their protection.

Milly worked at dressmaking mornings and afternoons, alternately her wedding gown and the dresses she was making for the mercantile. Each dress sold almost as soon as she brought it in, Mr. Patterson informed her. Milly was pleased to see her creations on the ladies of the town, and there were usually garments to be altered or mended waiting for her at the store, too.

While Milly sewed, her sister baked, both for the hotel and the mercantile. Both were pleased to watch the amount of money growing in their bank account.

At midday, Milly and Sarah interrupted their endeavors to drive the wagon into town, accompanied by one of the men, while the other kept watch over the ranch. While Sarah delivered pies and cakes to the hotel restaurant, Milly took her dresses to the mercantile, along with more of Sarah's baking. Then they took Nick and the rest of their men their noon meal, and sat down with them to eat.

The other ladies of the town were doing likewise for their men. Members of the Spinsters' Club stopped by to chat with Milly and Sarah about the wedding preparations and the upcoming Founders' Day celebrations. Caroline and Emily flirted with their beaus, who were working right alongside the rest of the town to build the fort. Sarah and the other Spinsters compared their letters and speculated about the men who had agreed to come meet the ladies on Founders' Day.

Dr. Nolan Walker, the man from Brazos County with whom Sarah had been corresponding, had written her three times. His letters were short, and he mostly responded to what Sarah had written about her doings, but he didn't offer many details about himself. The fact didn't seem to bother Sarah much—"Men just don't write long detailed letters," she told Milly. He claimed to be looking forward to meeting Sarah, and Sarah was satisfied with that, reminding Milly that he might decide he liked one of the other Spinsters better, anyway.

Her sister's calmness about the matter was typical of Sarah, Milly knew, but she thought it was a good thing Nick had just traveled to Simpson Creek and not corresponded with her first. She knew she would have plagued him with questions. Typical of all those in love who want others to feel that same joyous emotion, Milly hoped that the man from Brazos County would be the right man for Sarah.

Milly wasn't surprised that Bill Waters never came to the work site. Dayton and a few of the others participated from time to time, but when they did, they ignored the Brown brothers. There was no changing some people's hearts, Milly mused, but if they helped build the fort and caused no trouble, that was all that mattered.

It did her heart good to see how the rest of the town had come to accept Elijah, Isaiah, Caleb and Micah, greeting them as they rode into town and at the site. Mrs. Detwiler had made them her own personal concern, plying them with extra sandwiches and cookies. As a result, the Brown brothers had lost much of the wary tenseness that had marked their expressions and had begun to smile, laugh and exchange pleasantries with the townsfolk. They even seemed to walk taller.

Ada came to the work site but rarely, and was either accompanied by Harvey, who apparently considered himself above manual labor, or spoke of meeting him soon for some outing. There was a strained quality to her. Milly wondered if she was still unsure of the Englishman's affection.

A detachment of the Fourth Cavalry, led by the same Major McConley whom Nick and Milly had encountered before, paid a visit when the fort was halfway done. The arrival of blue-coated soldiers alarmed some in Simpson Creek, but after talking to the mayor, Nick and several others at the building site, McConley reassured them that the Federals had no argument with the citizenry being ready to defend themselves against Indian attacks. He even suggested features to include in the fort.

The fort rose in height, foot by foot, behind Mrs. Detwiler's house, as summer faded into fall. It was clear it would not be completely finished by Founders' Day, though it was nearly so. The stone walls stood two stories high, interspersed with narrow windows to fire through at the second-story level. These were reached by a stairway. There was no complete ceiling between the first floor and second floor, only narrow walkways. The heavy, metal-reinforced double doors had just been fitted into place. It could be bolted from the inside. There was a well in the center of the fort and a stone fireplace against the back wall. Beans and rice had been stockpiled against an interior wall in case of a prolonged siege.

By the week of Founders' Day, only the roof, which was to be tin so that flaming arrows could not set it afire, was not in place. The interior was big enough that everyone in town would fit inside, and all those who could reach the fort in time from the nearby ranches.

Milly was thankful as the building's completion drew near, but prayed the fort would never need to be used.

Founders' Day dawned bright and sunny. The intense heat of summer had metamorphosed into cooler nights and pleasantly warm days.

"I'm sure glad the original settlers didn't found this town in the middle of the summer," Milly remarked as she settled herself on the driver's bench of the wagon next to Nick. Sarah was already sitting in the wagon bed along with Josh; Bobby and the Brown brothers had mounted their horses and would ride alongside as they drove into town for the festivities.

"There's a nice breeze," commented Sarah, lifting her face to it as the wagon left the yard. She looked lovely today in a dress of cream-colored crossbar lawn sprigged with orange and yellow flowers. It had a lace-insert bodice and a matching shawl for later if it grew cool. A very fitting dress for Sarah to wear to meet her prospective beau, Milly decided, for naturally she had made the dress. It would accent Sarah's lovely golden hair.

Even if her sister wouldn't admit it, Sarah was nervous, Milly thought, though only someone who knew her well would have guessed it by the way she kept playing with her topaz earbobs and pendant necklace.

Milly wore a new creation, too. Her two-piece dress featured a shaped peplum and alternating wide and narrow stripes of moss green sprigged with autumn leaves and solid burned orange. She couldn't wait to see everyone.

Turning onto the road, Nick snapped the reins to quicken the horses' pace, then, after he had transferred the reins to one hand, Milly saw him rub his forehead.

"What's the matter?" she asked. "Are you all right?"

He nodded. "Bit of a headache, that's all. Sarah made me some willow bark tea for it before breakfast, before you came into the kitchen."

"You didn't tell me," Milly said, feeling a frisson of worry skitter up her spine. She'd spent longer than usual over her toilette, wanting to look perfect today at the festivities, for they were going to announce their wedding date, the Saturday after Thanksgiving, and invite everyone to the ceremony. "Are you sure you'll be okay? It's not—"

"Not malaria," he finished for her. "No, don't worry, Milly darling. Most times a headache is just a headache, even for me. I have my quinine, just in case," he said, pulling out a small flask from his shirt pocket.

"Most men who carry one of those would have whiskey in it," she said with a chuckle.

They went to the fort first, for the festivities were to begin with a dedication and blessing of the unfinished fort by Mayor Gilmore and Reverend Chadwick, respectively. A midday picnic on the church grounds would follow and then games for the children—a fishing contest on the banks of Simpson Creek, foot races and sack races. Supper was to be a barbecue sponsored by the hotel, and for those who still had stamina after all that, the day would end with a concert put on by the Fourth Cavalry Regimental Band—a neighborly gesture, Milly thought—and end with fireworks at dark.

Dr. Nolan Walker had written he would probably arrive in town by noon, so Sarah had arranged that he would meet her at the midday picnic. But Prissy Gilmore dashed up to them as the ceremony was beginning.

"He's here! They're all here, all three of the candidates! I just happened to be leaving our house when these three nice-looking strangers came riding by, and asked if I could direct them to the church, so of course I did, and then I found out who they were! And then we ran into Jane and Maude, so of course I introduced them and said I'd come find you!"

"Well, are you going to tell me what he's like?" Sarah demanded, grabbing Prissy's hand. "Is he good-looking? Does he seem nice?"

Prissy grinned. "Rather handsome in a craggy sort of way, I'd say, and yes, he seems nice…"

"But what? There's something you're not telling me, isn't there, Prissy Gilmore? What is it?"

Prissy looked mysterious, her gaze straying sideways. "Well…there *is* something surprising about him…"

"What's that?"

"I'm not going to tell you. You'll just have to come meet him," she said, grinning like the cat that swallowed the canary.

As Milly watched, Sarah's face went pale, then flushed as she clutched Milly's hands in hers. She was shaking. "Oh, Milly, this is it! Wish me luck!"

"Oh, I do…" Milly began, but Prissy was already pulling Sarah away with her.

"Come on, Nick, I want to see this man," she said, urging him after them.

"Easy, there," he said, pulling back. "Why don't we give your sister some privacy? I'm sure she'll introduce us to her beau, if she approves of him. Let's stay right here as we planned, and listen to the mayor and the reverend's speeches, and by the time we get to the churchyard, Sarah will be ready to introduce us to him, I reckon," he said, winking as he gave a fair imitation of a Texas drawl on those last two words.

Milly was torn, but she knew Nick was right, so she settled down to watch the fort dedication.

Sarah was standing by herself, clearly waiting for them, when they arrived at the church grounds. Even from a distance she looked mad as a wet cat.

Milly hurried forward.

"I'm so angry I could spit, Milly!" Sarah cried. "Can you imagine? Nolan Walker's a *Yankee!* That's what Prissy was calling 'surprising'! Of all the nerve—"

"But… She said he was nice…" Milly began. "Didn't he seem like a nice man?"

"Milly! There's no way I could consider getting to know a…a blue belly! A man who could have been the one who shot my Jesse! He *lied* to me, Milly!"

"Did he…are you saying Dr. Walker claimed to have fought for the South in his letters?" Milly asked, desperately trying to make sense of her sister's words. She'd never seen Sarah so furious.

"No! He mentioned being an army doctor, and tending the wounded, and that he'd even had to fight alongside the other men at times—he just didn't *bother* to tell me he'd worn blue, not gray—as if that wasn't important!"

"Sarah, dear, perhaps you should give him a chance…" Milly began uncertainly, taking hold of her sister's flailing hands. Sarah hadn't mentioned Jesse since that day in the church when Milly had first thought up the Spinsters' Club, so Milly had assumed Sarah had begun to accept her fiancé's loss, especially after she'd agreed to write to Dr. Walker.

"Not on your life! I'm not about to take up with any Yankee! Not after my Jesse died in the war and I'll never even know what happened to him! I couldn't bear to spend a moment in that man's company, from the moment he opened his mouth and started talking in that horrible Yankee accent! This is how he talks— 'Hello, Miss Matthews, I'm glad to meet you,' she said, mimicking an accent that sounded flat and nasally to Milly.

Sarah burst into tears, and went into her sister's waiting embrace, sobbing. "I told Prissy she could have him, if her standards were so low, or he could just ride back out of here on that horse of his!"

Chapter Twenty-Eight

Milly looked from her sister's tear-stained face to Nick. After proffering a handkerchief, he hovered by the two of them as if not certain what to do. Milly didn't know either. Ought she to encourage Sarah again to give the man a chance, against her sister's strongly held convictions, or just let her be?

Sarah finally wiped her eyes and cheeks. "I—I'll be all right," she said. "Don't worry about me. I don't want to spoil the day for you. I said all along we might not suit one another." She shrugged. "If you don't mind, though, I'm going to sit with you two rather than the others."

Sarah made a vague gesture toward the group standing next to the church, which included the three candidates, Prissy, Maude and Jane. Since Maude and Jane were each standing close to one of the men, Milly assumed the man standing by himself must be the rejected Yankee. Milly couldn't see him well, but from where she was standing Dr. Nolan Walker appeared tall and reasonably well-favored, and had hair that might have been brown or auburn—she couldn't be sure from this distance. Prissy approached him and seemed content enough in his company. As Milly watched, he offered Prissy his arm and the group of six strolled over to a spot on the lawn where Maude spread out a large table-cloth. So Sarah's loss, or rather rejection, might well be Prissy's gain, Milly decided, but then she saw Walker aim a glance in Sarah's direction. Even from so far away, she thought she could read regret on his face.

Milly urged Nick and Sarah over to an area near the bluff overlooking the creek, deliberately picking a spot to have their dinner that was as far away from the three couples as possible. They were soon joined by Josh, Bobby and the Brown brothers, who'd been visiting with some cowboys from the ranch beyond Waters's property, and Milly had been pleased to see the ready acceptance they were given.

They made short work of the delicious dinner Sarah had packed—fried chicken, biscuits and homemade jelly, apple pie and cold tea.

"I'm full as a tick on an ol' dog's ear," Josh said, when nothing was left but chicken bones and crumbs. He patted his stomach as he stretched out backward on the blanket.

"Me, too. Miss Sarah, you sure are a good cook," Micah said, and the others joined in the praise.

Nick put down his chicken leg, hoping Milly hadn't noticed how little he'd eaten, or how many times he'd surreptitiously rubbed his thumping head. He didn't want to spoil this special day. Perhaps if he stole away for a few minutes he could drink his quinine without any of them becoming the wiser. He still wasn't sure it was a malaria attack—those had always been heralded by headaches, but as yet he hadn't had any of the pre-monitory chills.

But the eyes of the woman who loved him missed little. "What's the matter, Nick?" Milly whispered so that the others wouldn't hear.

"That headache's being a bit stubborn about going away," he told her. "Don't worry about it. I'm sure it will fade in time."

"Nick, are you sure this is not your malaria?"

"I don't think so," he tried to tell her, but even to his own ears he didn't sound sure.

"We can go home, you know."

"I don't want to spoil the fun for the others," he protested. He'd been relieved to see Sarah laughing along with the others at some joke Josh had made.

"We don't have to," Milly argued. "We could take two of the horses, and whoever rode them could come back in the wagon."

"No, we wanted to invite people to our wedding, didn't we? I don't think it's the malaria, but just to be sure, I'll go ahead and take a draft of quinine. Let me just get a cupful of water from the church pump to wash that bitter taste down, and I'll be right as rain."

"Englishmen are every bit as stubborn as American men!" Milly retorted in exasperation. "At least let's go inside while you drink it, and get you out of the sun for a few minutes," Milly said, rising to her feet. "Sarah, we'll be back in a while. We're going to get a drink of water and then go around and tell folks about the wedding," she said.

But Nick's hopes of a few peaceful minutes alone

with Milly in the cool dimness of the sanctuary were to be frustrated. When they walked inside, Nick's eyes made out a huddled form in a front pew even as the sound of weeping reached his ears.

It was Ada Spencer. He had to smother the urge to groan aloud.

Milly rushed forward. "Ada? Ada, what's wrong?"

The woman started. Obviously she had been sunk too deep in distress to hear their quiet entrance.

Nick took in the other woman's disheveled hair and red-rimmed eyes as Ada looked up.

"What is it?" Milly asked gently. "Where's Mr. Harvey? Did you two have a quarrel?"

"He's gone," Ada said dully. "He left town about an hour ago..."

"But why?"

"Did he hurt you, Miss Spencer?" Nick said, stepping forward. "I promise you, if he did, we'll hunt him down and see that he's punished."

The woman shook her head, a weary gesture that spoke volumes. "No...not like you mean," she said, her voice raspy and cracking. "He didn't do anything I didn't agree to. But when I told him I was expecting his child, and I wanted to know when we were going to marry, he said he was leaving and going back to his post in Austin—maybe even back to England."

"We'll find him and bring him back," Nick said, promising himself he'd force the scoundrel to make an honest woman of Ada Spencer, even though he was sure Ada was better off without him, even if it meant bearing a babe on her own.

"No!" the woman cried, startling both of them with

the vehemence she was able to summon. "I don't want anyone that doesn't want me! I'll go away somewhere— tell everyone I'm a widow! But you can't tell anyone what he did, Milly, swear you won't..." She buried her face in her hands as a new paroxysm of sobs erupted from her.

Milly knelt by Ada's side and gathered the woman into her arms. "Of course I won't, Ada dear, but you mustn't think of leaving. No one in town will condemn you—"

Ada raised her head and opened her mouth, surely about to argue.

And then a shattering scream split the air from outside.

"Oh dear heaven, what can that be?" cried Milly. Ada jerked bolt upright, her sorrows momentarily forgotten, and all three of them ran to the door as the screaming went on and on.

When they reached the outside, it was all too plain what had caused someone to scream—a winded horse stood there, its flanks heaving. A man slumped over the horse's neck, his back pierced with multiple arrows. He was tied on the saddle by a rope binding his hands around the horse's neck and tying his feet to the stirrups.

"It's Blakely!" screamed Ada, and fell over in a faint.

"Milly, stay with her!" Nick shouted, and ran to the horse. Everyone else who had been picnicking had jumped to their feet, but seemed riveted to the spot with horror.

He was certain Harvey must be dead, but when he reached the horse, he saw the man was still breathing.

"Harvey, can you hear me?" Nick hoped the man had passed out, for surely he must be suffering untold agony if he was conscious.

To his astonishment, the man turned a milk-white, blood-spattered face toward him. "Comanches… coming…they killed Waters…" he managed to say, and then his eyes rolled back as a last breath rattled through him and he died.

And Nick heard the pounding of hooves in the distance.

"The Comanches are coming! We've got to get to the fort!" he shouted. He ran back to where Milly was stooping over Ada, trying to slap her awake, and with one swift motion moved Milly aside and scooped up the unconscious woman.

"Milly, can you run?"

Wordlessly, her eyes wide, she nodded. "But where's Sarah?" Her eyes searched the lawn.

Both saw Sarah at the same time, running toward them alongside Elijah. The other Brown brothers, Bobby and Josh flanked them. Sarah's gaze met Milly's, and she beckoned for Milly to hurry, then ran to the street.

Milly took off, running alongside Nick.

All around them, parents snatched up their little ones, the children wailing in confused protest at their suddenly interrupted fun. Women screamed and men drew their guns as they ran. They became like a sea of ants, all streaming toward the fort in the middle of town.

Then over all the cries and turmoil came the whoops and shrieks of the charging Comanches on their mounts splashing across Simpson Creek behind the churchyard.

A panic-stricken woman collided with Milly, and Milly nearly fell, saved only by Nick's extended hand. Arrows and bullets whooshed and whined past them as they fled, past the livery, past the mercantile, past the hotel, past the general store... Dear God, surely they must be near the fort!

Nick heard Milly panting for breath, and he breathed a prayer as he ran with his unconscious burden. *Please, Lord, let Milly make it to safety, and Sarah. Take my life if You will, but save this woman and the others.*

Some men had already reached the fort and the wagons parked outside it, and had grabbed rifles to set up a covering fire at the Comanches galloping so closely behind the last of the townspeople. Their firing slowed the attackers' charge long enough, Nick thought, as he ran inside with Ada and Milly, for the townspeople to make it to safety—at least those who hadn't been felled as they ran. He'd seen at least a couple go down, but he'd dared not stop to help them.

As soon as he laid Ada down inside the fort in Milly's care, he dashed back outside, grabbing the rifle that Josh tossed to him from the wagon. Together they fired at the front line of the mounted Comanches until the last men ran inside. Then they, too, jumped inside, and rammed the door bolt home.

Men were already perched on the inside second-story walkways, firing out of the narrow windows as the whoops of the Indians and the whinnies of their horses circled the square stone fort. Nick joined them even as the first chills racked his body. The malaria would have to wait.

Below him, he saw that Milly had turned over the care of Ada to Mrs. Detwiler, who was already clucking over her charge as if a hundred murderous savages weren't whooping outside. As the older woman sponged her face with a damp cloth, Ada blinked and raised her head, only to bury her face against Mrs. Detwiler's body as war whoops floated in through the windows, joined by a bloodcurdling scream and thud outside as a settler's bullet found its target.

In a moment, Milly had joined him at an adjacent window, firing with a rifle he didn't recognize. *Lord, save us and make me always worthy of this brave woman!* Looking to both sides, he saw Josh, Bobby and the Brown brothers, all firing out at the attackers. Between Elijah and Caleb stood the Yankee Sarah had rejected, shooting a Winchester carbine out the narrow window with deadly accuracy.

He could hear Reverend Chadwick and several others below, praying aloud for their deliverance, and added his silent prayers to theirs.

Where was Milly's sister? Then he spotted her, one of several women huddled over wailing, terrorized children against the walls as flaming arrows rained in with hissing sounds from the roofless top of the building. These embedded themselves harmlessly in the dirt floor, where the fires soon hissed out. The echoing yelps and screams rose upward to rattle around inside Nick's skull with the hammer and anvil already jammed inside there. He stiffened his body to try to control the chills that threatened the accuracy of his aim.

Just a little longer, Lord. Let the fever hold off a little longer... As he watched, their coppery skins and contorted, screaming faces became the faces of warring Punjabis and the town's buildings became the northern plains of India. He fired again, and had the satisfaction of seeing a Punjabi—no, a Comanche—about to loose a flaming arrow fall off his horse with a hoarse cry instead. As he looked, his blurring vision caused the crumpled body on the ground to become two.

And then, blessedly, they heard a bugle in the distance, and more pounding hooves. As Nick watched through blurry vision, horsemen in blue galloped around the corner, heading straight for the fort, as Comanches scattered left and right, fleeing the oncoming cavalry.

Chapter Twenty-Nine

When Nick woke, he was lying in a strange bedroom and Milly was sponging his forehead with water that felt blessedly cool.

"Where am I?" he asked, staring up at the lovely face of his beautiful Milly.

She smiled down at him. "Ssssh! I don't want her to know you're awake just yet, so I can have you all to myself. You're in Mrs. Detwiler's spare bedroom, and she's out in the kitchen making broth for you. She wouldn't hear of us taking you home in the wagon until you came around. But I wouldn't be the least bit surprised if she insists you stay longer. I think it's been a long time since she had anyone to ply with calves' foot jelly and tea."

"I...I take it the Comanches have been routed?"

She nodded. "Put to flight, the few who survived the crossfire between our fort and the cavalry."

"Thank God," he said soberly, to which she said, "Amen."

"It'll be a long time before they try to attack Simpson

Creek again, the major said, now that we have a fort," Milly continued.

"Have the others been back to the ranch yet? Is it all right?" he said, hardly daring to hear the answer. If Waters had been killed and his ranch burned, it was always possible the Matthews ranch had been hit, too, and the livestock stolen.

"Untouched. We've been so blessed."

"Indeed, we have. Thank You, Lord." He straightened up in the bed. "The last thing I remember was hearing the cavalry bugler sounding the charge, and the cavalry galloping into sight."

Milly grinned now. "That's when you swooned."

He glared at her with all the ferocity he could muster—which wasn't much, considering the headache he still had. "I did not *swoon,* woman, I'll have you know. Men do not swoon. Females swoon."

"Very well, you fell unconscious," she said reasonably, but mischief still danced in her eyes. "Whatever you did, you slept nearly around the clock. It's Sunday now."

"Did we…lose very many townspeople?" Nick had guessed from Milly's calm demeanor that Sarah and their ranch hands must be all right, so now he could ask about the others.

Her expression sobered. "Doctor Harkey. He didn't make it to the fort. He must have been behind us."

"That's a shame. Poor Maude…"

She nodded. "Blakely Harvey, of course… And the major said they found Bill Waters and a couple of his hands killed and the ranch house burned to the ground."

Nick nodded, unable to find anything to say. No one deserved to die that way. He only hoped Waters and Harvey had had time to cry out to God before they died.

"Other than those, no one was killed, though several got arrow or gunshot wounds, and there's an assortment of cuts and bruises."

"And the town's without a doctor, because Doctor Harkey is dead."

Milly shook her head. "In God's providence, no, it's not. Remember, the Yankee who was corresponding with Sarah was a doctor? Right now he's busy as a barefoot boy on a red ant bed, as Josh would say."

"How does Sarah feel about that? Before the attack, I'm sure she was hoping he'd ride back out of here when the day was over."

Milly grinned. "I'm sure she realizes he's a very essential man to have around right now. I think she's worried he'll decide to stay, though, now that the town needs a doctor." She chuckled. "I met him, and I liked him. I think he might just turn out to be exactly what my sister needs. If Prissy Gilmore doesn't snap him up, that is."

"It'll be interesting to watch."

She nodded. "He's been to check on you, though of course you wouldn't remember it. He's brought some more quinine from Doctor Harkey's supply. He expects taking the quinine when you did will considerably shorten this attack."

"I feel quite a bit better already."

From somewhere beyond the bedroom a clock began to chime.

"Church will be over soon," Milly remarked. "We'd better get you shaved for the visit."

"Visit? Who's visiting?"

"The mayor was planning to stop by after the service at church—they were going to give thanks for the town's deliverance," she said. "He says the town's going to proclaim you a hero. I believe he's commissioning a medal to be made."

"I? As I recall, every man in the fort was firing at them, and the bravest woman I know, too," he said, reaching up to cup her cheek.

"If it weren't for you, that fort wouldn't have been there just when we needed it. And we'd still have been giving in to the demands of bullies wearing hoods and making threats."

He smiled, warmed by the love and admiration he saw in her eyes. "And all because one plucky woman decided to advertise for husbands." He raised his head and met her lips. "I love you, Milly Matthews. Being your husband is going to be an adventure."

* * * * *

Dear Reader,

As I was trying to decide what to write for my next submission to the Love Inspired Historical line, and hoping to find an idea that could possibly extend into a series, I remembered the advice of a wonderful former agent of mine, who's now retired, Alice Orr—something to the effect of "Take an idea that's popular and twist so it's new." Mail-order bride stories are popular (I certainly love them), and a staple of Western historical romances. But I couldn't remember ever seeing a mail-order *groom* story. And so was born Milly and her Spinsters' Club, formed by my enterprising heroine in a Texas town with no single men. Since I met my husband, Tom, online, it's a story that's near and dear to my heart, and I hope you like it, too.

My next book will feature Milly's shy sister, Sarah, and the man she finds to love—who should have been the last man she'd ever consider.

As always, I love to hear from readers, either via my website at www.lauriekingery.com or on Facebook.

Laurie Kingery

QUESTIONS FOR DISCUSSION

1. Have you ever been afraid to begin something that's never been done before, as Milly is when she starts the Spinsters' Club? Were you afraid of what people would say? How did you handle it?

2. Would you say you are more like Milly or more like Sarah? How would you describe the differences in the sisters' personalities?

3. If you lived in mid-1800s America, would you be brave enough to settle in an area in which Native-American attacks are possible, or would you remain in a safer area?

4. Are you fully using the talents that God has given you, as Milly and Sarah did by the end of the book? If not, what's holding you back?

5. Have you ever had a "Mrs. Detwiler" in your life? What was your response? Have you tried to or been able to change his or her mind by what you did?

6. Have you ever kept secrets from someone you loved? Why or why not? What was the effect?

7. What was the townspeople's response to the Circle's actions and threats? Why did it change?

8. Why is Nick so afraid to reveal his secrets to Milly? What problems could Nick have avoided by trusting Milly sooner?

9. Do you think God guides us in our choice of mates? Why or why not?

10. If you had to plan a sermon around your favorite Bible verse, as Reverend Chadwick did with Micah 6:8, what verse would you choose?

11. Do you think it's all right for someone who wishes to marry to take action to meet someone, as Milly does, or should he or she wait for the Lord to send him or her the right person? What role does prayer play in the choice of the right mate?

12. Do you think Sarah should have been more willing to consider getting to know the Yankee doctor?

HISTORICAL

TITLES AVAILABLE NEXT MONTH

Available December 7, 2010

REQUEST YOUR FREE BOOKS!

2 FREE INSPIRATIONAL NOVELS
PLUS 2
FREE
MYSTERY GIFTS

Love Inspired.

HISTORICAL

INSPIRATIONAL HISTORICAL ROMANCE

YES! Please send me 2 FREE Love Inspired® Historical novels and my 2 FREE mystery gifts (gifts are worth about $10). After receiving them, if I don't wish to receive any more books, I can return the shipping statement marked "cancel". If I don't cancel, I will receive 4 brand-new novels every other month and be billed just $4.24 per book in the U.S. or $4.74 per book in Canada. That's a saving of over 20% off the cover price. It's quite a bargain! Shipping and handling is just 50¢ per book.* I understand that accepting the 2 free books and gifts places me under no obligation to buy anything. I can always return a shipment and cancel at any time. Even if I never buy another book, the two free books and gifts are mine to keep forever.

102/302 IDN E7QD

Name	(PLEASE PRINT)
Address	Apt. #
City	State/Prov. Zip/Postal Code

Signature (if under 18, a parent or guardian must sign)

Mail to Steeple Hill Reader Service:
IN U.S.A.: P.O. Box 1867, Buffalo, NY 14240-1867
IN CANADA: P.O. Box 609, Fort Erie, Ontario L2A 5X3
Not valid for current subscribers to Love Inspired Historical novels.

Want to try two free books from another series?
Call 1-800-873-8635 or visit www.morefreebooks.com.

* Terms and prices subject to change without notice. Prices do not include applicable taxes. Sales tax applicable in N.Y. Canadian residents will be charged applicable provincial taxes and GST. Offer not valid in Quebec. This offer is limited to one order per household. All orders subject to approval. Credit or debit balances in a customer's account(s) may be offset by any other outstanding balance owed by or to the customer. Please allow 4 to 6 weeks for delivery. Offer available while quantities last.

Your Privacy: Steeple Hill Books is committed to protecting your privacy. Our Privacy Policy is available online at www.SteepleHill.com or upon request from the Reader Service. From time to time we make our lists of customers available to reputable third parties who may have a product or service of interest to you. If you would prefer we not share your name and address, please check here. ☐

Help us get it right—We strive for accurate, respectful and relevant communications. To clarify or modify your communication preferences, visit us at www.ReaderService.com/consumerschoice.

LIH10R

HARLEQUIN®

A *Romance*

FOR EVERY MOOD™

Spotlight on

Classic

Quintessential, modern love stories
that are romance at its finest.

See the next page
to enjoy a sneak peek from
the Harlequin® Romance series.

See below for a sneak peek from our classic
Harlequin® Romance® line.

Introducing DADDY BY CHRISTMAS by Patricia Thayer.

MIA caught sight of Jarrett when he walked into the open lobby. It was hard not to notice the man. In a charcoal business suit with a crisp white shirt and striped tie covered by a dark trench coat, he looked more Wall Street than small-town Colorado.

Mia couldn't blame him for keeping his distance. He was probably tired of taking care of her.

Besides, why would a man like Jarrett McKane be interested in her? Why would he want to take on a woman expecting a baby? Yet he'd done so many things for her. He'd been there when she'd needed him most. How could she not care about a man like that?

Heart pounding in her ears, she walked up behind him. Jarrett turned to face her. "Did you get enough sleep last night?"

"Yes, thanks to you," she said, wondering if he'd thought about their kiss. Her gaze went to his mouth, then she quickly glanced away. "And thank you for not bringing up my meltdown."

Jarrett couldn't stop looking at Mia. Blue was definitely her color, bringing out the richness of her eyes.

"What meltdown?" he said, trying hard to focus on what she was saying. "You were just exhausted from lack of sleep and worried about your baby."

He couldn't help remembering how, during the night, he'd kept going in to watch her sleep. How strange was that? "I hope you got enough rest."

She nodded. "Plenty. And you're a good neighbor for

HREXP1210

coming to my rescue."

He tensed. Neighbor? *What neighbor kisses you like I did?* "That's me, just the full-service landlord," he said, trying to keep the sarcasm out of his voice. He started to leave, but she put her hand on his arm.

"Jarrett, what I meant was you went beyond helping me." Her eyes searched his face. "I've asked far too much of you."

"Did you hear me complain?"

She shook her head. "You should. I feel like I've taken advantage."

"Like I said, I haven't minded."

"And I'm grateful for everything…"

Grasping her hand on his arm, Jarrett leaned forward. The memory of last night's kiss had him aching for another. "I didn't do it for your gratitude, Mia."

Gorgeous tycoon Jarrett McKane has never believed in Christmas—but he can't help being drawn to soon-to-be-mom Mia Saunders! Christmases past were spent alone…and now Jarrett may just have a fairy-tale ending for all his Christmases future!

Available December 2010,
only from Harlequin® Romance®.

HREXP1210

Love Inspired®

When Karen Imhoff
finds a beaten man lying
unconscious in her Amish
community, she doesn't
hesitate to help. "John Doe"
needs a place to stay while
he regains his memory,
and he quickly proves
invaluable around the
farm. But the handsome
Englisher wreaks havoc
with her emotions....

An Amish Christmas
by
Patricia Davids

*Available December
wherever books are sold.*

Fall in love with
Amish Country with the last
book in the miniseries

BRIDES OF
Amish Country

Steeple
Hill®

LI87637